Doctored Images

ROBERT SHERRIER

abbott press®
A DIVISION OF WRITER'S DIGEST

Abbott Press books may be ordered through booksellers or by contacting:

Abbott Press
1663 Liberty Drive
Bloomington, IN 47403
www.abbottpress.com
Phone: 1-866-697-5310

Because of the dynamic nature of the Internet, any web addresses or links contained in this book may have changed since publication and may no longer be valid. The views expressed in this work are solely those of the author and do not necessarily reflect the views of the publisher, and the publisher hereby disclaims any responsibility for them.

Any people depicted in stock imagery provided by Thinkstock are models, and such images are being used for illustrative purposes only. Certain stock imagery © Thinkstock.

ISBN: 978-1-4582-1311-2 (sc)
ISBN: 978-1-4582-1310-5 (hc)
ISBN: 978-1-4582-1309-9 (e)

Library of Congress Control Number: 2013921801

Printed in the United States of America.

Abbott Press rev. date: 01/02/2014

ACKNOWLEDGEMENTS

First and foremost, I need to thank my wife, Carol, for reading the many drafts of this book and answering countless "what if's" without too much eye rolling. I love you.

I want to give a big thanks to my early readers for their helpful suggestions and words of encouragement: Fred Blume (who's not responsible for any geological blunders), Mike McBride, Jim Semple, Bud Richards, Berta and Greg Parrott. Thanks to my triathlon buddies Dan Miller and Kat D'Angelo for their useful training tips. And special thanks to my son Bob and daughter Karen (who would be a great editor) for their plot recommendations.

I want to acknowledge Dr. Gil Brogdon, considered by many as the father of forensic radiology. His work with Dr. Paul R. Algra on the radiology of drug smuggling sparked my nefarious imagination.

Finally, I want to express my heartfelt appreciation to all the radiology technologists whom I've worked with over my 20-year career. You toil thanklessly behind the scenes to provide our patients with the best possible images. Thanks.

This is a work of fiction. Any similarity to people I've known might be intentional. You know who you are.

CHAPTER

1

Monday, July 5
Cabo San Lucas, Mexico

eath arrived at dawn.

Marisol cowered in the corner of her tiny bedroom, smothering her baby with fear. There was no way out, no escape. Car doors slammed, and boots crunched on broken shells in the driveway. How many were out there?

The bungalow shivered as the killers climbed the porch steps.

She hugged Arturo tighter and leaned forward to kiss the last few strands of his baby hair.

The front door splintered open, and the men stormed in.

"No!" she screamed as the thugs ripped Arturo from her grasp. Two men carried him away, the bewildered child clutching the soft blanket Marisol had made with scraps from the sewing plant.

The leader stood before Marisol. A cigarette dangled from his wrinkled face. He pointed a gun at her head. "Stand up."

The faded tattoo under his left eye confirmed her worst fear: she was indebted to the Mexican mafia, the Sureños, the most powerful gang in the Baja. She wondered how many lives he'd taken to earn the teardrop under the other eye and prayed her husband, Hector, wasn't one of them.

The man lit the cigarette and inhaled deeply. "Do you wish to see your husband and son again?" he asked as smoke streamed around his face.

Trembling, Marisol stood and nodded.

"Then you must deliver this shipment." He explained how she would swallow cocaine-filled condoms—*bolitas,* he called them—and travel to the United States, where his friends would meet her.

He grabbed Marisol's hair and shoved her into the front room. The men gave her a sour liquid they said would stop her bowels from moving. Then they started feeding her the dry packages of rubber out of a dirty, metal bucket. One by one, she forced herself to swallow the packages. When her stomach revolted and she slowed, the man with the gun slapped her to the ground.

"Swallow the rest now, or we'll kill the little one."

She heard Arturo wailing in the kitchen.

Marisol couldn't bear to look at the man anymore, disgusted by the smell of tequila and onions drifting from his pores. She stared at the carpet, peppered with his black spit, and willed her stomach to cooperate.

"Swallow." He kicked the bucket under her chin and pushed her head down. Marisol blinked away the tears and watched the few remaining bolitas roll to a stop. She could do it. She reached in, grabbed one, and gagged as the dry condom stuck in her throat.

When she finished, they stripped her to her underwear and laughed at her swollen stomach. They dressed her in a "sundress" (as the tourists at the hotel called them), and shoved her into the backseat of their SUV. The man with the gun sat next to her, his breath revolting, his hand wandering up her thigh.

"Stop," she pleaded when his clawing got too close, and she felt his breath quicken. A bump in the road jerked his hand closer, and she gasped. The men laughed.

At the airport, Marisol fought the nausea that had built up during the long drive. The Sureños pushed her forward, and she straightened up, stifling the retching sensation. They walked her past leering security guards and customs agents, slipping pesos into their pockets.

At the gate, the leader said, "Talk to no one."

She took her seat on Frontier Flight 76 to Denver International Airport. When they were airborne, she looked out the window, searching for Arturo in the town below and wishing there had been another way.

CHAPTER

2

Monday, July 5
Denver, Colorado

D r. Bo Richards stared at the MRI images on the bank of monitors in front of him. He squirmed in his chair, tense from the silence of the roomful of doctors behind him. Finally he said, "I don't see anything wrong with this patient."

The senior resident next to him winced, and Bo's anxiety mounted. It took a lot to intimidate Bo. Only a year ago, he had survived a grueling surgical internship at Duke University, with the daily horror of ruptured intestines and amputated limbs. But he never felt the pressure he was now feeling. He sat in the darkened sanctuary of the neuroradiology reading room, surrounded by images of brain tumors, aneurysms, and spine diseases. Dr. C. R. Sylva, full professor of radiology at the University of Colorado Medical Center, had written the leading textbook in the field. If only he'd read it.

Bo studied the images of the four-year-old boy with new seizures. The clarity of the hospital's new MRI scanners offered almost unlimited diagnostic possibilities. Bo calmed himself and again searched for an abnormality. *There has to be a tumor lurking somewhere on these images. But where?* He worked his way from the frontal lobe to the cerebellum to the brain stem and still couldn't find the cause of this kid's problem.

"What if I told you the patient was right-handed?" Dr. Sylva asked.

Bo started to sweat. *How's that supposed to help me?* He felt like everyone in the room knew the answer except him. His oldest brother, Matt, would have already solved the puzzle. Hell, he would have already operated and saved the kid's life. But Bo didn't need to think about his brilliant brother now. He could do it himself. He just needed to try harder.

As much as Bo loved radiology, loved figuring out why people were sick or in pain, he still didn't like this method of teaching. Even after a year in the residency he hated being in the hot seat. Learning in surgery was so much easier: watch the operation, perform one under supervision, and then teach the next one. But in radiology, knowledge was acquired under pressure—like today. An unknown X-ray displayed on a monitor, with the professor taunting the hapless resident in front of a group of doctors glad it wasn't their turn.

"Would anyone like to help Dr. Richards?" Sylva asked, looking around the room for volunteers. More silence. The smell of stale coffee lingered. The phone rang.

Seizing the opportunity for a diversion, Bo answered the phone. "Neuro reading room."

"This is Rosie in MRI. I have a patient on the table who's short of breath. Can someone come over and take a look at her?"

"I'll be right there," Bo said. Bo stood, his lean frame stiff from this morning's run, and said, "Minor emergency in MRI. I'll be right back." He opened the door, thankful for the interruption, but curiosity prevailed and he turned around. "I give up. What's wrong with that patient?"

Dr. Sylva peered over his glasses. "Nothing, Bo. He's normal."

Nervous laughter filled the room.

"I don't like the new residents to start out too confident." Sylva smiled.

Bo chuckled politely and then hurried down the hall mumbling, "Asshole."

—◦◦◦❖◦◦◦—

The university had opened its luxurious MRI center six months ago. Unlike the rest of the hospital, which was starting to show its age, this facility was an architectural marvel. The waiting room reminded Bo of a hotel lobby, complete with water fountains, plush carpets, and relaxing couches. It even had a Starbucks in one corner. Valet parking was available to cater to an upscale outpatient clientele. It was clearly a major revenue center for the university.

Bo rushed downstairs to the basement and got lost in a maze of corridors. He stopped twice to ask directions before finally finding the hallway that connected the main hospital to the new imaging center.

"It's about time," Rosie said when Bo entered the control room. "I'm getting worried about this patient."

"Sorry. I got lost," Bo answered. "What's going on?"

Sharply dressed in clothes more suited to a businesswoman than a hospital employee, the MRI technologist said, "Mrs. Adcock is a breast cancer patient with back pain. She was doing fine until I gave her the injection of dye. She asked to come out to catch her breath. That's when I noticed her labored breathing and called you."

"Maybe it's just a panic attack."

"I hope so. And don't forget to take the metal out of your pockets."

Bo placed his beeper and keys on a desk and followed Rosie into the magnet room.

The patient turned her head at the sound of Rosie's high heels clicking across the tile floor. Mrs. Adcock's loose-fitting clothes did little to hide her gaunt appearance. A flowery scarf attempted to cover her bald head. She smiled at Bo with swollen, bluish lips. "I'm having trouble breathing," she said. The slurred words got Bo's attention. "And my tongue," she said, pointing to her open mouth, "feels too big."

Bo placed his hand under her neck and looked into her mouth. Her tongue was swollen twice its size and was blocking her airway. Bo felt his pulse quicken. He turned to Rosie. "She's having a reaction to the contrast. I need the radiology nurse, epinephrine, and some oxygen, quickly."

Rosie rushed to the phone. Bo turned back to Mrs. Adcock. "Just relax and take some slow, deep breaths." He reached for her thin wrist and felt a rapid pulse. Her chest heaved with each wheezy breath. She was running out of time.

Come on. Where's the epinephrine?

He patted her hand, trying to reassure her. She looked up at him with desperate eyes, and for a moment, they connected. He'd met her only minutes before, but somehow, on some level, he felt like he knew her and the fear she was experiencing. He remembered a professor in medical school who told him he'd never be a good doctor because he cared too much.

Mrs. Adcock seized his arm. "I can't get any air," she croaked, and then she blacked out.

"Shit," Bo muttered. "Call a code," he yelled to Rosie.

The first rule of all emergencies is to establish an airway and give oxygen. Bo searched the counters and drawers. He scanned the walls for oxygen tubing. Nothing.

"Where's all the emergency equipment?" Bo tried to hold back the panic. "You can do this," he said to himself. He remembered passing oxygen tanks on his way to the MRI center. He rushed into the control room and heard Rosie calling the code. He ran out of the MRI suite and into the hallway, where he spotted a cart of the familiar green cylinders. Bo picked one up like a football and rushed back to his patient. Suddenly Bo felt a strange tug on the tank in his arm and briefly thought Rosie had bumped into him. As he took one more step toward Mrs. Adcock, the canister was ripped out of his hands.

A shriek pierced the air as the room went dark. "You idiot," Rosie shouted. "That oxygen tank wasn't supposed to come in here."

Bo couldn't believe his bad luck. Of course he knew that some oxygen tanks were ferromagnetic and could be sucked into the powerful magnet, but he never imagined they would be right outside the MRI room. He cringed when he saw Mrs. Adcock's left leg bent at an awkward angle. If she had been any further in the gantry, the tank would have killed her.

Bo shook off his stupidity and came to the aid of the dying patient. Reacting out of instinct, he pulled the unconscious Mrs. Adcock onto a stretcher, supporting her broken leg. He grabbed an oral airway off the crash cart and inserted it into her mouth, pushing the swollen tongue out of the way. Rosie brought in the correct tank, and Bo started manually administering oxygen as they rushed down the hall to the ER. The code team met them in the hallway and took over.

Bo slumped against the wall and watched until they turned the corner.

Vince Flickinger, the "golden boy" chief resident came running down the hall. "Jesus, Bo, what the hell were you thinking? Were you sick the day we learned about magnetic field strength?"

"Sorry, Vince," Bo said, "I screwed up."

Vince's stern expression and red face contrasted with the laid-back, California surfer-dude image he usually portrayed. "You're damn right you did. I want you off the MRI rotation this instant."

The chief resident's nostrils flared, and spittle formed in the corner of his mouth.

Bo thought Vince was going to hit him.

"Get out of my sight. Just get out of the hospital," Vince said. "I need to talk to the chairman. Meet me in my office after lunch."

CHAPTER

3

On the plane, a large man wedged Marisol against the window and stared at her legs. She watched the clouds and fought the waves of nausea that kept erupting on the bumpy flight. She pulled out her rosary beads—thankful that one of the thugs let her take them—and prayed for Arturo after each round of Hail Marys. The smooth, black beads contrasted with the chipped, scarlet nail polish on her fingers.

Once during the flight, she rushed to vomit in the cramped toilet. She worried that the rubber balls might block her intestines. Would she need surgery to remove them? This might be better than the alternative, though. The man with the gun warned her that she would have to wash and reswallow any "accidents." Marisol returned to her seat and squeezed past the man who seemed a little too happy to help her scoot over his lap.

The landing petrified her. She closed her eyes as the plane roared to a stop and the seatbelt pushed against her swollen stomach. She didn't realize she was holding her breath until she gasped for air. She watched the passengers deplane, afraid to get out of her seat. She shivered and rubbed her thighs, focusing on the Sureños's instructions. She would be brave. She would not fail Arturo.

Marisol finally shuffled off the plane into Denver International Airport. The cramps slowed her progress down the long corridors. She turned down the wheelchair offered by a nice man, entered the long customs line, and took a deep breath. She clutched the passport the men had given her, afraid it would slip out of her sweaty hands.

9

Policemen with dogs roamed the room. They were looking at her. Could they tell she was a smuggler? Did they see her distended belly? She took another breath, but the air wouldn't fill her lungs. Her chest tightened like she was drowning. The room darkened. She shook her head and inched forward. She came to the yellow line and waited.

Her legs wobbled. The Sureños told her what she was supposed to do. They had it all worked out with the officials, they said. Marisol's breathing quickened and again she couldn't fill her lungs. She noticed the customs agent wave to her. She could do this. He motioned Marisol to his desk. His eyes were black and cold, and Marisol hesitated. She looked down at her new sandals and the tan lines from her old flip flops.

Another breath. A little more air.

She walked toward the customs agent and prayed. A halo of light started to form around his head and Marisol felt reassured. Maybe it was a sign from God. Then his head exploded into a ball of fire and Marisol noticed she was falling as the bright light turned to darkness.

CHAPTER

4

Vince, still fuming after Bo's screwup in MRI, cut off an elderly couple as he stormed out the front of the hospital. He hoped the brisk morning air and postcard view of the Rockies would relax him. For the last couple of weeks he'd been short-tempered and on edge. He didn't like it. He took a circuitous route and wandered through the patient tranquility garden, and by the time he entered the atrium of the MRI center, the pressure in his chest had begun to ease. Maybe he was just nervous about dinner tonight.

The lobby of the MRI center bustled with families and patients. The facility also maintained an attached surgical suite, run by his friend Dr. James Vanderworst, a gifted young neurosurgeon and medical director of the facility. Ever since the article on Vanderworst's new laser technique for disc herniations, business had boomed; the surgical schedule was so full they had to cancel their regular Thursday night club hopping. Vince was tempted to break the bad news about the MRI accident to James but decided to check on the damage to the scanner first.

He found Rosie in the magnet room, sullen-faced, staring at the gravity-defying green cylinder attached to the side of the magnet. She flashed Vince a disgusted look, as if he needed a reminder that their short, romantic relationship had ended badly last month.

"What exactly happened, Rocio?" Vince asked.

Rosie smirked at the use of her formal name. "I was on the phone calling a code when Dr. Richards slipped into the gantry room with the oxygen tank. There was nothing I could do."

"Why were the ferromagnetic tanks out in the hall in the first place?"

"Wait a minute. You're not going to blame me for this. It was your resident."

"I'm just trying to get the facts straight. The chairman is going to grill me about this."

"No you aren't, Vince. I know you better than that. You twist everything around so you look good—the great Vince Flickinger. Even when I found that bimbo in our bed, you—" Rosie's face reddened and she dropped to one knee.

Vince knelt next to her and put his arm around her. "I apologized for that a long time ago, Rosie."

"No. It's not that." Rosie gasped and clutched her chest, her eyes widened in panic. "I can't breathe. My chest hurts." She looked up at Vince with a bewildered expression before collapsing.

Vince knelt to feel her pulse when he felt an uncomfortable sensation in his own chest, like a band tightening around him. He couldn't take a deep breath. His vision started to blur. He looked back at Rosie—her eyes were closed and she wasn't moving.

His mind sluggish, Vince had the sense to glance at the monitor across the room. The blurry readout confirmed his suspicion: the oxygen level in the room was plummeting. They had to get out of here fast. He grabbed Rosie's leg and started to pull her toward the door, but his weak muscles wouldn't cooperate.

"Come on. Help me out, Rosie," he urged, but she remained motionless on the floor.

He tugged harder, and the chief tech started to move. He gradually inched her toward the door, his strength fading with each step. The room darkened; the exit loomed far away.

"Vince?"

He heard the voice and turned his head as he slumped to the ground.

Thank God, Bo is back. "Help." Vince gasped for air and pointed to the oxygen monitor.

Bo dashed into the room, grabbed Vince's arm, and dragged him into the control room.

A minute later Rosie lay beside him and Bo returned with an oxygen tank.

Vince latched on to the mask and devoured the air. His vision gradually returned and the chest pain eased.

"I think it's time Rosie got some of that, Vince."

"I need more brain cells than she does," Vince mumbled.

Bo wrenched the mask away and placed it over Rosie's mouth.

CHAPTER

5

Marisol opened her eyes and panicked. A large, dark man in a uniform leaned over her, holding a bag over her mouth. She looked up at his serious eyes and a crowd of onlookers staring at her and she screamed. He took the bag away from her mouth. She sat up and noticed the wetness between her legs.

Once, when she was sixteen years old, she collapsed in church on a hot Sunday morning. Her friends still remind her of that embarrassing day. One moment Marisol was standing in front of the priest, her mouth open and tongue ready for the communion wafer, and the next moment she was lying on a couch in the sacristy, drenched in sweat and feeling nauseated, looking at her mother's worried face. The doctor said she was dehydrated, but her friends joked that the Lord had punished her for kissing her boyfriend on Saturday night.

The black man picked Marisol up and placed her in a wheelchair. He pushed her down a corridor to an empty room, and she was glad to be away from the prying eyes and the noise of the passengers.

"Stay here," he said and left her alone.

Marisol looked around the tiny room and waited. She recognized a portrait of President Barack Obama on the wall behind a large shiny wooden desk. Paperless and uncluttered, only a phone interrupted its smooth surface. The room was barren except for a couple of chairs around the desk. She imagined this is what a jail cell would feel like and she began to panic again. What would the Americans do to her when they found out about the cocaine? Send her back to Mexico? Put her in prison? She'd never see Arturo and Hector again.

She jumped when two officials entered the room. She remembered the man with the angry, black eyes. He took a seat behind the desk and looked at her passport. A female official in the same uniform sat next to Marisol and smiled. Marisol admired the graceful way the woman crossed her legs and placed her manicured hands over her knees.

"Do you speak English?" the man asked, looking up from the passport.

"Yes, pretty well," Marisol said.

The woman handed Marisol a blanket before asking her about the purpose of her visit to the United States. The Sureños had prepared Marisol for these questions. She told the officials that she was visiting family in Denver for a couple of days. No, she didn't have a return ticket yet since she didn't know how long she would be here. No, she wasn't carrying drugs and she didn't have any luggage.

The angry man didn't look convinced. He picked up the phone and mumbled something Marisol couldn't hear. His greasy fingers smeared the shine on the desk as he glared at her. The silence was overwhelming. She knew she was going to jail.

The door opened and a woman entered. She wore colorful, baggy clothes that Marisol had only seen in the hospital when Arturo was born. The yellow top was covered with pictures of birds and the orange pants slipped below her waist, held by a loose string. She might have been pretty except for the dark circles under her tired eyes.

"My name is Melissa," she said, tightening the string around her pants. "I'm here to take an X-ray of your belly."

Marisol tensed. The Sureños told her not to worry about X-rays, but what if they were wrong? What if the X-rays could see the drugs? She'd be thrown in jail and never see her family again.

Melissa stood there waiting for Marisol to respond. "Do you understand?"

"Yes," Marisol said, "X-ray picture."

"Right. Now I need to know if you are pregnant."

Marisol shook her head.

Melissa wheeled her out the door, and the customs officials followed them into a big room, empty except for a skinny table in the middle. A gray box hovered from the ceiling, and three thick cords snaked under the table. Marisol took off her sundress and wet panties in the changing room and put on a pink paper gown. Melissa helped her onto the cold surface, moved the scary contraption over her belly, and told her to stay still. Marisol looked away from the machine and watched the technologist walk into the next room and stand behind a glass barrier. The pungent disinfectant on the table made her feel nauseated again. She closed her eyes and prayed that the Sureños were right—that the coins they'd made her swallow would block the X-rays and hide the cocaine.

Marisol felt a motor whir under the table and heard a short beep.

"Great," Melissa said, returning to the room. "Why don't you put on these old scrub pants until you can get your clothes cleaned? I don't need them anyway."

"Thank you," Marisol said. "God bless you."

"After you're changed, come back to the wheelchair. It could take a few minutes to get these X-rays read."

Marisol pulled on the dry cotton pants, thankful for Melissa's generosity. Maybe everything would turn out okay. She stood up, wobbled, and sat back down. She didn't want to black out again. She took a couple of deep breaths and slumped into the wheelchair. She started to relax. She thought of the first time she met Hector, at a soccer party on the beach. She could still remember the easy way his muscular legs glided over the sand, darting around the defense, and the nervous smile he gave her after each goal.

She was startled as a siren pierced the sterile quiet and the official with the angry black eyes stormed in, gun drawn, and pointed it at her.

Marisol shrieked, jumped out of the wheelchair, and ran.

CHAPTER

6

B o hesitated outside the door to the chief resident's office and stared at the gold-embossed name plate, "Vincent P. Flickinger, MD." He felt like a grade-schooler being sent to the principal's office and berated himself. He had made an honest mistake. He was trying to save the patient's life, after all. He finally opened the door and walked in.

Vince was talking on the phone and motioned Bo to the couch.

The chief residency is a unique position of honor and prestige in the medical training hierarchy, one rung below the assistant professors. The chief provides a buffer between the overworked residents and the administration. And more importantly, the chief controls the schedule, including the onerous night call and has the potential to be the resident's worst enemy.

Dr. Musk, chairman of the department of radiology for as long as anyone could remember, selected the chief resident from the upcoming fourth-year residents in an elaborate ceremony each May. Years of speculation and competition ended on that day. The chairman wanted a bright, hardworking, and personable chief, and most years there were many candidates. They all wanted the powerful position and the lucrative job offers that accompanied it. Private practice groups boasted about the former chief residents in their partnerships like law firms who hired chief justice clerks. Signing bonuses were common.

Bo sat on the couch, disturbed by the quiet. He sneaked a look at Vince: the chief resident tugged a clump of hair and glared back at

Bo. *Okay, this isn't going to go well,* Bo thought. *Better just apologize and get out of here.*

Vince dominated the race for the chief residency since his first year of training. He started the program with a fund of knowledge that usually took years of reading and practice. His speed and accuracy were legendary. Medical and surgical residents sought his advice. Before they were finished describing their patients' symptoms, Vince would have the diagnosis. And then he'd tell them how to treat their patients, which antibiotics or interventions worked best. Vince was the shining star of the program. Musk had selected him to represent the radiology department at the stressful grand rounds with the other departments. Perhaps it helped to have been a competitive surfer braving the pounding, dangerous waves, but Vince never faltered under pressure. No one had ever seen him lose his cool. At least until now.

"That was Musk," Vince said, slamming the phone into the receiver. "I've never heard him so upset. You're lucky he's out of town."

"Vince—" Bo started to say before being cut off.

"Wait. I know that oxygen tank shouldn't have been in the building, much less outside the scanner. I'm going to look into that. And I owe you my life." The phone interrupted Vince, who stared at it for few rings before answering, "Yes, sir."

A surprised look turned to anger and he shouted, "I told you I'll have it by Saturday." Vince's face turned scarlet. Ignoring Bo, he moaned and walked into his private bathroom.

Stunned, Bo sat and waited. Several minutes passed. He heard water running. He looked over at the muted television, replaying this morning's stage of the Tour de France. Until moving to Colorado, he had never lived in a place where anyone cared about a professional bike race, much less watched it. His long bike rides in North Carolina were interrupted by rednecks in pickups throwing crushed beer cans at him. Sometimes, if they hadn't finished the beer, they'd sneak their trucks up behind him, blare their horns, and laugh at his startled reaction.

The bathroom door opened and Vince returned. He looked flushed. His face was damp. He said, "The oxygen tank damaged the scanner when it was sucked into the magnet. The damage caused the magnet to quench. You know what that is, don't you?"

Bo nodded. The worst thing that could happen to the magnet and anyone in the vicinity was a quench. He had seen pictures of an explosion in Georgia during an installation. Luckily the machine was in the parking lot and no one was seriously injured. He didn't completely understand the physics, but the MRI magnet was able to keep its strength, even after the power was turned off, by the cooling effects of liquid helium. If the MRI machine heated up, even a little, the liquid helium turned into a gas and an explosion could occur in seconds.

Vince continued. "Fortunately, the magnet didn't blow up. But it did break the ventilation system, which eliminates the helium from the room. That's why Rosie and I collapsed and nearly died."

Bo suppressed the urge to apologize again.

"Look, Bo, I know this has been a tough day for you. Cory died a year ago today, right?"

"I'm surprised you remembered."

"I really liked your girlfriend. I was stunned when she was killed. Why don't you take the afternoon off before your night shift? Take a break and get your head together."

"Thanks, Vince."

"I'll work on Musk. He wants a meeting tomorrow morning. Let's hope he doesn't fire you."

CHAPTER

7

The wheelchair rolled into the changing room as Marisol darted away. She entered the control room, pushed Melissa out of the way, and hurried to the door. Marisol pulled the handle and froze with terror when the locked door didn't budge. She turned back to the door, looked at the bewildered X-ray tech, and slid to the floor crying.

The alarm stopped blaring and the customs lady walked over and looked down at Marisol. "It was a false alarm. I'm sorry it scared you," she said, offering her hand.

Marisol stood up and returned to the wheelchair, feeling stupid and embarrassed. Surely they must suspect her of smuggling after her crazy behavior. Why else would she run? Marisol pulled out her rosary beads and prayed while she waited.

About twenty minutes later, the two customs officials entered the room.

Marisol looked up and tried to read their faces. Were they about to arrest her and send her to prison, never to see Arturo and his pink cheeks again?

The woman handed Marisol her passport and said, "Your X-ray is clear. You are free to leave. Sorry for the inconvenience."

Marisol blinked in dismay. They were letting her go? Maybe she'd get through this after all.

The official was still looking at her. "Are you okay to walk, or do you need the wheelchair?"

"I'll be okay." Marisol stood up. She followed the two officials out of the dark X-ray room and squinted as she entered the main terminal. They walked past the passengers in the customs line, led her to an escalator, and pointed out the exit. She got on the moving staircase, steadied herself on the handrail, and waved back at the officials. As she ascended, her spirits rose too, and she felt that her prayers had been answered.

She whispered, "I'll be home soon, Arturo."

Marisol stepped off the escalator and waded through a sea of waiting friends and family members. She looked around, overwhelmed at the enormous room and the throngs of people all talking on cell phones. Two older men in cowboy hats gave directions. She saw signs for baggage and stepped around moving carts filled with luggage.

As she moved around an elderly couple she felt a tug on her arm. A skinny, pale-faced man grinned at her. Her eyes caught a jagged scar under his chin and she hesitated.

"I'm Miguel," he said, grabbing her elbow firmer, and she followed him outside. He led her to the backseat of a large black limousine, sat beside her, and shouted for the driver to hurry up. With shaking hands the skinny man fidgeted with the wires of his headphones before managing to get them into his ears. As his head started rocking to an unknown beat, the scar turned blood red and Marisol turned away from the sight. The black car sped out of the airport.

She looked out the window, dry swallowing to stop the nausea. She spotted tall mountains with white peaks in the distance. She'd only seen photos of them when she dusted off the big picture books at her part-time hotel job.

The car left the highway and drove down crowded streets. She craned her neck but couldn't see the tops of the buildings surrounding her. Rich people in fancy suits walked between the skyscrapers, oblivious to Marisol's pain. Waiting at a stoplight, she noticed a statue of Saint Francis of Assisi outside a church and mumbled a silent prayer. At the next corner, the car turned on to a deserted street. A huge door stuttered open and they drove into a warehouse.

A group of young men were smoking, and they stared at Marisol as she stepped out of the car. They yelled at her and laughed, but she didn't hear what was so funny.

Miguel led her to a windowless room and told her to sit and wait. Black and green mold covered the cinderblock walls. Her feet stuck to the floor, and a gooey liquid oozed into the drain in the middle of the room. A single anemic fan did little to improve the putrid smell, and Marisol ran through the open bathroom door to vomit in the seatless toilet.

Miguel returned accompanied by a huge, bald man. "I'm going back to the airport," Miguel said. "Hugo will show you what to do."

Without warning, Hugo shoved Marisol back into the bathroom. She tripped and sprawled onto the disgusting floor. Hugo entered and bent over to pick her up, and Marisol spotted a red-blue birthmark on the top of his smooth scalp. Hugo pointed out the "seat" and explained how she was to evacuate the bolitas. He said he'd be back soon, that she should hurry up because El Jefe needed the cocaine tomorrow.

Marisol walked to the corner and looked at the disgusting contraption. She pulled down the scrub pants Melissa had given her at the airport, sat on the hard wooden surface, closed her eyes, and tried to relax.

CHAPTER

8

Bo drove from Denver, past his condo in Boulder, and up the windy road to Estes Park. He never found out why his girlfriend, Cory, had been driving out here that day. He parked his truck in a pull out next to a couple of Subarus and climbed down the boulders to the St. Vrain River. He shuddered at the thought of his her car tumbling down the embankment. He crossed a well-used running trail and sat on a rock beside the river.

Bo had never been to the scene of Cory's accident and had been dreading the one-year anniversary. He'd been at a medical conference, lounging around the pool after one of the sessions, when he got the call. He should have invited Cory to the meeting, and the guilt had been eating him up for the past year.

Bo looked at the photo he brought for the occasion. It was his favorite memory of their five-year relationship, taken at a rock quarry the day after they met. The night before, at a party Bo and his second-year medical student roommates hosted, he was surprised to find himself chatting with this petite nurses' student with toned, tanned arms and a short skirt that accentuated her runner's legs. And he was even more surprised that this beautiful woman accepted his invitation to join him at the quarry.

When Cory arrived with her roommates on that sunny August day, Bo and his friends were already swimming in the cold, deep water and warming up on the rocks. She looked stunning in a bikini and more toned than Bo realized from the previous night. Her friends were lively and funny and the afternoon passed quickly.

At the end of the day the group gathered at the top of the quarry, daring each other to jump off the thirty-foot ledge. Despite his confidence in the water, Bo didn't like the idea of leaping into the dark, ominous pit with unknown hazards beneath the surface. One by one, he watched his friends disappear over the edge with a yelp and a splash. Bo inched his way to the rim and peered down at his waving buddies. He stepped back a few feet to get up his courage. Cory was right behind him. She kissed him, grabbed his hand, and the two of them flew off into space hand in hand.

The picture captured them in midair: muscles taut, eyes wide with excitement, mouths open in a silent, endless yell. Bo said a silent prayer as the picture blurred with his tears. Finally he got up, stretched his stiff neck from side to side, and headed back to the trail. Time to get back to work.

It happened so fast Bo didn't have time to react.

A black blur darted out in front, tripping Bo and sending him sprawling to the ground. He rolled away from the animal, terror setting in.

A woman's voice screamed out, "I'm so sorry. Are you okay?"

Bo struggled to a sitting position and wiped the gravel off his knees and hands, not sure what just happened. "Yeah, I guess so."

"That was Lucy. She was chasing a squirrel. I thought she was doing better on voice control. I feel terrible." The black lab sauntered back to her owner, tail wagging, oblivious to the havoc she had caused.

Bo's picture skittered away toward the river. The runner ran after it and grabbed the photo before it reached the bank. She stared at the picture as she walked back.

Her eyes widened with surprise and she said, "Oh my God! Are you Bo?"

Bo looked at her for the first time. She was young, probably late twenties, thin—not gaunt like a marathon runner—and very tan. An auburn ponytail, pulled through a Colorado Buffaloes cap, sparkled in the late afternoon sun. She held an empty leash in one hand and a water bottle in the other and looked down at Bo with apologetic, hazel eyes that shimmered in the reflected light.

"Do I know you?" Bo asked, standing up and taking the picture.

"I was here the day she died," the runner said, pointing to the picture. "I haven't been able to get it out of my mind since then. That's why I'm running here today."

Bo didn't know what to say. He had so many questions.

"I held her hand while the paramedics climbed down the rocks."

"My God. Was she still alive?"

"She was in and out of consciousness."

"How do you know my name?"

"Her last words," the runner hesitated, struggling with the words. She wiped her eyes. "I'm sorry. It still upsets me."

"What did she say?"

"Tell Bo I love him."

CHAPTER

9

Sheri Masterson looked up from the computer monitor when Bo entered the reading room. She was one of his best friends in the residency and an actual Southern belle who grew up on a tobacco plantation in eastern North Carolina.

"You're as white as a Klan rally," Sheri said in her southern drawl.

"I just came from the scene of Cory's accident."

Sheri stood up and hugged him. "Sorry. I forgot today was the day. Do you want me to do the night shift for you?"

"No. It'll keep my mind occupied. Besides, after my screwup this morning, Musk might fire me tomorrow."

"For that little MRI thang?" Sheri batted her eyes.

"It's no joke, Sheri. I almost killed the patient. And I damaged the new MRI scanner. It's going to need some major repairs."

"Ouch. If you do get fired, could we have one quickie before you leave?"

Bo rolled his eyes.

"Come on, Bo. You know I'm just trying to help. This will blow over. You're the smartest resident in our class. You've got to screw up a lot more than that to get fired. It's not like you chopped off the wrong leg or put in the wrong heart. Come to think of it, weren't you at Duke for the famous hydraulic fluid fuckup?"

"Do all Southern belles have trash mouths?"

Sheri smirked.

Bo remembered the incident. During routine cleaning of the elevators, the used hydraulic fluid was collected in an unmarked industrial-sized drum. A custodian placed the drum on the loading dock the same day as an incoming shipment of surgical cleaning fluid, and the unthinkable happened: surgical equipment was immersed in the oily hydraulic fluid, and it wasn't until surgeons started dropping instruments on a regular basis that the problem was discovered. Fortunately, no patients were harmed, but a public-relations nightmare ensued and the national media camped outside the hospital for weeks.

"Let's hope the newspapers don't get wind of my screwup."

Sheri logged off the computer and started gathering her books. "Well, I've got a hot date with my anatomy book. Maybe I'll stop by later with some old-fashioned southern cooking."

"You're too nice, but I'll be fine, Sheri."

Sheri left, and Bo settled in for a long night in the reading room. A computer workstation dominated one wall, and four large monitors provided the only light in the room. Well-worn books filled the shelves to the right, and a threadbare couch on the opposite wall stood ready if Bo got a break tonight. An automatic coffee maker, a gift from the hospital auxiliary, completed the sparse furnishings and was conveniently located next to the bathroom.

Despite the terrible hours, Bo enjoyed the action of the night shift. At six each night, as if a factory whistle blew, the faculty and residents hurried to the parking deck. One junior resident remained to cover the urgent X-rays, CAT scans, and MRIs. The volume of work could be overwhelming at times, but Bo liked the challenge and importance of the decisions. It got to the core of his decision to enter radiology: figuring out what's wrong with the patients. Is Joey's arm broken? Does mom have appendicitis? Has grandpa's cancer spread? Is the star quarterback's season over with a torn ACL? *Is it a stroke, Doc?* Bo loved answering the questions; he relished the challenge and the opportunity to make a difference.

He really hoped he still had a job tomorrow.

CHAPTER

10

Vince leaned back in the plush chair, cradling a glass of fine port as the waiter scraped away the few crumbs from the starched-white tablecloth. The sun had long-ago descended below the Rockies, and the streetlights sparkled through the spotless windows of Ralph's Bistro. In contrast to the humble name, this was downtown Denver's finest restaurant, the waiting list months long.

To his left, he heard muffled tones of serious business negotiations; on the right was a more boisterous yet refined birthday celebration. He turned toward a joyous shriek as a young man on one knee presented to a beautiful woman a box that would change their lives forever.

The waiter refilled the water glasses, leaving Vince alone with his dinner partner.

The succulent shrimp appetizer, tender prime rib, and crème brûlée had been spectacular; the conversation effortless. Best of all, D. Arthur Hammond, MD, president of Radiology Associates of Southern California (RASC), the most prestigious radiology group in the state, was smiling. Vince had been waiting for this moment his entire life. He relaxed and listened as Dr. Hammond extolled the virtues of working at RASC. But Vince already knew them. Every resident in the country wanted this job and hundreds had applied. Over the last sixty years, RASC had acquired multiple outpatient imaging centers in the best locations in Orange County, catering to the well-insured populace. Salaries were exorbitant; partners retired in their fifties.

"You know, Dr. Flickinger, it's been five years since we added our last partner. Positions open up so rarely at RASC," Hammond said. He wiped an imaginary crumb off the table and added, "In fact, no one has left our group except for retirement."

"Sounds like *The Firm*," Vince joked.

Hammond laughed. "I haven't heard that before. However, at RASC, we don't need the mafia. We make money the old fashioned way: we earn it—and lots of it, I might add."

Hammond reached into his briefcase and removed a manila envelope. Placing it on the table, he crossed his hands over the document and smiled at Vince. "I have good news, Dr. Flickinger."

This is it, Vince thought. *I'm going to get the job.*

A shout from the front of the restaurant interrupted Vince's attention and he lifted his eyes over the left shoulder of the senior partner. His stomach tensed and he stifled a gasp; a sip of port caught in his windpipe and he coughed.

This can't be happening. Vince tried not to panic. No way was that jerk arguing with the maître de going to ruin his life. Vince had worked too hard to get here. For the last nine years after college, while his university buddies bought condos and cars, he'd been busting his ass studying in the library and spending endless nights on call in the hospital. The man had to be stopped.

"Before you start," Vince said, straining to keep his voice calm, "could you excuse me for a second? I guess I'm overhydrated."

As soon as Hammond nodded, Vince slid his chair back and hurried to the front of the restaurant, straight toward the ridiculously dressed man arguing with the maître de.

"That's the guy." The man pointed to Vince. Tacky gold necklaces nestled in the abundant gray hair that sprouted from the vest of the man's leisure suit. Despite the platform shoes, Vince could see the bull's-eye bald spot in the center of his greasy hair.

The owner, Ralph himself, who must have sensed a brewing altercation that wouldn't help his restaurant ratings, came over to assist.

"I'll take care of this," Vince said to Ralph as he grabbed the intruder's polyester coat and pushed him into the bathroom.

"What the hell do you think you're doing, Ramón?" Vince shouted and shoved the man against the urinal. "I'm in the most important meeting of my life."

"Not my problem, Doc. I got my own priorities, you know." Ramón dusted off the suit. "The people I work for don't care that you're some big shot doctor."

Vince reached into his pants. "Here's $500. You'll have the rest on Saturday." Vince watched Ramón count the money before shoving it inside his coat pocket.

"Saturday might be too late," Ramón said. "But I know where to find you, Doc."

Vince watched the man leave. He washed his face with cold water and walked out to the restaurant. With a reassuring nod, Vince smiled at the owner and rejoined his dinner partner.

"Sorry about the interruption, sir," Vince said in his most polite voice, straining to keep the inner rage at bay. "Where were we?" He hoped the partner would continue his acceptance offer.

"Are you feeling all right, Dr. Flickinger?"

"Yes. Why do you ask?"

"Your nose is bleeding."

CHAPTER

11

"Trauma team activation, five minutes."

The overhead speakers blasted, startling Bo from his daydream. The night had been slow and he must have dozed off. He picked his head off his drooled-wet arm, stood up, and hustled down the short hallway to the ER control station.

Nurses, X-ray techs, and respiratory therapists assembled, alerted by the announcement, ready for the ambulance to arrive.

Bo spotted Vonda, the CT tech for the emergency room, and asked, "Do you know what's going on?"

"Two-car collision, three victims," she replied.

Dr. Sal Martinez tied the straps of his yellow gown around his thin waist, slipped the plastic splash shield over his face, and strode out to the loading dock. In the trauma rooms, ER techs stood by with IV fluids, EKG leads, and a portable ultrasound machine. The hospital remodeled the emergency room last year, striving for efficiency and safety. X-ray tubes hung from the ceiling, ready for rapid pictures of the seriously injured patients. The digital images appeared on computer monitors in the room—no more waiting for films to be developed in the dark room. A new CT scanner across the hall accommodated the more seriously ill patients.

Bo had watched the paramedics wheel the three accident victims into the ER. An elderly couple lost control of their car on I-70 and crashed into a Ford Escape driven by a sixteen-year-old high school boy. Dr. Martinez moved from patient to patient, making a quick assessment and ordering studies.

Bo listened to the sounds of modern medicine: the slicing of scissors through jeans; the whirring and beep of the X-ray generators; the squeaking shoes of scurrying nurses; the soft groaning of the patient strapped to the backboard. The efficiency impressed Bo. He'd moonlighted in several rural ERs in North Carolina, and the process there had been anything but smooth.

The elderly male driver sustained a head injury and was disoriented. Vonda wheeled him over for a head CT, which Bo read as normal. The man's wife moaned in pain, and Bo winced in sympathy when he saw her dislocated hip.

The sixteen-year-old had suffered the most severe injuries. According to the paramedics on the scene, the elderly couple's car had impacted the driver's side door. The fire department had to cut the car door to extricate the kid. Bo stood outside the room with Sal, waiting for the X-rays to be displayed on the computer monitor.

"How's he look?" Bo asked.

"Not great. His pulse is weak, but his vital signs are holding steady. He'll probably need a CT." Looking up at the monitor, Sal asked, "What's that?"

Bo pointed out several left rib fractures and a collapsed lung. As if on cue, Dr. Mark Nicolai, the attending general surgeon, blustered in out of breath. Nicolai was a large, round, balding bully with a reputation for belittling OR techs and throwing instruments around when things didn't go his way. Bo heard the stories but hadn't met the man until tonight.

"This better be important," the surgeon said to Sal, ignoring Bo, as he looked up at the X-rays on the monitor. After reviewing the films and examining the patient, Dr. Nicolai inserted the chest tube with the ease and precision of an experienced plumber installing a pipe fitting. In fact, as Nicolai bent over to insert the tubing into the kit on the floor, his pants slipped down, giving Bo a visual he didn't need.

Bo remembered the first chest tube he put in as a new surgical intern; it didn't go as smoothly as this. The trick was to apply just enough pressure to pierce the stubborn tissue between the ribs, but not go too deep and puncture the lung inside. Bo had thought he was pushing hard enough—the patient was writhing in pain—but couldn't get through the darn ribs. Finally his senior resident backup pulled him aside and encouraged Bo to be more aggressive, to just go for it. With this reassurance, Bo had set aside his fears and popped between the ribs and was met with the satisfying rush of air.

Nicolai came out of the room and said, "Are you the radiologist?"

"Yes, sir. Dr. Richards. Nice to meet you."

"Get this kid over to CT. His belly feels rigid and I'm worried about him. He might have a ruptured spleen."

Bo helped Vonda transport the boy down to the CT room. They slid the moaning teenager on to the table and connected the dye injector to his IV. Vonda typed in the scan parameters, and twenty seconds later—the speed still amazed Bo—images of the boy's head, chest, and abdomen appeared on the screen. Vonda moved aside so Bo could sit down and study the hundreds of individual sections through the body. He asked Vonda to page his senior backup, Roger Simons.

Dr. Nicolai strutted into the CT suite complaining that his night was ruined. He pulled up a chair and joined Vonda and the ER nurses looking over Bo's shoulder. Bo felt the tension rising. He wished he could read as fast as Vince, his chief resident, who'd been known to look at five hundred to one thousand images in seconds with amazing accuracy.

"What's that?" Nicolai yelled, despite the close quarters. Bo caught a faint scent of scotch on the surgeon's breath.

"I just started looking at the images. Could you please give me a minute?" Bo tried to block out the hovering surgeon and concentrated on the images before him, reminding himself to look at every organ; he didn't want to miss anything.

The ER nurse looked over at the patient monitor. "Dr. Nicolai, his blood pressure is dropping! What do you want to do?"

"I want this damn radiologist to tell me what's wrong with this kid. In the meantime get him back to the ER and increase his fluids. And get some blood from the lab for a possible transfusion." Nicolai looked back at Bo, slurring his words. "Well, what's it going to be, son?"

Bo didn't look up from the computer screen. He had shuffled through the images once and was starting on his second look. *This guy is plastered. And where the hell is my backup?*

"All right," Bo said, wishing he had more time to analyze the images. "He has multiple rib fractures. Your chest tube looks good and his lung is almost completely re-expanded."

"Tell me something I don't know."

"I see a small amount of blood in his abdomen but I'm not sure where it's coming from. His liver and kidneys look okay. His spleen looks a little unusual to me. It's kind of splotchy and I'm worried about laceration through this part of the spleen, but I'm not sure. Could we wait a couple of minutes for my senior resident to see if he agrees?"

"No," Nicolai shouted with a volume out of place for the small CT control room. "I need to know right now. I'm not going to sit on a ruptured spleen while you damn radiologists can't make up your mind."

Bo felt the acrid taste of his last cup of coffee rising in his throat and swallowed hard. He glanced up from the monitor, looked through the leaded glass window, and watched the ER tech move the teenager back onto the gurney. Streaks of dark blood covered his muscular arms, and his lips were swollen to grotesque proportions. Poor kid. He squirmed on the backboard and tried to free himself from the restraints, too disoriented to realize they were for his protection.

"What's it going to be, Dr. Richards?" the surgeon taunted.

I'm not going to let this kid die. "I'm worried about the spleen. That's all I can say now."

Nicolai stumbled out of the room fuming. "Get the OR ready."

"What a jerk," Vonda said as the surgeon left the room.

"These images are hard enough to read without that arrogant bastard standing over my shoulder. Did you get a whiff of anything funny?"

"That's single malt. Everyone knows he has a drinking problem." The techs always knew the inside scoop on the doctors. "Ever since his divorce, he's gotten worse. He used to just be rude, now he's drunk and belligerent. We've written him up a few times, but the hospital administration never does anything. I think he's drinking buddies with half the board of directors."

Bo returned to the reading room and plopped down on the couch. The adrenalin rush from the trauma patients had worn off, replaced by exhaustion. He laid back and closed his eyes.

When he opened them again, Roger Simons stood over him. "What's up, Bo? I just got your page."

Bo looked at his watch. He'd been asleep for more than an hour. "We had a multitrauma come through the ER a little bit ago," Bo said, sitting up. "I had trouble deciding about a teenager's spleen. Dr. Nicolai was pressuring me and didn't want to wait for you." Bo stretched his arms and yawned. "And I think he was drunk."

Roger moved over to the computer. "Yeah, he's got a problem. But he's a technically gifted surgeon and hasn't had any complications, at least yet. Let me have a look at that case."

Bo joined Roger at the workstation. After a quick review of the images, Roger said, "I see what you mean. The spleen does look a little weird. But sometimes, when the contrast goes in quickly, it can look like that."

The reading room door swung open and Nicolai barged in red-faced and breathing hard. The surgeon looked enormous in the extralarge white scrubs, reminding Bo of the Pillsbury Dough Boy. He marched in and stood close to Bo, preventing him from standing up. "Hey, Richards. What are they teaching you here? There was nothing wrong with that kid's spleen. Maybe you should go tell his parents why he'll have a scar for the rest of his life."

Bo pushed his chair to the side so he could stand up. He wasn't going to be intimidated by this guy, even if he was a senior surgeon. "Dr. Nicolai," Bo said, trying to keep his composure, "I told you I wasn't sure about the spleen. I wanted a second opinion from Dr. Simons."

"Sometimes we can't wait while you guys sit back and drink coffee. We've got patients to take care of. The kid's pressure was dropping and something had to be done." He walked away from Bo, and before leaving the room said, "I'm going to have a chat with your chairman, Dr. Musk, tomorrow morning."

CHAPTER

12

Marisol sat and strained on the disgusting seat, hoping to pass the bolitas. She spent the night pacing, squatting, and praying for the one bowel movement that would take her away from all of this, back home to Hector and Arturo. So far she had expelled only half of the packages. Throughout the long night, she cursed herself for not being more forceful with Hector. If she had only stopped him, none of this would be happening.

When Hector first mentioned the trip, she was suspicious. She knew the Sureños were involved, knew they controlled the drug traffic and prostitution in the Baja, and knew the stories of ruthless killings. But Hector insisted this was different. His friend Pedro, a soccer player from his childhood, had ridden the route many times without problems. He only needed help this one time since his driver was sick.

Hector and Marisol had missed the last three rent payments, and the landlord was getting nasty. The chicken plant remained closed, and Hector couldn't find another job. Marisol took night shifts at the sewing factory after working at the hotel all day, but the bills kept mounting. Pedro's offer would cover all their debts and allow them to stay in their home.

Pedro picked up Hector the next morning, and Marisol kissed him before they drove away.

"You don't have to do this, Hector," she reminded him.

"I'll be back tonight. I love you."

Marisol worked at the sewing factory that evening, her mind distracted with worry. Twice she was reprimanded for daydreaming. When she got home Hector still hadn't returned. She ate alone, put Arturo to bed, and waited on the dark porch. She must have dozed because when she opened her eyes, Hector was standing before her, hands bloody, arms scratched, jeans ripped. And he was shaking with fear.

"Oh, Marisol. I'm in trouble," he said and dropped to the floor.

Marisol picked him up, bathed him, and bandaged his wounds. She waited for Hector to explain.

"Everything started out so easily," he said and told Marisol about the terrible trip. They had picked up the packages by noon and were heading back home on the beach road when Hector heard a couple of loud pops. One of the front tires blew out and the truck started to spin out of control, but Hector managed to bring it to a stop without crashing into the sea. That's when he saw Pedro slumped forward, held in place by his seatbelt, blood pouring out of his head. In the side-view mirror Hector saw men with rifles approaching the truck. He grabbed Pedro's pistol, jumped out, and ran to the front of the truck and waited, trying to decide what to do. There was nowhere to run. On the beach side was a rocky cliff with a forty-foot drop into the rough sea. On the other side were sandy dirt bike trails, where he'd be exposed.

Hector fired Pedro's gun to stop them and ran to the cliff. He leapt into the air, bullets ricocheting off the rocks, and dropped into the rough water, barely missing a rock. He sank deep into the sea, spinning and turning, trying not to panic when he couldn't tell which way was up. Finally he surfaced, gasping for air. He looked up and saw the men searching for him. After hiding behind a big boulder and getting thrashed around, he spotted a cave. He timed the waves, swam as fast as he could into the narrow opening, and rested on a ledge.

"I was never so scared in my life. All I thought about was you and Arturo. I'm so, so sorry Marisol."

"Did the men come down there?"

"No. I waited in the cave until the tide rose and climbed back up the rocks. The truck and the men with guns were gone."

"Poor Pedro."

"They threw his body onto the rocks before they drove off."

"What about the Sureños?"

"They're going to be mad about the truck. And the lost merchandise. The Sureños boss in the states, Mateo 'El Piojo' Sanchez, is going to send his men after me, I'm sure."

"El Piojo?"

"Pedro told me one of the rival gangs nicknamed him 'The Louse' because he looks like the bloodsucking parasite."

The next day Hector didn't come home, and the Sureños forced her to swallow the condoms. And now here she was, sitting on this disgusting seat, trying to expel the drugs so she could get back to her family.

The door squeaked open and Marisol covered her private parts with her hands, embarrassed.

Hugo stood at the doorway, his nose scrunched. "Finished?" he asked.

"Not yet. Maybe halfway; it's slow."

"Get up and follow me," he demanded. "Don Mateo wants to meet you."

Marisol stood, pulled up her scrub pants, and followed the man out the open door. He led her upstairs to a nice, clean-smelling room complete with a kitchen table, couch, and refrigerator. She noticed a soccer game on the large television, a Spanish announcer yelling. The bald man stood next to the door and motioned for Marisol to sit at the table.

Mateo Sanchez entered the kitchen. He wore a purple shirt under a shiny dark suit. Not a single lock strayed from his slick, jet-black hair, and the strong scent of cologne followed him as he crossed behind Marisol and sat next to her. His eyes were a little too far apart, and with his thin, pursed lips, she could see how he got his parasite nickname.

"A delivery has been promised." El Piojo paused to cross his legs, revealing expensive, spotless black loafers. He looked at his gold watch and continued. "You will give us the drugs today."

"I am trying, señor."

"I understand that. But we have priorities. So we might need to explore other options." He folded his manicured hands together and said, "First I want you to eat and drink this morning. Help yourself to the food in the refrigerator. We'll give you a couple more hours—"

Sanchez stood, pulled out an enormous knife, and jammed it into the table. Staring into his eyes was like looking down long, dark tunnels.

"—before we cut them out of you."

CHAPTER

13

H all lights brightened, fresh-faced nurses carried coffee and bagels to their posts, and scrub techs wheeled the first group of patients to the operating rooms: the night shift had ended.

Bo walked through the radiology department and stepped into the antechamber of the chairman's office and stopped to adjust his eyes to the dim lighting. Wood paneling, brass fixtures, electrified candles, and even statues recessed into the walls confused him. Had he entered the chapel by mistake? Bo thought of his years as an altar boy, putting on his robes in the vestibule with the priest before services. Only the pictures on these walls weren't religious.

Bo looked around the sanctuary—or maybe he should call it a shrine to the ego of Dr. Theodore Musk, professor emeritus, and chairman of the department of radiology at the University of Colorado. Diplomas with more Latin than English covered one wall: summa cum laude at Yale University, Harvard Medical School, and radiology residency at Columbia. The Ivy League must be proud. Bo knew the rest: full professor before forty and the youngest chairman in the history of the University of Colorado. Over the past twenty-five years he had worked his way up to the administrative committees and was now untouchable—at least for the next five years until mandatory retirement. But maybe he'd change that.

Emily, Musk's long-time personal assistant, stood up to greet Bo. Her naturally gray hair was pulled back into a tight bun, and her reading glasses dangled on a gold chain as she led Bo to the chairman's door. "They're waiting for you, Dr. Richards."

The door opened and the chairman filled the doorway. A sneaky smile breached his round face. Short and overweight, he could have been the shorter twin of Dr. Nicolai.

Bo followed him into the room and was startled to see Vince Flickinger and Dr. Dick Dunner, the vice chairman, already seated.

Bo sat in the empty chair. Musk walked around his massive desk and sat on his throne, and Bo wondered if it really was elevated a few inches to give a negotiating advantage, as the rumors went.

Vince had mellowed since yesterday. He relaxed in his chair with a smug confidence that annoyed Bo. Granted, he was brilliant, had already secured a lucrative job in southern California, and had every available female in lust over him. But did he have to flaunt it?

In contrast, Dr. Dunner—never Dick—sat upright and emotionless. Bo hadn't figured him out yet. The residents said he was a genius, dazzling the orthopedic surgeons with his vast knowledge of sports injuries. While dull at work, Bo heard rumors of an alter ego outside the hospital, partying with his beautiful wife at the local clubs.

"Dr. Richards," Musk said.

"Sir," Bo replied.

"I've spoken with Dr. Vanderworst, the medical director. He's in surgery and isn't able to be with us today. Perhaps you could explain what transpired in the MRI suite yesterday?"

Bo collected his thoughts and began. "I was called to the MRI center for an emergency. A patient was having difficulty breathing from an allergic reaction to the MRI contrast. I examined the patient. Her tongue was swollen, her face was red, and she was struggling to breathe and swallow. I immediately called for the radiology nurse as well as epinephrine. While the technologist was initiating these procedures, the patient suddenly blacked out. I looked around for oxygen and, not seeing anything in the room, remembered a tank outside the MRI center. I grabbed the tank and brought it into the room to aid the patient. Unfortunately, the tank must have been ferromagnetic, and it was sucked into the magnet, injuring the patient in the process. After my initial shock, I stabilized the patient and got her on a stretcher, and the ER code team arrived to take over."

"Did you attend the MRI safety lectures last year?" Musk asked with a pained look.

No. I went skiing, Bo was tempted to say. Of course he had attended the mandatory lectures. The powerful force of the magnet—greater than thirty thousand times gravity—had caused many accidents since the scanners were introduced in the 1980s. Some were tragic, like the death of a young boy in New York who was killed by a canister of oxygen brought into the room by the anesthetist. Physicists estimated the tank was hurtling at forty miles an hour when it struck the boy. But some of the situations were comical, like the janitor who brought a steel bucket into the MRI room. Almost everything imaginable had been sucked into the magnet—pens, knives, guns, even stretchers.

"Yes, sir. I know and understand the rules about metal in the scanner. It was an honest mistake in the process of saving the patient's life. I'm very sorry."

"I'd say you almost killed the patient, not saved her life."

"Again, I'm sorry, Dr. Musk. I will apologize to Mrs. Adcock."

Dr. Dunner spoke up. "Now don't go doing that and screwing things up even more. We've already spoken to the legal department and are trying to control the situation. They've advised against any contact between you and the patient. Sometimes good intentions get translated into big malpractice settlements. The hospital will certainly cover her surgery and compensate her for any lost time from work. Let the lawyers work this out."

Bo nodded, wondering how common courtesy had been lost from the medical profession. Traditionally, doctors were taught never to apologize for an unexpected outcome for fear this would lead to an admission of negligence in a malpractice suit. Bo never liked this attitude. If a doctor makes a mistake, he should admit it and explain what happened. Patients want their doctors to be human, not perfect.

Musk stood up, walked around his desk, and sat on the edge looking down at Bo. "The oxygen tank cracked the casing of the MRI machine, and it started to quench. Helium gas leaked into the room and almost killed Dr. Flickinger and the chief technologist, Rocio Garcia."

Musk stopped for emphasis. Bo readied himself for a lecture on the economics of the MRI business and how much money the department is now losing during repairs.

"One good thing has come out of all of this, Dr. Richards," Musk continued. "The ventilation system was improperly installed and needs to be redesigned. According to the engineers, the hospital was fortunate the magnet didn't explode."

"That's good." Bo said, and then regretted it.

"Good?" Musk asked. His round face turned a bright red and Bo noticed his clenched fists. "Don't forget this is a business I'm running. Each of the new MRI machines will be down for a week. I hope I don't have to tell you how much money we'll be losing during all of this." Musk worked himself up into such a fury that Bo wondered if smoke would shoot out of his ears.

Bo sat in stunned silence. He couldn't think of an appropriate response. Nothing he could say would help pacify the chairman.

Musk continued to fume. Dr. Dunner and Vince looked away.

A beeper broke the tension.

Vince, quiet throughout, looked at his pager and stood. "I need to get this, Dr. Musk."

Dunner also stood. "We're almost done here, Dr. Flickinger." He turned to Bo. "Dr. Richards, we've decided to pull you off of the MRI rotation for now. Starting tomorrow, I want you in the emergency department reading room with Flickinger. Shadow him, learn from him, and stay out of trouble. Don't think we're not taking this seriously. Consider this a working probation."

Musk added, "We're also going to have our physicist give a new safety lecture. I want you in the front row."

The meeting ended, and Bo walked through the shrine into the hall.

Vince caught up with him and said, "I've never seen Musk so upset. You're lucky he didn't hear about your imaginary spleen rupture last night or he might have had a stroke in front of us."

"Look, Vince. I'm doing my best, all right? Nicolai was so drunk last night he probably doesn't even remember it." Bo had never spoken to a chief resident like that. But he was tired and grumpy. "I really don't need any more crap from you right now."

"Who do you think you're talking to?" Vince's eyes flashed with anger, his chest expanded, and he shoved Bo backward. The chief emitted a guttural sound and raised his right arm. Bo held his stare and tensed for a fight. The approaching footsteps of Dr. Dunner caused Vince to relax his fist but he continued scowling at Bo. "I'll see you in the ER reading room tomorrow morning."

Bo could hardly wait.

CHAPTER

14

What's wrong with me? Vince thought as he walked away from his confrontation with Bo. He'd almost hit a resident. Vince's beeper flashed again. He ignored the page from his dealer—he didn't have the money anyway—and walked over to the chief resident's office. "Just one more hit to get me through the morning."

Now, standing in front of the mirror in his private bathroom, waiting for his nose to stop bleeding, he tried to remember when this all began. A year ago, he was, well, "in-Vince-able," he used to joke to himself. He had been named chief resident, was about to secure the best job in southern California, and was one year away from a high six-figure salary. The cushy chief resident job afforded time to moonlight at a local hospital to pay off some of his bills. He had traveled a long, hard road from the goddamn children's home, and it was about to start paying off.

It started with a woman: a captivating and ravishing woman. Vince couldn't even remember her name anymore. It might have been Tracey, or Tara, or Tina. He met her at The Med in a blur of fusion music and multicolored lights dampened by his alcohol buzz. He'd been on call the night before and should have been home sleeping off the twenty-four-hour shift, but he needed some new female company that night. And not a lonely intern or resident this time.

He'd finished a couple of vodka martinis and sank deeper into the plush couch, letting the beat of the music vibrate through his bones. When he opened his eyes she stood in front of him, smiling.

She held out her hand and led him to the dance floor. Vince could still picture her dancing to the rhythm of the music, the subtle, erotic sway of her hips, her wavy blonde hair flowing over her sultry eyes. She was gorgeous and knew it and every guy in the club knew it. Vince savored the jealous stares, grabbed her supple waist, and matched her tempo beat for beat.

Later, on his balcony overlooking the skyline of Denver and the starry headlights leaving the Pepsi Center, she removed the bag of cocaine from her purse. Vince had never had an interest in the stuff before. Alcohol and an occasional joint had always been enough. But tonight, sitting naked with this captivating woman, the sweat from their lovemaking evaporating in the cool mountain air, it felt right. She took the powder, placed it on a small mirror, made two neat white lines, and snorted. She'd moaned with delight, leaned back, and rested her soft hand on his thigh, handing him the remaining line.

Vince could still remember that first rush: the intensity, the euphoria. He'd been awake more than thirty hours now but felt as alert as he'd ever been in his life. He felt the neurons in his brain firing, synapses exploding. His muscles bulged and his heart swelled, straining against his confining ribs. He'd been fully aroused and she was insatiable, unlike any woman Vince had ever known. Tasha—maybe it was Tanya—took him right there on the balcony, slowly at first, and then, sensing his urgency, faster and faster until everything, even the tiniest hairs on his arm, had exploded with his release.

Vince returned to the club a couple of times after that amazing night, but he never saw her again. Not that he expected to. She was a goddess, a once-in-a-lifetime phenomenon, who'd come down from the heavens to grace Vince with her charm and beauty. Vince wanted the sensation of ecstasy and the ferocity of the lovemaking that he had never experienced before. He waited a couple of days, hoping the feeling would fade, but the urge grew stronger. He called an old girlfriend who had access to a dealer, and for a small favor that Vince was happy to oblige, he bought his first bag of cocaine.

Fifteen months and countless bags of cocaine later, Vince still savored the exhilaration of the drug, but it never matched the sensational moment on his balcony that night. He began taking hits in the morning before work and at night before cruising the clubs. He never needed much sleep anyway. He was able to study until ten each night, party until one or two, and still be sharp in the morning. He didn't think he was addicted. He could stop anytime he wanted. He just didn't want to yet.

Money was the only problem. His credit had dried up, and the dealer was getting restless and more threatening. The other residents envied his lifestyle and thought he'd been born into wealth. He'd never told them the real story.

The beeper buzzed again.

Vince ripped the damn contraption off his belt and threw it across the room. He shook his head, dismayed at his temper. He didn't know where the rage came from, but it scared the hell out of him. He picked up the phone and dialed the unknown number. Vince listened to the incensed drug dealer, and anger washed over him like a rogue wave. "I told you last night, you cretin. You'll have the money by Saturday." He slammed down the phone.

Vince walked back into the bathroom for a quick check. He straightened his tie, wiped a dried spot of blood off his upper lip, and shook his head. Talking to the dealer reminded Vince of the embarrassment last night at the restaurant. The senior partner of RASC accepted Vince's lame story of a recent sinus infection and they rescheduled the meeting for next week. That had been a close call. Maybe it was time to stop. He had too much to lose.

CHAPTER

15

Bo drove away from the hospital angry and confused. What a twenty-four hours from hell. First he almost killed a patient on the MRI scanner, and then he let that surgeon Nicolai bully him into making a call he wasn't comfortable with. *Working probation?* Dunner's words replayed in his head. What the hell was that? Was it all about money, the lost revenue because of the damage to the scanner? Or did Musk need to show the hospital president that MRI safety issues were taken seriously?

What bothered Bo the most was that woman he met at the river yesterday, the last one to see Cory alive. He was so shocked by Cory's last words that he didn't even remember the runner giving him her number until he emptied his pockets last night. Lisa Folletti, the card read. Bo needed to talk to her about Cory. Maybe that's what he needed to move on with his life.

Bo looked down at his fingers, white from clenching the steering wheel, and realized he was going way too fast for the crowded streets of downtown Denver. He eased his foot off the pedal and tried to relax. The probation was only a month, after all. He could handle it.

Bo glanced at his watch and realized he could make the late-morning swim practice at the YMCA. Exercise was the best way to escape his troubles. Besides, he had a half-Ironman triathlon to train for.

He entered the locker room and was greeted by a group of high school swimmers getting ready for their morning practice.

"Hey, Doc, you gonna swim with us?"

"You sure you want me to show you up?" Bo liked these kids. Most of them were from the projects. Donations helped support the team and provided the suits and goggles their parents couldn't afford. They were a dedicated and talented group of kids who swam every afternoon and most mornings at five thirty. During the summer, the coach gave them more sleep with ten o'clock practices.

When Bo first joined the Y, he swam in the morning in the open lane next to the team. He gradually got to know the coach and was invited to train with the kids. Bo loved the tough interval workouts and the camaraderie of the group. He liked joking around with the kids between the sets.

Many were being raised by single mothers. Occasionally, when Bo's schedule allowed, he took a couple of the kids out for breakfast. They told him about problems at school and troubles with the gangs. It was a new world for Bo. Growing up in the suburbs of New Jersey, Bo's biggest worry was getting a date for the prom.

Today was sprint day. The coach spread them out on the pool deck in groups behind the starting blocks. He put Bo in the first group of eight swimmers, and Bo loosened up for the challenge. He would be racing the fastest kids. Bo was never a serious year-round swimmer like these kids. He swam on his high school team but didn't practice in the off season. His technique didn't improve until medical school when one of his classmates, Doug, a former swimmer from William and Mary, gave him lessons. Every day at lunch time they would rush out of the last lecture, race across the Duke campus, and swim in the natatorium for an hour. Doug taught Bo about body position, streamlining off the walls, and flip turns. Bo was a better swimmer after a couple of months with Doug than he had ever been in high school.

Bo swam the first two races at a moderate pace. They were doing ten 100-yard sprints and he needed to conserve his energy. He picked up the pace for the next two and was finishing just behind the leaders. At the start of the fifth race he looked over at the swimmers and gave the challenge, "Eat my bubbles," and took off.

The first two laps felt great and Bo had a slight lead, but he could sense the faster swimmers closing the distance. He concentrated on pulling all the way through the stroke, maintaining his power, and maximizing his efficiency. It started to work. On the last flip turn Bo stretched his long arms in front of him, hands clasped in a perfect streamlined position, and dolphin kicked until his lungs burned. He popped up halfway down the pool and finished the last few strokes a split second ahead of the fastest swimmers.

"Nice race, Doc," Ernesto said. He was entering his senior year of high school and was the captain of the team. Bo had written a glowing college recommendation for him last week. "Now let's see what you've got left."

Bo didn't have anything left. He gasped for air. His arms felt like lead. He finished off the last group of sprints well behind the leaders. He was pulling himself out of the pool when the coach came running up to him, out of breath.

"Bo, come quick. We've got an emergency in the locker room."

The coach led Bo to the showers where Raul, one of the older swimmers, was sitting on the floor, back to the wall, bleeding onto the tile. He had a five-inch knife wound to his upper thigh. Blood pulsed out of the gash. A sickening smell of blood and chlorine filled the room.

He was going to die in seconds if Bo didn't act fast.

Bo dived to the floor and covered the wound with his hands. Warm blood oozed around his fingers and he pushed harder. He couldn't let this kid die. Raul was like a little brother. His mother brought Bo a breakfast burrito after Wednesday-morning practice every week.

"I don't want to die," Raul cried, eyes wide with fear. He was so pale.

"That's not going to happen, buddy."

Bo turned to the coach. "Call 911 and have one of the kids get my medical bag from the back of my truck."

Bo felt for the femoral pulse above the wound and pressed down with all his strength on the artery. *Where's my bag?*

"I can't feel my leg, Dr. Bo," Raul moaned before his head slumped to his chest.

"Come on. Come on. I need my bag," Bo urged the coach.

Finally his medical kit arrived. Bo showed the coach where to hold pressure while he dug a scalpel out. He sliced through the skin, expanding the wound, so he could get a better look. Raul didn't even stir. Bo spread the tissues with a hemostat until he could see the torn artery.

He opened up a clamp and gingerly slid the metal around the vessel. "Steady now," he said to calm himself. "You're almost there."

Bo heard a crash, and a gush of blood filled the wound and spurted in his face.

"What?" Bo looked up, confused until he saw that the coach had slumped over and cracked his head against the tile.

"Shit." The cavity was rapidly filling with Raul's blood. Blindly, Bo squeezed the clamp and prayed that he was in the right spot.

The bleeding slowed!

He opened up a suture and passed it under the clamp until he could feel the free end. He tied a knot and breathed a sigh of relief when the bleeding slowed to a trickle. The paramedics arrived and Bo held the wound as they hoisted Raul onto the stretcher.

Bo stopped to check on the coach. He was sitting up, rubbing his head, embarrassed. "I'm sorry, Doc. I can't believe I passed out."

Bo rode in the back of the ambulance, watching the efficient paramedics start a large-bore IV to push fluids and give morphine for pain.

Raul drifted in and out of consciousness. Once he looked up at Bo and said "stupid gangs," and fell back to sleep.

They arrived at the university ER, and Bo helped move Raul into the trauma room. The paramedics had called ahead, and Dr. Sal Martinez, one of Bo's favorite ER physicians, along with a surgical resident Bo didn't know, met him.

Bo explained what he had done. "Take good care of this kid. He's a great swimmer and a nice guy."

"Sure thing," the confident surgeon said as he wheeled Raul down the hall to the OR.

Bo remained in the trauma room with Sal. His hands were sticky with Raul's blood, he was exhausted, and he suddenly realized he was wearing only his Speedo. A small crowd of gawkers had formed outside the room, and Bo felt naked and awkward.

A camera flashed, he heard a catcall, and someone mumbled, "Nice package, Doc."

Jan, one of the ER nurses, handed him a lab coat.

"Thanks," Bo said.

"My pleasure," Jan said, her downward gaze lingering.

CHAPTER

16

Marisol heard a coin clink into the toilet. She had finished! The laxative and juices had worked. The condoms were finally out! She danced around the room, overjoyed. Even the smell didn't bother her anymore. She was ready to go home, anxious to be reunited with her husband and child.

The door opened and Sanchez entered the room, stepping around the wet drain. The Sureños boss looked inside the makeshift toilet and turned back to Marisol.

Marisol said, "I'm finished. They're all out except a couple of coins I swallowed at the end."

El Piojo nodded and left the room. Marisol waited. He came back with some of the men Marisol saw standing around yesterday when she arrived. *They must clean up the cocaine,* she thought.

"Come with me," Sanchez finally said to her.

Marisol followed him into the warehouse. "Are we going to the airport now?"

He turned and looked at her without emotion. Sanchez walked over to a black car and spoke to Miguel, the skinny man who'd met Marisol at the airport. The scarred addict pushed her in the car and slammed the door.

Marisol waited. She started to worry that the Sureños wouldn't keep their promise. She had done her part—she'd delivered the drugs. Now it was time to go back to Mexico.

The front door opened and the same driver from the airport got in. He was more frightening than she remembered. Muscles bulged in his tight shirt as he turned and leered at her with two gold front teeth. "We are going to have some fun now, eh, señora?"

Marisol looked away from the horrible man. The back door opened and the skinny man slid in next to Marisol. The driver laughed.

"Are we going back to the airport?" Marisol asked.

No answer.

"The men in Cabo said I would fly back after I was done."

The car backed out of the warehouse and the large door closed. "Well, I believe Sanchez has other plans for someone as beautiful as you." He stroked her leg and licked his colorless lips. "If you know what I mean."

Marisol pulled her leg away and looked out the window. She realized these men would never let her go. They would use her for sex or worse and throw her away when they were done. Just like the other women in her village who never came back. Why did she think she would be any different? How could she be so stupid? Damn Hector!

As the car turned onto the street Marisol heard a beep and watched Miguel pull out his cell phone and read a text message.

"Stop, Juan," the nervous addict shouted. Glaring at Marisol, he said, "The bolitas count might be wrong." Miguel opened the car door and said, "Let me check this out. I'll be right back."

Marisol couldn't believe it. She didn't count the disgusting packages in the bucket but she figured the coins would come out last. What would Sanchez do to her?

The driver turned around with a leering smile and said, "While we're waiting, how 'bout we start now, honey? I could use a little action." He reached over and grabbed Marisol's breast.

She twisted free and he slapped her. "I'll bet you like it rough, huh?" Juan's cell phone rang and he turned back toward the front.

Marisol tried the door but it was locked. She had to get out of here before these men raped her. She had to run. She had to do something before the skinny man returned. But what?

She reached inside her pocket and pulled out the rosary beads. She kissed the cross and prayed. She clasped her hands over the beads, remembering how proud her mother looked when she'd handed Marisol her Confirmation present. Marisol had carried the rosary with her every day since, except for the time the brown cord snapped and had to be replaced. That was it! The cord; the man at the repair shop said it would never break again. Marisol shivered at the sudden thought. Could she do it?

The driver shouted into his cell phone and slammed his hand on the steering wheel. The skinny man would be back any second.

Now!

Marisol flipped the rosary over the angry driver's head, wrapped it around his neck, and pulled as hard as she could. His head snapped back and he dropped the cell phone. "Wha—" he tried to say.

Marisol pulled and twisted. She pushed her feet against the back of the seat and pulled again. She heard a gurgling sound. The man reached in his pocket for his gun but couldn't turn around now. Marisol twisted some more. Years of cleaning hotel rooms had strengthened her hands.

She grimaced as the cord dug into her palm. The man thrashed from side to side but Marisol wouldn't let go. She grunted and howled. She thought of the pain of Arturo's birth and Hector's gentle touch as she struggled to push her baby out. She had to get back to them.

A swollen tongue protruded from the driver's purple face. The gun was out and he was firing wildly. Marisol ducked behind the seat and twisted some more. The firing stopped and the man slumped forward. She had killed a man!

She turned and saw the skinny man running back to the car.

She had to hurry. She crawled over the front seat and flopped onto the dead driver, now aware of the putrid scent of his feces. She fought the urge to vomit. She opened the door locks, grabbed Juan's gun, and jumped out of the car.

The skinny man yelled.

Marisol fired the gun into his belly and ran.

She bolted down the deserted street—the businessmen must have gone home. She reached the next intersection and hid behind a building, trying to decide her next move. She didn't have much time before Sanchez and his thugs would come after her and kill her. She remembered El Piojo's knife and the casual way he talked about cutting her open.

Marisol spotted the statue of St. Francis of Assisi and sprinted down the block. The church lights flickered through the stained-glass windows. She stumbled on the uneven sidewalk and opened the large, cracked wooden doors. A small group of parishioners sat in the pews on the left. Marisol ran down the aisle. She was about to cry for help when a woman stepped out of a small doorway and Marisol realized the people were here for confession. Marisol ignored the stares as she cut in front of the next person in line and stepped into the dark confessional.

The panel slid back. Marisol took a deep breath. "Forgive me, Father, for I have sinned."

CHAPTER

17

Bo woke to the obnoxious ringing of his phone. With the curtains closed, he couldn't tell what time it was or how long he'd been asleep. He barely remembered driving back to his Boulder condo after picking up his truck at the YMCA. After the intense excitement in the ER last night and then again this morning at the pool, he collapsed into bed exhausted as soon as he got home.

"Dr. Richards," he answered, forgetting he was at home and not on call.

"Aren't you formal?" a voice Bo didn't recognize said.

He stalled, hoping he'd remember. "I'm just waking up, sorry."

"This is Lisa. From the river yesterday. I thought we were meeting for coffee."

Did he really make plans with the runner?

"You forgot, didn't you?" she asked.

"I, uh …"

"It's all right. I only half-expected you to show up. You looked kind of dazed yesterday."

"You're right. I didn't remember. But I can be ready in a few minutes."

"Don't worry about it."

"No. I really want to talk to you. I'd like to know more about what happened. How about tomorrow?"

"You can join me for a run, if you'd like. I'm running up Chautauqua tomorrow."

"I won't forget this time."

CHAPTER

18

The headache woke Vince. Eyes still closed, he rubbed his temples over the throbbing pain bouncing around his skull. He needed aspirin or something stronger. *What happened last night?* He tried to sit up but his body wouldn't cooperate; his head felt glued to the bed. A ray of sunlight pierced his closed eyelids, stabbed his retina, and sent a wave of pain through his brain. Through the fog of his hangover, Vince realized it was morning. He had to get to work.

He struggled to turn his head toward the nightstand on his right, managed to open one eye, but didn't see his alarm clock. "Where am I?" He turned his head to the left and closed his eyes until the room stopped spinning. He heard rhythmic breathing. Vince opened both eyes and rubbed them. A milky white form came into focus. A breast? The sunlight shifted and reflected off the nipple ring, sending another wave of agony through his brain.

Who the hell is she? Vince struggled to remember where he'd gone last night. He tilted his throbbing head back to see her face. She was young and gorgeous. Stringy blonde hair wrapped around her long neck. That neck! The night started to come back to Vince.

Vince wanted to be alone last night. He was confused and upset about his recent temper outbursts. Even in the most stressful situations, Vince had always managed to stay calm, his sharp, deliberate mind a step ahead of everyone else. Two stunning blondes had joined him at the bar while Vince finished his shrimp scampi. A couple of martinis later they invited him to a party. He remembered a penthouse suite crowded with writhing bodies, endless lines of coke, and overly friendly women. He remembered the blonde with the succulent neck and the invitation to a private party. He didn't remember the rest.

Vince felt a smooth, soft hand on his chest. She was awake. She smiled as she straddled him, her long blonde hair tickling his chest. She massaged his scalp, twisted her long legs around his, and began to sway from side to side. Vince's head felt better as blood rushed below. Sensing his arousal, she glided over him, letting him enter her pleasant wetness. Gently rocking, she moaned, "Good morning."

Satisfied, she rolled off Vince and fell back to sleep. Vince spotted a clock and realized he was already an hour late to work. He was supposed to meet Bo for his ER orientation. "Shit!"

He jumped out of bed, too quickly, apparently, and a wave of nausea hit him. He stumbled past his clothes littering the living room and managed to make it to the bathroom before vomiting. Staring into the toilet in a stranger's apartment, stomach retching, he vowed to stop the drinking and the drugs. He opened her medicine cabinet in search of mouthwash, pushing away the prescription medicine. He read the label on the bottles, annoyed that he'd forgotten her name. He rinsed with mouthwash, got in the shower, and let the scalding water run over him until his head stopped pounding. Stepping out and toweling off he felt a little better, and he left the bathroom to collect his clothes.

She was sitting unabashedly naked, cross-legged on the plush couch, arranging a neat line of coke on the table. She looked up and smiled. "Hey, Vince. How 'bout a little kick start to your day?"

"I've got to get to work. I'm already late."

"I think it'll help. You look kind of sluggish."

It probably would help, Vince thought, forgetting his recent vow to stop. *And God she's sexy, sitting there so invitingly.*

"Let me make a phone call," Vince said. He removed the towel and joined her on the couch.

CHAPTER

19

B o sat beneath the large display monitors in the reading room, waiting for the daily medicine conference to begin. He loved this conference; it was the radiologist's chance to shine. The medical students described the patients who were admitted the previous day, outlining their symptoms and lab results. Bo would show their imaging studies. Some of the cases were easy, such as a routine pneumonia, and Bo pointed out the nuances of the X-ray findings. The university also attracted tough cases—patients the local doctors couldn't figure out—and Bo relished the opportunity to make an impact in their treatment.

Bo woke up refreshed and arrived at the emergency reading room early, determined to get off to a good start with Vince, but the chief resident hadn't show up yet. Worse, Vince was supposed to be his backup for this conference too, so Bo hoped he'd show up soon.

Bo turned his chair to face the room and watched the medical team trickle in. Even though he'd never met them, he knew their position in the pecking order. First, the fresh-faced medical students sporting short, clean white coats, pockets filled with reflex hammers and unused stethoscopes, walked up to the front. The interns came next, bleary-eyed from admitting patients, running tests, and resolving crises all night. They leaned against the wall, half-asleep, scrubs stained with unthinkable bodily fluids. Finally the residents, wearing longer white coats and much less sleep-deprived than the interns—they actually had time to think, not just react—took their usual place in the back of the room.

Bo readied the list and displayed the images of the first patient while half-listening to the fragmented conversations around the room. The chatter abruptly stopped when the guest of honor, the medical attending, strode into the room. Dr. Perfect—Bo couldn't believe it when he first heard the name—vice dean of the medical school, tenured professor of cardiology, one of the first doctors in the country to perform angioplasty—took his position next to the residents. His starched, knee-length white coat covered his thin frame. The shiniest stethoscope Bo had ever seen dangled from his neck, adding credence to the rumors that his medical students polished it.

Dr. Perfect nodded and the conference began. The first couple of cases were straightforward. A middle-aged smoker presented with a new cough and thirty-pound weight loss. Bo described a large mass on the chest X-ray, which was almost certainly lung cancer, and a biopsy was scheduled. Next, a college student arrived in the emergency room with knee pain and fever. His MRI showed fluid and cartilage damage, and Bo suggested checking the fluid for gonorrhea, the most common cause of a single swollen joint. After some chuckles, the intern thanked Bo and jotted notes on her index card.

Bo was on a roll, in his own radiology zone, pointing out abnormalities and offering diagnoses when the last patient came up. The case started with a presentation by a stunning brunette medical student who was more appropriately dressed for a cocktail party than hospital rounds.

"I'm Cindy Strong," she said, flicking a stray hair off her flawless face. "The patient is a fifty-year-old ski instructor who's getting progressively short of breath." Cindy stopped, adjusting her clipboard and books under her right breast. "He'd been perfectly healthy until two months ago. Now he can't breathe without supplemental oxygen."

Dr. Perfect, quiet until now, looked over at Cindy with interest. Either he was intrigued by the case or he was a dirty old man. "Any recent travel outside the country? Any family members sick?" Perfect asked.

"I didn't ask that."

"Don't you think that might have been useful?" Apparently he wasn't looking for a date, after all.

"Could it be high-altitude pulmonary edema?" one of the other med students asked. "He works in the mountains."

"Wrong time course, but interesting thought," Perfect added. "Why don't we see what our radiology colleague has to say?"

Bo tensed. He didn't like the insincere tone of "colleague." Perfect trained in an era when internists were truly mavericks. They not only examined the patients but drew and analyzed blood, looked at their own X-rays, and performed their own procedures. They didn't rely on consultants, particularly radiologists.

Bo said, "The chest X-ray shows hazy densities in both lungs, pretty nonspecific. We see this with pneumonia and heart failure, but it could be many things."

"That's helpful."

Jerk. Bo ignored the sarcasm and racked his brain for additional diagnoses. *What else could this be?* He looked up at Perfect and saw a familiar look, the look that never failed to weaken his confidence. It was the same look the teachers in grade school gave him when they said, "Well, your brothers didn't have any trouble with these problems." He hated when this happened. He'd read the textbooks; he was prepared.

"What about the CAT scan, Dr. Richards?"

"The normally black lungs are almost completely filled with a hazy white substance that looks like ground glass."

Dr. Perfect smirked and nodded before turning to his senior resident. "Any ideas?"

"Could be infection. We should make sure he's not HIV-positive."

"Good," Perfect said. "Let's get sputum for culture and start him on antibiotics."

The team prepared to leave when a familiar voice called out from the back of the room. "You might want to start him on steroids, Dr. Perfect."

Perfect turned to the voice, annoyed at the interruption. "And why is that?"

Vince Flickinger stepped around the crowd and bumped his way to the computer monitors. He leaned over and whispered an apology to Bo before turning around, revealing his perfect blond hair, sharp eyes, and knowing smile.

Like an actor delivering a dramatic soliloquy, he said, "I see that the patient suffered a clavicle fracture—a couple of months ago by the looks of it. I heard Ms. Strong say he is a ski instructor. I've known a few myself, and they don't make very much money. To keep working through the pain, I suspect he spends a lot of time in the hot tub—both before he goes out into the cold and after a lesson."

Vince turned to Cindy and gestured like a magician to his assistant.

"Uh. Yeah," she stammered. "He did mention something about that. His stomach can't tolerate Motrin."

Vince continued. "Ladies and gentleman, this is a textbook case of hot tub lung." Vince bowed and rested his hand on Cindy's shoulder. She actually blushed.

"We'll take that under consideration, Dr. Flickinger," Perfect said in an annoyed tone. He ripped his stethoscope off his neck, shoved it in his coat pocket, and stormed out of the room.

As the medical team began filing out, Bo stood up and shook Vince's hand. "That was an amazing call."

Vince shrugged. "You know what they say, Bo: the answer is always on the film. The clavicle injury was the key and the rest just followed. Most people don't know that hot tubs can harbor a strain of bacteria that causes an allergic reaction in the lungs."

"I'll see you in the ER reading room?" Bo asked, but it was too late. Vince had caught up with Cindy, had his arm around her waist, and Bo heard him say, "Speaking of hot tubs ..."

CHAPTER

20

Bo hurried back to the ER reading room, excited by the last patient from the medicine conference and laughed as he remembered the stunned look on Dr. Perfect's face when Vince gave him the diagnosis. Maybe the stuffy old internist would respect radiology now.

Sheri met Bo in the hall. "Well, aren't you the happy one? You get lucky last night or something?"

"I never kiss and tell." Bo winked. "But that's not why I'm smiling. I was struggling with this case at conference. The esteemed Dr. Perfect was baffled as well and was intimidating me with that supercilious look of his. Have you seen it?"

"He's a pompous jerk," Sheri said.

"Luckily Vince came to the rescue. He came up with the diagnosis from the back of the room. It was awesome."

"Oh, Vince the Great. The God of Radiology. I thought he tried to slug you yesterday."

"How did you know that?"

"We women have our ways."

"You and Vince"—Bo hesitated—"don't have a thing going on?"

Sheri recoiled in mock disgust. "Come on, Bo. I don't want to be another notch on his beeper. Why would I want a guy like that anyway—rich, smart, good-looking, great job—when I could have a simple guy from New Jersey?"

"Was I just insulted?" Bo's beeper rang. "It's the ER. I'd better go."

Bo walked over to the ER and pressed the button for the automatic double doors. A potpourri of alcohol, blood, and disinfectant assaulted his senses. The minor trauma rooms were filled with broken bones and lacerations waiting for treatment. The opposite room reeked of an alcoholic sleeping off a binge.

Bo found Dr. Sal Martinez coming out of another room and asked, "Did you page me, Sal?"

"Yeah. What a morning!" He walked over to the sink and washed his hands. "I need your help with this patient in Room 3. A priest brought her in a little while ago. She was complaining of abdominal pain. I gave her some morphine and she got a little better, but now she's acting crazy. Anyway, I sent her over for a head CT scan. She already had an abdominal X-ray. Could you look at them and give me a call? Her name's Marisol Hernandez."

"Sure. Did you say a priest?"

"He says she showed up hysterical in his church last night. He thinks she's homeless or a prostitute. He kept her overnight in their shelter."

Bo walked to the ER reading room and booted up the computer. Of course Vince wasn't there. He was probably still hitting on that cute medical student from conference. *The guy never stops.* Bo pulled up the X-ray on Ms. Hernandez and studied the abdomen. He immediately saw several coins on the right side of the belly and thought that was funny. The air in the intestines looked okay—no blockages. He didn't see any kidney stones. As Bo continued to search the film for abnormalities he noticed an unusual oval density in the left lower quadrant. *Maybe it's just stool,* he thought. But the air in stool was usually more irregular, and this was very linear.

He paged Vince to get a second opinion as the CT tech called him. "Dr. Richards, I think you'd better look at this head CT."

Bo got up and walked over to the CAT scan room. He glanced through the glass partition at the young female patient resting on the table. He looked at the images and saw a small hemorrhage.

Bo picked up the phone and called Sal. "Your homeless lady has a small bleed in her head. And her abdomen film looks weird. I'll come by and—"

"Doctor," the CT tech yelled, "I think she's seizing."

"—you'd better get over here, Sal." Bo hung up and rushed into the scan room.

Her body jerked and flopped on the table. Bo caught Marisol before she fell off. He turned the convulsing body on her side and held on tight. Sal came running in, ordered Valium, and helped Bo restrain her. As quickly as it began, Marisol stopped seizing and the nurses took her back to room 3.

Bo walked Sal into the control room and showed him the hemorrhage on the head CT.

Sal nodded. "Well, that's why she's seizing."

"Let me show you her abdomen X-ray." Bo turned to another computer. "First of all she swallowed a couple of coins. And look at these curvy black lines in the left lower quadrant. They don't look like stool."

"This case is getting screwier and screwier."

"You said she's a prostitute. Is she a drug addict? You can get brain hemorrhage from cocaine, you know."

"Yeah. I know. I'm not sure she's a prostitute, and there aren't any needle tracks on her arms."

The ER nurse ran into the room. "Dr. Martinez, her blood pressure is sky high."

After Sal hurried out of the CT suite, Bo continued to stare at the X-ray, bothered that he'd seen this before. Then it dawned on him: the conference on drug smuggling. Bo remembered an interesting lecture last year about body packers stuffing drugs into their rectums and mules swallowing huge amounts of cocaine-filled condoms.

Bo ran out of the room and caught Sal in the hall. "Wait. I've got it." Bo's eyes lit up with excitement. "She's a drug mule. I've never seen one before, but I've heard about them. They swallow cocaine packets that look exactly like stool. The density is the same. And some swallow coins thinking the metal will bend the X-rays or something."

Sal looked at Bo. "If you're right, then that packet is leaking and she'll be dead in minutes."

"I'll page Vince again to see what he thinks. You'd better call the surgeon."

Bo waited outside room 3 as the ER team worked on the patient. Bo shuddered as Dr. Mark Nicolai strutted down the hall and entered the room. Of all the surgeons at the university, it had to be him. *I hope he's sober today*, Bo thought.

"What's going on?" Nicolai blustered.

"A young female from a shelter came in with abdominal pain, Mark. Now she's seizing. She's got a small bleed in her head on CAT scan, and Bo thinks she might be a cocaine mule with a leaky condom."

Nicolai peered over his glasses at Bo and snarled, "Like the leaky spleen, Dr. Richards?"

Bo ignored the insult and pulled up the X-ray on the monitor. "Look at this. There's some weird air surrounding this oval density. It's too smooth for stool."

"She's in V-fib, doctors."

Sal grabbed the shock paddles as the nurse charged them up. After two attempts, Marisol was back in normal rhythm. But her blood pressure was out of control.

"Give her nitroglycerin. I'll call the OR," Nicolai said.

"There's no time, Mark. If she's leaking cocaine, she'll be dead before you get in the OR."

"You want me to cut her open right here based on this radiologist's impression? He's never even seen a bolita before."

"I think he's right," Sal said.

"Wait," Bo said, "here's Vince."

Vince entered the crowded room, hair mussed and face flushed. "What's going on?"

Bo showed Vince the X-ray as Nicolai paced impatiently behind them.

"What's it going to be, Vince?" the surgeon asked.

"Cut her, Mark," he said and walked out of the room.

The nurses removed Marisol's shirt and Nicolai poured a liberal amount of Betadine soap over the belly.

"Where's anesthesia?" Nicolai yelled. The scalpel hovered over Marisol's abdomen.

"On the way. She's already heavily sedated, Mark."

"She's going to arrest," the nurse shouted as she looked at the monitor. "Hurry!"

Nicolai didn't hesitate. The blade sliced through the skin and Marisol wailed.

Bo couldn't believe it. He'd never seen an operation without anesthesia. But he knew there wasn't any time. If he was right and the cocaine package was leaking, she'd be dead of an overdose in seconds.

Marisol writhed in pain and wrenched her head to the side.

Bo grabbed her hand and Marisol turned toward him, eyes frightened and pleading. "It'll be all right," Bo whispered and knelt on the floor to keep eye contact. "Just squeeze my hand."

Marisol kept her eyes fixed on Bo and started mumbling.

Bo leaned closer and realized she was praying. His Spanish was rusty—it had been eight years since he'd volunteered with a church mission in Peru—but it sounded like the "Our Father." He stroked her hair and joined the prayer with his limited Spanish until the anesthetist finally arrived and put her to sleep.

Bo stood up and looked down at the pink, quivering loops of bowel dangling from the surgeon's arm. Nicolai systematically squeezed and kneaded the tangled intestines.

"I think we've got something here." A sly smile appeared between his puffy jowls. Nicolai cut through the wall of the small intestine, and a rubbery condom popped out.

"Bingo," Nicolai said, looking up at Bo. "You were right this time, Dr. Richards. Good job."

Bo examined the condom. A pasty white gel oozed through a small hole along one side. "That's incredible," he said shaking his head.

Bo looked back at Marisol's peaceful face, and his eyes started to tear. He turned away, embarrassed. The fine line between life and death was never so apparent. And it all balanced on one X-ray. It was too much to grasp.

CHAPTER

21

After the drama in the ER, Vince dragged himself back to his private office, desperate for a nap. He wanted to watch Nicolai operate but was too exhausted to stand up. His quiet and comfortable call room beckoned. If he could get an hour of shut-eye, he'd be good for the rest of the afternoon. He kicked off his shoes, loosened his tie, and opened the door to the sleep room.

The scent of perfume confused him. Was he in the wrong office? He looked at the bed and saw a shape, covers up to her chin, hiding everything except a seductive smile: Cindy, the med student he flirted with after conference this morning. How did she get in here?

"I wanted to thank you for helping me at conference this morning." Cindy said.

"It was nothing."

"You really saved my ass from that jerk Dr. Perfect. Thanks," she said, pulling the covers down, revealing soft, shapely curves.

"And a very nice ass at that," Vince replied, removing his clothes to join her. His nap would have to wait.

The annoying beep of his pager woke Vince. He groaned as he reached for his pants on the floor. He was alone except for the lingering scent of Cindy's perfume. Vince struggled to sit up and rubbed his eyes to read the number on the pager. He punched the buttons on his bedside phone and waited. His dealer answered. Shit!

The pusher threatened Vince in a mixture of Spanish and English. When was he going to get his $5,000? He needed to pay off his suppliers, you know. Vince listened, his anger growing. Did this high school dropout know who he was talking to?

Vince exploded. "I told you yesterday I'm working on it."

"I need the money today."

"Listen up, you fucker. I've made you a lot of money. I can't pay you until Saturday." Vince slammed the phone and cradled his head with shaking hands. Blood raced up his neck and pounded his temples.

Vince picked up his clothes and stormed into the bathroom. He turned on the shower, hoping the hot water would relax him before he had a stroke.

Vince didn't have many options. He didn't have the money. Christ, he only earned $4,000 a month. His bank accounts were overdrawn and credit cards maxed out. He needed to come up with something, and fast. The dealer had some nasty friends Vince didn't want to meet. He'd try another bank today. And if that didn't work, he had one more option, his last resort, and he hoped it wouldn't come to that.

With his temper under control, Vince dressed and walked over to the ER reading room to check on Bo. He sat on the couch and waited for Bo to finish reviewing a chest X-ray with one of the ER docs. Bo had real potential, Vince thought as he listened to the discussion.

When they were alone, Vince asked, "What happened with the lady in the ER? Sorry I couldn't stay."

"It was unbelievable. Nicolai found a leaky cocaine condom in her small intestine."

"Great call, Bo."

"Yeah, well thanks for backing me up. Nicolai didn't believe me, especially after the other night."

"Is she okay?"

"She survived the surgery. Nicolai is a gifted surgeon, even if he is an asshole."

CHAPTER

22

The ER slowed down in the mid afternoon, leaving Bo with time to research drug smuggling. Not finding much in textbooks, he turned to the Internet and found a wealth of information. The body packers went to amazing lengths to stuff cocaine, heroin, or marijuana into every orifice imaginable. Most mules take drugs to induce constipation, thinking the feces will hide the drugs from X-ray detection. Unfortunately, the longer the condoms stay in the bowel, the greater the chance for a rupture, and the rapid absorption of the heroin or cocaine into the blood stream is usually fatal. The smugglers take the risk because even a single mule can carry as much as two hundred bolitas—Spanish for "small balls"—worth more than $200,000.

Bo read with interest about the detection methods that customs officials have developed and the ingenious techniques the smugglers use to hide the drugs. Sometimes the drugs are put into wax pellets. Other smugglers mix the drugs with aluminum foil or carbon paper to make them look more like stool. The major international airports have X-ray capabilities to screen for drug mules. If a passenger is suspected of smuggling, they are given the choice of an X-ray or to pass three drug-free stools. Bo laughed out loud as he read about the "drug-loo"—the contraption to collect and filter the stool.

At precisely 5:00 p.m. the ever-punctual Dr. Wu, the radiology attending, came by to officially sign off on the films. Dr. Wu was a legend in the department. A radiologist in China, he escaped the Cultural Revolution and was granted political asylum in the United

States. He'd been working at the university for the last forty years. An old-school radiologist, not as adept in the newer modalities such as CAT scans or MRIs, he was a virtuoso with plain X-rays. He was a slight man, quiet and self-effacing, who loved teaching residents the subtle shadows and lines on chest X-rays. His astute observations astounded the clinicians.

Once, as resident lore goes, he stared at a film of a patient and turned to the residents saying, "The patient is six feet, three inches, smokes Camels, drives a yellow Ford Mustang, and walks with a limp." The residents sat in stunned disbelief, looking at the film and wondering how Wu could deduce all of that from a simple X-ray.

Finally, stumped, one of the residents asked, "How did you figure all that out, Dr. Wu?"

"I saw him drive up a little while ago." Wu smiled.

Dr. Wu pulled up a chair next to Bo and they reviewed the day's films. Vince rushed in, face flushed, and apologized. As usual, Wu pointed out a couple of findings that Bo and Vince had missed, and Bo made the corrections to his reports. Bo displayed the abdomen X-ray of Marisol Hernandez and told Dr. Wu about the excitement this morning.

"Wow. Great job, Bo," Wu said and gave Bo more information on drug smugglers and the university's program with Denver International Airport.

"See that icon there next to her name?" Wu asked, pointing.

"I didn't notice that before."

"Click on it. She had an X-ray at the airport two days ago."

"What?" Bo looked at Wu. "I didn't know that."

Bo opened up the file, and the three of them looked at Marisol's airport X-ray.

"There must be one hundred bolitas," Bo said, "and those are the same coins I saw today."

"This is a great case. Maybe you could show it to the residents at morning conference," Wu suggested.

"Sure. But I don't understand why she wasn't arrested two days ago," Bo said. "Don't all the airport X-rays get interpreted here at the University?"

"Yes," Wu answered. "Open up the report."

Bo displayed the X-ray interpretation, and the three of them sat speechless.

"Normal?" Vince asked. "That's ridiculous. How could anyone not see all of those bolitas?"

"Scroll down to the bottom. Let's see who read this," Wu said.

They looked at the signature and then each other.

"Ouch. Sorry, Bo," Vince said.

Bo stared at the electronic signature on the bottom of Marisol Hernandez's X-ray: "Bo Richards, MD."

CHAPTER

23

Vince arrived at Dr. Dunner's office, knocked, and walked in. The vice chairman looked up from his desk and motioned for Vince to sit. Vince watched him flipping over papers, entering numbers into a small calculator, shaking his head in frustration. Vince started to get worried.

He knew Dunner better than any faculty member in the department. Perhaps sensing Vince's gift for radiology, Dunner spent extra time with him, teaching him the finer points that were beyond the grasp of the other residents. Dr. Dunner and his wife, Susan, had invited Vince over to their house for dinner several times. Dunner portrayed a stern, serious posture in the department. Most of the residents thought he was aloof and unapproachable. But Vince got to see the relaxed side of Dunner. He had a witty sense of humor, and the dinners at his house sometimes turned into all-night partying.

Dunner was the team radiologist for the Denver Broncos. He took Vince along when he reviewed the players' MRIs with the orthopedic surgeons. He introduced Vince to the athletes and showed him how to inject steroids into inflamed joints. The responsibility was mind-boggling—deciding if a multimillion dollar athlete could play the next weekend—and Vince reveled in it.

Vince opened up to Susan and Dick Dunner like the parents he never had. They were the only ones who knew about his rough childhood, his foster care problems, and his juvenile record. Vince never trusted anyone before. He realized early in life that if he wanted to accomplish anything, he needed to do it himself and not rely on other people. But with the Dunners' caring nature, he began to open up, to confide in them, and it felt good.

"I'm having a little trouble understanding these numbers," Dr. Dunner said, looking over the top of his reading glasses.

This is trouble, Vince thought. Wiping a bead of sweat off his forehead he replied, "What's wrong?"

"The expense sheet you submitted with your chief resident credit card. It doesn't add up."

Vince realized he was holding his breath. "Let me see," he said. He didn't think anyone would notice the extra charges he used to pay his dealer last month. He thought the bills would slip through unchecked. Vince pretended to pore over the charge slips while trying to think of a reasonable explanation. He started to feel nauseated.

"I must have left out some of the receipts. I threw a couple of parties for the new residents. I'll check tonight and get back to you, okay?"

Dunner didn't look convinced. He took off his reading glasses and leaned back in his chair. "I'm worried about you, Vince. Is everything all right?"

"Sure. I just have a lot going on right now, that's all."

"You look tired. And it looked like you were about to hit Dr. Richards the other day."

"It was just a misunderstanding."

"If you need to talk, come on over. It's been a while. And bring Rosie. She's such an interesting woman."

"I'm fine, Dick. And Rosie and I are over." Vince left Dunner's office and hurried down the hall to vomit in the bathroom. After all Dunner had done for his career, he couldn't let the vice chairman find out the truth. He had to come up with a reasonable explanation for those phony charges.

CHAPTER

24

o drove back to Boulder, anxious about his run with Lisa, and trying to forget how he could have missed such an obvious abnormality on X-ray. He passed Louisville on Highway 36 and started the descent into Boulder. The expansive beauty before him reminded Bo why he preferred to live here rather than Denver, despite the forty-five-minute drive. He loved it all: the picture-postcard views, the unlimited biking and running trails, kayaking in Boulder creek. The red-roof buildings of the University of Colorado spread out before him. On his left, the famous flatirons, triangular peaks from the massive uplift that formed the Rocky Mountains and the symbol of Boulder, pointed to the azure sky. In the distance, snow remained on top of Long's Peak, one of Colorado's fourteen thousand-foot mountains that Bo and Cory climbed a few weeks before her death.

Bo parked his truck at the ranger station in Chautauqua and found Lisa leaning against the gray-white bark of a quaking aspen tree, stretching her calves. A multicolored running skirt and matching sports top accentuated her perfect figure. A petite fanny pack hung below her smooth, flat stomach.

Lisa turned and delivered a smile so radiant against her deeply tanned face that Bo's heart skipped a beat, and he felt like an awkward teenager. He never had a steady girlfriend in high school and only dated sporadically in college, too busy concentrating on his studies.

Bo smiled back and managed to say, "Sorry I'm late."

"I just got here, myself," Lisa said.

"Where do you want to go?"

"I like the Royal Arch trail. It's beautiful this time of year. It's a pretty good climb though, about twelve-hundred-feet elevation gain. Is that okay?"

"Sure. I need to get in shape for the 5430."

"The 5430?"

"It's a half-Ironman that starts at the Boulder Reservoir in August."

"Nice. I've always wanted to do a triathlon. I suck at swimming, though."

"That's the only thing I'm good at."

Lisa pointed the way and they set out side by side, jogged past the ranger cottage and onto Bluebell Road, directly toward the towering flatirons. They climbed across a meadow, skirting the swordlike leaves of the yucca plants and butterflies resting on the fiery red and pink flowers of Indian paintbrush. The trail narrowed and Bo dropped behind Lisa, admiring her effortless stride.

When the path widened again, Lisa slowed down so Bo could catch up. She chatted, no more out of breath than at a tea party, about growing up in Boulder, attending the University of Colorado on a track scholarship. Injuries had forced her to stop running. "At that level of intensity, everyone on the team got stress fractures—it was only a matter of time before I did—and I decided to give it up."

"When did you start up again?"

"A couple of years ago. I had an office job after college, got out of shape, and missed it. I just run for fun now."

When the trail narrowed to single-track, Bo said, "If you could give me any running technique tips, I'd appreciate it." He moved in front, concentrating on keeping a steady pace and relaxing his upper body. He felt self-conscious, stumbled on a couple of rocks and tree roots, and slowed to avoid falling.

"When the trails are uneven like this," she said from behind him, "resist the urge to look down. Focus your eyes on a spot a little ahead of you so you know what's coming up. It's similar to mountain biking in that you need to pick a line and commit to it."

He concentrated on Lisa's instructions and was surprised that he was running easier when he didn't look down at the rocks. He was a lot less sloppy than when he started. The altitude and pitch of the hill strained his legs and lungs, but he had enough stamina to keep a steady pace.

"Good," he heard her say. "Now try to shorten your stride and take smaller steps. Think baby steps."

Bo took her advice. His pace quickened with the shorter steps but he didn't feel any more tired. He ran like this for another quarter mile until he arrived at the top of the mountain, an exquisite twenty-foot-high rock arch in front of him.

Bo stepped into the opening and gawked at the stunning, panoramic view of the city of Boulder below. "Wow. This is beautiful. I can see Folsom Field down there."

"The Royal Arch is like a frame." Lisa stood at the base of the rock formation, holding her hands like a camera. "And the picture changes depending on which direction you face."

Bo sat on a ledge under the arch and faced Lisa.

"I took a geology course when I was at CU," she said. "This place is so amazing. It's more than two hundred million years old, part of the Ancestral Rockies. The flatirons"—Lisa pointed north through the arch—"were flat once but got pushed up in the air like that during tectonic plate shifts. Before that, they were actually covered by the sea, which formed all this sandstone we see around us."

Lisa unzipped her fanny pack, took out a power bar, and wandered around a small outcropping out of view.

Bo stood and looked back through the archway. He thought about Cory and how much she would have liked this view.

A rustling noise behind him interrupted his daydreaming, and Bo turned to the sound.

Lisa knelt on one knee.

She was holding a large handgun.

And it was pointed right at Bo.

Just before he heard the explosion, a split-second after the flash, Bo realized how little he knew about her.

CHAPTER

25

Marisol sits on the porch with Hector and his parents. The afternoon sun, a brilliant ball of light, descends over the horizon, filtering through the screen. A soft breeze from the overhead ceiling fan cools Marisol's bare shoulders. Her initial nervousness over meeting the Hernandezes has faded with the smiles and easy conversation. Hector, quiet and handsome, holds her hand. She's so happy to have met him. Mrs. Hernandez goes into the kitchen and returns with a large pot of steaming soup. The aroma of tomato and basil smells delicious, and Marisol realizes how hungry she is. Mr. Hernandez grins as he watches Marisol dip her spoon into the bowl and take a sip.

The rubbery texture gags her.

What's in this? She spits it out and looks down at the bowl. It's filled with condoms shaped into little rubber balls.

Marisol gasps.

Hector's mother glares at Marisol. "Eat," she insists.

"I can't."

"Eat," she says again, shoving a spoonful down Marisol's throat. Marisol chokes and retches, but no sound comes out.

"You must eat, you wretched girl!"

Marisol has to get out of the house. She tries to stand up but she's stuck to the chair. Mr. Hernandez stands behind her, pulling her hair and holding her head back. "Stop!"

Now Hector looms in front of her. His face is changed: an ugly tattoo surrounds his left eye. Thick blood oozes down his bare chest.

"You must eat, Marisol," Hector snaps, picking up a knife from the table, "or we will have to kill you."

"Heeeeeeeeeelp!" Marisol screams but only hears a gargling sound.

———∘∘⊰❂⊱∘∘———

"Relax, Relax." Someone shook her. "Relax," the voice said again. Marisol opened her eyes and a woman stood over her, touching her shoulder, talking to her. She was blonde and very pretty. And then Marisol remembered the soup. Her panicked eyes flitted around the small room. Hector and his parents were gone. She tried to sit up, but an intense pain ripped through her stomach. She yelled but again no sound came out. A tube was stuck in her throat and she couldn't breathe. She was trapped.

"Shush, shush," the pretty lady whispered. "You're in a hospital."

Hospital? Marisol struggled to understand. She couldn't concentrate. And then the memories flooded back to her: the mean Sureños drug dealers; the airport; the pain in her belly; the priest; the nice doctor praying with her.

A man in a white coat joined the blonde lady and spoke to her in Spanish. "I'm Dr. Wilson. You're in a hospital. Try to relax." He took out his stethoscope and put the cold metal plate on Marisol's chest, closing his eyes as he listened.

"We're going to take that tube out of your mouth. This is Karen," he said pointing to the nice lady. "She's going to help me, okay?"

Marisol nodded.

Karen reached over and turned off the machine. She grabbed the plastic tube and pulled it out of Marisol's mouth. Marisol coughed and gagged. She couldn't catch her breath.

"Breathe slowly," Dr. Wilson encouraged.

After several tries, Marisol was able to breathe again. "God bless you," she tried to say, but her hoarse voice was unintelligible.

"Try not to talk. Your throat will be sore for a little while."

Marisol understood. The nurse took a syringe out of her pocket and grabbed one of the loose tubes and squirted the clear liquid. Marisol closed her eyes and drifted back to sleep, back to her dream.

———∘∘∘⧏◉⧐∘∘∘———

This time the soup is really soup, and it's delicious. Hector calls Marisol the next day and invites her to the beach. They swim and talk and walk along the shore. He embraces her in the water and kisses her for the first time, gently at first, but then deeper and deeper until Marisol's lips and tongue are one with his. It is beautiful and exciting, and on that lovely afternoon Marisol knows she wants to spend the rest of her life with him.

CHAPTER

26

Bo grunted when he hit the ground, the gunshot blast echoing around him. Reacting out of instinct, he rolled to the edge of the mountain and grabbed the woody base of a juniper bush to stop his fall, surprised he didn't feel any pain. From above, an agonized howl pierced the thin air, and the largest cat he'd ever seen thumped to the ground.

Lisa approached cautiously, her gun hand outstretched, and circled the animal like an Amazon huntress until she was satisfied it was dead. Bo took a couple of deep breaths and climbed back up. The dead mountain lion leered at him.

"That was close," Lisa said.

Bo stood dazed and picked the spiny needles out of his shirt.

"Are you okay?" she asked when Bo didn't reply.

"What ... who ... are ... you?"

"Don't worry. I have a license to carry this guy," she laughed, gesturing with the gun. "I'm an officer with the Boulder Police Department." Lisa returned the gun to the fanny pack. She took a sip from her water bottle and offered it to Bo, who gulped it down. The cool liquid brought Bo back to reality.

"I never even heard it," Bo said, looking down at the mountain lion.

"I was lucky I spotted him. He was poised to attack. There wasn't time to warn you."

"Do you always carry a gun when you run?"

"Up here I do. Ever since a mountain lion pulled a kid right out of his father's hand last year, I don't take any chances."

As they prepared to run back down the mountain, Lisa gave Bo instructions. "On the way down, try to keep your head up again. It's a little scary, but you have to trust it. Also, keep your nose over your toes so you don't kill your quads."

Bo had more on his mind than running, but he tried to pay attention to his technique.

Lisa flew down the rocky trail and was soon out of sight. He finally caught up with her at the bottom. She was on the grass stretching when he arrived.

"Thanks for saving my life," Bo said.

"No problem. I only wish …" Lisa's words trailed off.

"… You could have saved Cory?" Bo finished her sentence.

"Yeah."

"Me too. We were a good team. She was a runner too—not as talented as you of course."

"Would you like to have dinner with me and talk about it? It might help both of us."

Bo hesitated. What would Cory think?

Lisa noticed his hesitation. "Or not. No big deal."

"No," Bo finally replied. "I'd love to. How about Friday night?"

CHAPTER

27

B o felt different when he returned home after his run with Lisa. The condo didn't seem as quiet as usual. He took Cory's nightgown off the back of the bathroom door, pressed it to his cheek, and folded it. Baby steps.

After a quick shower and dinner he poured a glass of merlot and logged on to his computer. He jotted down a few notes about drug smuggling for his upcoming lecture and decided to search for more examples. All the doctors at the university had Internet access to the X-ray department. After entering his username and password, Bo searched the database for recent films performed at Denver International Airport. He was surprised at the number of suspected smugglers—some days as many as five passengers were screened— and it didn't take long to accumulate examples for his presentation. Bo winced at the sight of an enormous condom inserted into a smuggler's rectum; the pain must have been terrible.

Most of the positive cases had swallowed the drugs like Marisol, taking their chances that the packages would be obscured by their constipation. The more cases he examined, the quicker Bo recognized the characteristic crescent of air between the drugs and packaging material. If nothing else, at least he wouldn't miss another case of drug smuggling again. After an hour, Bo had thirty cases to show the residents. He printed the reports so he'd have the names handy for his talk.

He stood up to pour another glass of wine and noticed it was getting late.

Bo returned to his desk and pulled out the pile of customs X-ray reports. He started to read them and almost dropped his wine. All but five were reported as normal. It was just like Marisol Hernandez. These were all obvious cases of bolitas—impossible to overlook. There was no way anyone could miss this many cases. And page after page was signed "Bo Richards, MD."

CHAPTER

28

It took Bo a long time to fall asleep after his discovery of all those fake customs reports. He knew he couldn't have missed them all. Someone was setting him up.

The damn phone woke him.

"Hello?"

"Dr. Richards?"

"Yes, who is this?" The digital clock read 3:30 a.m. Bo groaned.

"It's Rosie Garcia. I'm sorry to call you at this hour."

"Rosie?" Bo's sleepy brain couldn't place the name.

"From MRI."

That woke Bo up. His eyes snapped open as he remembered the oxygen cylinder hurtling through the air.

"Are you calling to tell me I'm an idiot again?"

"No. And I'm sorry about that. Vince Flickinger showed up at my apartment last night. He passed out as soon as I let him in. His respirations are really shallow, and I'm worried that he'll stop breathing."

"Why don't you call 911?"

"As much as I despise Vince, I don't want him to lose his medical license. Could you come over and check him out?"

Bo stumbled out of bed, popped a pod into his coffee maker—he loved those new one-cup systems—and headed to the bathroom. He threw cold water over his face and grabbed the steaming mug on his way out the door.

Twenty minutes later Bo arrived at Rosie's apartment. She met him in her bathrobe. "I still can't wake him," she said. "I can barely see him breathing."

He followed Rosie into the bedroom, where Vince lay sprawled across the messy bed. He was on his side, a foamy drool cascading from his mouth to a large orange stain on the bed. His blond hair was covered in vomit, littered with unidentifiable objects. Boxers covered his flabby, naked body. Bo had thought Vince was in better shape.

He shook Vince, shouting and clapping. No response. He pinched his clammy skin between his fingernails, and Vince opened his eyes. *That's a start,* Bo thought. Bo peeled back Vince's eyelids and shined a pocket light into his pupils. They were reactive but pinpoint.

Bo looked up at Rosie, asking, "Were you guys doing any drugs last night?"

"Not me. Vince didn't show up here until after midnight and he was already slurring his words and acting crazy. I almost didn't let him in."

Bo opened his medical bag and took out an IV set. He pumped up Vince's right arm with a tourniquet, inserted the catheter into a vein, and hung a bag of fluids. He removed a vial of Narcan and injected it into the tubing.

He turned to Rosie and said, "I've given him Narcan—it counteracts narcotics like heroin or Vicodin—and usually works pretty fast."

Within seconds Vince's eyes shot open and he twisted his head, looking around the room. "Wha ..." he tried to say, and his head fell back to the bed.

Bo took his vital signs before turning to Rosie. "His blood pressure and pulse are normal. His respirations are still shallow, but I think he'll be okay."

"Thanks for coming over," Rosie said.

"We're going to have to watch Vince for a while. Do you have any coffee?"

"Coming right up," she said and walked out of the bedroom.

Bo followed her into the living room and looked around at the sparse furnishings before sitting on a stained leather chair.

Rosie came back with coffee, noticed Bo had moved to the living room, and said, "Not too stylish, is it?"

Bo shrugged.

Rosie explained, "I'm working on paying back my student loans before I buy anything nice. But this is actually a big step up from the projects where I grew up."

They sipped the coffee in the quiet apartment.

"I'm sorry I called you an idiot that day with Mrs. Adcock," Rosie said.

"I deserved it, I guess." Bo dropped his head. "But those tanks shouldn't have been there."

"You're right."

Vince moaned, and they moved back to the bedroom. He rubbed his arm and tried to pull out the IV.

Bo said, "Stop, Vince. It's your IV."

Vince opened his eyes and noticed Bo and Rosie staring down at him. Looking shocked, he reeled back, pulled his legs up to his chest, and wrapped his arms around his knees. "What's going on?"

Bo explained. Vince's first reaction was denial. "I was just a little strung out."

"It was a little more dramatic than that, buddy," Bo said, and helped Vince into the shower.

When Bo returned to the bedroom, he saw that Rosie had stripped the bed and was cleaning the spot on the mattress with a steamer.

Fifteen minutes later Vince came out of the bathroom, this time apologetic. He looked a little better. "I'm sorry for the trouble, Bo. I owe you one, man." He walked over to shake Bo's hand but staggered and fell to the floor.

Bo picked Vince up, wrestled him outside into the truck, and managed to get him over to his condo and into his own bed.

"I owe you, man," Vince said again before passing out. "More than you know."

CHAPTER

29

B o only had fifteen minutes to get to work. He rushed through the corridors and past the hospital gift shop, stepping around the stuffed animals cluttering the hallway, to the radiology locker room. He took a quick shower, put on the spare clothes he kept in his locker, and hurried over to the ER reading room.

The pitiful scene in Rosie's apartment replayed in Bo's mind. How could Vince—golden-boy chief resident, most likely to succeed, Mr. Personality—put himself in that position? He almost died of an overdose. It didn't make any sense. Bo knew the statistics—10 percent of doctors were impaired from drugs or alcohol—but he couldn't believe it included Vince. Perhaps it was a one-time binge, a mistake. He would talk to Vince today.

At precisely 8:00 a.m. Bo opened the door to the ER reading room to find Sheri half-asleep on the couch. She opened one eye and groaned. Twenty-four-hour-old makeup smeared her exhausted face while errant strands protruded from her matted hair at gravity-defying angles.

"Tough night?"

"Unbelievable," Sheri replied, her Southern drawl thicker this morning. "I think the whole city of Denver stopped by the ER last night. I've never seen so many accidents and strokes and gunshot victims."

"Sorry. Well, get out of here and get some sleep."

"I can't. Fucking Dunner hasn't come by for readout yet."

"Why don't you go home? I'll go over your films with Dunner. I'm sure you didn't miss anything. If there are any discrepancies, I'll take care of it."

Sheri strained to get off the couch. "I owe you, Bo." And with a feeble attempt to add sexual innuendo, she flapped her streaked eyelids like a cheap hooker and said, "If there's *anything* I can do for you …"

"Actually there is."

"You're finally going to date me?"

"Do you have any boyfriends in the IT department? I have a computer question for an expert."

"I might know someone," Sheri said. "I'll talk to at you at Expectations. You're going, right?" The local beer and pizza restaurant had become a Thursday-night ritual for Bo and his group of second-year residents.

"Wouldn't miss it."

Sheri grabbed her purse and ever-present two-liter bottle of Diet Coke and started to leave. She fumbled with the door and dropped the soda. "Now I know why they say staying up all night is the equivalent of being legally drunk."

"At least you live close enough to walk home."

Dr. Dunner moped into the ER reading room an hour later, looking as sleep-deprived as Sheri. Bo hadn't seen him since the "probation" meeting in Dr. Musk's office the other day. He looked ten years older, his white lab coat thrown on to hide his wrinkled shirt. An amoeba-shaped patch of unshaven stubble oozed to life when the vice chairman grimaced.

"Sorry I'm late, Bo. I assume Sheri has left."

"Yes, sir."

It didn't take long for the uninterested vice chairman to review Sheri's work and sign off on her reports. Dunner's malaise solved one of Bo's problems. After last night's discovery of the misinterpreted X-rays from the airport, Bo debated his next step. He considered approaching Dr. Dunner, who coordinated the program between the

DIA customs officials and the university's radiology department. But considering the vice chairman's current somber mood, Bo decided to wait for a more receptive opportunity.

On his way out the door, Dr. Dunner turned to Bo and said, "Oh. I almost forgot. Dr. Flickinger called in sick this morning. I'm arranging another senior resident to supervise you."

The ER was slow this morning, and Bo had time to attend the medical conference. Yesterday's clean-shaven, energetic interns now struggled to stay awake as the medical training cycle continued. Cindy Strong was there, not as well-dressed as yesterday, and presented the follow-up on the ski instructor. The steroids were working and his lungs were starting to clear up on chest X-ray.

After conference, Dr. Perfect came up to Bo and asked for Vince. The cardiologist was disappointed that Vince was sick and asked Bo to pass along his appreciation for a remarkable diagnosis.

Bo cleaned up a few ER X-rays—his senior resident still had not shown up—and decided to visit his swimming high school friend, Raul. He heard that the surgery had gone well and Raul might be discharged in a couple of days.

Bo called the hospital operator to get Raul's room number and took the elevator to the third floor. As he walked down the surgical floor, the assault on his senses reminded Bo of his own surgical days. In one room a nurse was obviously changing a colostomy bag, and in the next, the percolating sounds of a chest tube bubbled. Further down the hallway, the pungent combination of Betadine and bedsores trailed Bo like a toxic cloud as he entered Raul's room and closed the door. Raul was sitting up watching television, his left leg resting on an ottoman.

Raul smiled. "Hey, Doc. How ya doin?"

"That's what I'm supposed to ask you. You look good, man," Bo said sniffing, not recognizing the scent in the room.

"You like that smell?" Raul noticed Bo's confusion.

"What is it?"

"I call it 'au de pool.'" Raul laughed. "That nasty smell next door was making me sick. I asked the coach to bring me something to mask it. He came in yesterday with this fan filled with chlorine water. He said it would motivate me to get back in the pool."

"Funny. I'll bet you'll be back in as soon as the stitches come out."

"I hope so. I don't want you kicking my butt."

Bo and Raul sat quietly for a while, looking at the television, making small talk.

Bo got up to leave. "I guess I'd better get back to work."

"Hey, Doc. Thanks for saving my life. It was pretty damn scary that day."

"No problem. I needed to keep you alive so I have someone to beat in the pool."

"Keep dreaming."

"Did you ever figure out who did it?"

"Oh, I know who did it. This dude, Filipe, from the Norteños gang, I know him from the 'hood. My brother Roberto had some problems with him before he got sent to jail. I should have been more careful."

"I don't know that much about gangs, Raul."

"All you need to know is that the Sureños are part of the Mexican mafia and they control the Limon prison where Roberto is locked up. Didn't you see that movie *American Me* with James Earl Jones?

"No."

"They're some mean motherfuckers," Raul added. "And since they control the inside, they think they can control the streets."

After leaving Raul's room, Bo walked to the nurses' station and looked at Raul's chart. Everything looked good. No fever or other signs of infection. Raul was scheduled for discharge tomorrow. When he put Raul's chart back into the rack, he noticed a loose chart on the nurses' work table and recognized the name Gloria Adcock, Room 325. Bo decided to walk down her hallway.

The door to room 325 was open and he peeked in as he passed. Mrs. Adcock was alone, resting in bed, reading a book. He wanted to apologize to her but hesitated, remembering Dr. Dunner's warning. Then he remembered the brief connection they'd shared before she stopped breathing. She deserved an explanation. Screw hospital policy. It was the right thing to do.

Mrs. Adcock sensed his presence and turned to him. After a couple of tense seconds, Bo saw her look of recognition and said, "Mrs. Adcock, I'm Dr. Bo Richards. From MRI."

"Yes, I remember you."

"I wanted to say how sorry I am about the oxygen tank. I had no idea it was dangerous and I feel terrible about it."

Mrs. Adcock smiled weakly, and then her eyes shifted to Bo's right. Sensing a change in her demeanor, Bo turned to see a large man in a Circuit City shirt staring at him.

"Hello, sir. I'm Dr. Richards from radiology."

Bo held out his hand and the man started to reciprocate when he suddenly pulled it back as anger flashed across his face. "Wait a minute. You're the moron who broke my wife's leg. What the hell are you doing here?"

"I wanted to apologize."

"Well, apologize to this," Adcock said while his fist swung into Bo's abdomen. The punch knocked Bo down on one knee, and intense pain seared through his liver. He gasped for air but his lungs spasmed. Panic set in. The room darkened. He couldn't stop the next punch coming down on his head and braced for the blow when Mr. Adcock unexpectedly jerked to the side and stumbled backward. A crutch was pressed against his chest, driving him back to his wife's bed.

Raul was swearing at him in Spanish. Then he looked down at Bo and said, "Let's go, Doc."

"Yeah. Get the hell out of here," Mr. Adcock said. "You'll be hearing from my lawyer."

Bo stumbled out of the room and doubled over, panting. Raul looked worried, asking, "Are you okay?"

The pain subsided and Bo straightened up, holding on to the wall. "Thanks, Raul," he managed to say. "I don't know where you came from, but thanks."

"I was taking a walk down the hall when I saw that dude sucker-punch you."

"I owe you one."

"I don't think so, Doc."

CHAPTER

30

Vince parked his BMW in the Wells Fargo lot and tried to compose himself. He needed this loan to get the dealer off his back and balance the chief resident credit card before Dunner asked any more questions. He would work weekend shifts at a hospital in Fort Collins to pay it off. And money wouldn't be a problem next summer when he started his new job.

He rubbed his arm where the IV site still itched. He'd almost died last night, for Christ's sake. Bo and Rosie had to clean him up and carry him home like he was some seedy wino in the gutter. How embarrassing. After spending the whole day in bed, Vince had to rush to his appointment.

Vince checked his watch. He had five minutes before his appointment and twenty minutes before the bank closed. He needed the extra confidence. Vince opened the glove compartment, looked around the nearly empty parking lot, and slipped out the plastic bag—the last cocaine he would ever buy. A violent snort delivered the powder into his left nostril. He tilted his head back and closed his eyes, waiting. He pictured the drug covering his mucous membranes like a light snow, melting into the bloodstream and traveling to his brain, locking on to the pleasure receptors. Oh, those lovely receptors. He heard a chuckle and realized he was laughing. He was the man!

Vince walked into the bank brimming with confidence.

"Dr. Flickinger?" The loan officer stretched out his hand, and Vince was surprised at how young he looked. "I have your file right here," he said, pointing to a thin manila folder.

Vince followed the loan officer into his office, sat down, and looked around. The banker had the typical accoutrements of the profession: white button-down shirt; unobtrusive tie; day-planner perfectly centered on the mahogany desk. His suit jacket, which he probably only wore while walking from the car to his office, hung neatly behind him. Vince spotted the obligatory picture of a wife, kid, and dog. *How depressing.*

"After you called me this afternoon," the banker said, opening the manila folder, "I did some checking. Your credit cards are charged to the limit. And you have no assets to speak of."

If I had the money I wouldn't be here, moron. "I'm a resident— my salary is pretty meager right now. But this is only a temporary problem. I have a moonlighting job worked out to help pay back the loan. And next summer, I start a high six-figure job."

"So you said on the phone." The banker tapped his pen on the folder and waited. "I'm sorry, but I'm not authorized to issue you a loan."

Vince looked across the desk at the banker, unbelieving. This loser was denying him the loan? Vince struggled to remain calm. "Then who is authorized? Maybe I should speak to him."

"What I meant was the bank is not in a position to extend you credit."

"Do you know who I am?" Vince stood up, chest swelling, face red. Without waiting for the answer he continued. "I am the chief resident in radiology at University Hospital, one of the top five programs in the country. I manage thirty-six residents and sit on the executive committee of the hospital. While you were struggling through Accounting 101 and partying with your frat brothers, I was busting my butt in the hospital all night saving lives. Sure I don't earn as much as you right now, but that's all about to change. Now give me the fucking loan or let me speak to someone who will."

Vince followed the banker's eyes to the desk. The shiny manila folder was dotted with blood. He wiped the frothy mucous from his lips as the loan officer stood up, stepped back, and inched closer to the door.

"Well?" Vince crossed his arms over his chest and stared at the nervous banker.

"I'll be right back."

"It's about fucking time," Vince replied and sat down. He glanced out the window and saw the sun setting over Mount Evans, beautiful sparkles of light dancing over the summit. Two years ago, Vince competed in the Evans ascent bike race, winding up the road to the fourteen thousand-foot top. Now he couldn't remember the last time he rode, preferring the quick euphoria from the cocaine over the sweaty grind of the pedals.

He heard footsteps and turned around in time to see a large security guard enter the room, trailed by the cowering banker. The guard marched up to Vince with his nightstick out and ready.

Vince tried to look around the brute. "What the hell is going on? I thought you were going to get someone who had the authority to give me a loan."

"Sir," the security guard said. "I'm going to have to ask you to leave the building."

"I'm not going anywhere until this weasel gives me a loan."

"Sir," he repeated, raising the nightstick and flexing his muscles.

"All right, all right. Get out of my way."

The guard stepped aside, allowing Vince to pass. Vince looked at the annoying picture of the wife, dog, and kid and knocked it to the ground, breaking it.

CHAPTER

31

Bo returned to the ER reading room shaken, scared, and sore. All he had wanted to do was apologize to Mrs. Adcock. He sensed understanding in her eyes before her brute of a husband came in. Why couldn't Mr. Adcock appreciate that Bo was just trying to help?

Bo slumped into his chair, put his head on the desk, and cursed his fate. He hoped the chairman didn't get wind of this.

Dr. Wu entered quietly and cleared his throat to get Bo's attention.

Bo jerked his head up and apologized. "It's been a crazy day, sir."

"No worries, Dr. Richards. Let's look at the X-rays, shall we?"

Dr. Wu was calm and deliberate, and Bo relaxed. A rhythm developed as they worked through the queue of patients: Bo displayed the films on the computer monitor, described what he saw, and listened to Wu's helpful comments and advice. The next hour raced by as Bo got lost in the work. Bo showed Wu one case of a patient with chest pain and a normal-looking X-ray. He was about to go to the next patient when Wu stopped him and pointed out a subtle widening of the heart.

"I think she has a pericardial effusion," Wu said.

"Wow," Bo said. "I'd better call the ER and see what happened to her."

Bo picked up the phone and discussed the findings with the ER attending, Dr. Sam Carter. Luckily, the patient was still in the ER waiting for lab results to come back. When Bo alerted Jones to the possible buildup of fluid around the patient's heart, he got excited.

"No wonder we're having trouble controlling her blood pressure," Carter said. "I'll call the cardiologist."

As Bo and Dr. Wu finished the rest of the work, Bo decided he would tell Wu about the series of misses he had found last night. He felt comfortable with Wu and trusted his advice. Bo rolled his chair back to face Dr. Wu. He described his research on bolitas and how he decided to get some examples from recent X-rays at DIA. Wu was shocked at the number of cases of drug smuggling and was even more astounded when Bo told him that his name was on the reports of all the missed cases.

"I wasn't even working on some of those days," Bo said. He pulled up one of the cases. "Look how obvious this is. There's no way I could have called it normal."

Bo waited while Wu sat still, thinking. Wu asked to see a couple more cases before standing up, shaking his head, dismayed.

"I will speak to the chairman about this, Bo," Wu said. "Leave it up to me. For now, I wouldn't tell anyone else."

"Okay," Bo said as his pager went off. Looking at the number, he sighed and said, "I've got to go to Dr. Vanderworst's office. I'll keep quiet about this until I hear from you."

Bo trudged over to the neurosurgeon's office in the MRI center, taking the outdoor route, hoping the afternoon sun would cheer him up. Vanderworst, the youngest surgeon to be promoted to full professor, had recently been appointed director of the MRI facility. His new laser technique removed disc herniations without damaging the tissues and had catapulted the young neurosurgeon to instant success. He had more money than he could spend and the power to go with it. He even got Musk to agree to let him interpret his own patients' MRIs, so the money kept flowing. Bo passed the spotless black convertible with the vanity plates and walked into Vanderworst's office.

Bo was met by Jodi, Vanderworst's secretary of the week. She looked like a hooker with her miniskirt, tall white boots, and tight, tight top. Bo wondered why the university didn't demand a dress code for such an important position. Vanderworst probably found her at a night club. His after-hours activities were legendary: exotic vacations, beautiful women, fancy cars.

"Dr. V. will be right with you," she said, admiring her perfect manicure. She walked over to the corner to fill up a coffee mug, and Bo had to admire the MRI director's taste. The miniskirt barely covered her perfect bottom. When she turned around with her filled mug, her bountiful top didn't move, and Bo wondered if her breasts were real.

"Yes, they're real, Dr. Richards." Was he that transparent? "But if you'd like to use your medical training …" The door opened in time to save Bo from Jodi's invitation.

"Dr. Richards, come in," Dr. Vanderworst said. The diminutive surgeon looked more like a hobbit than a ladies' man. Even his hands were hairy. Bo guessed the easy flow of money made up for the pointed ears and plump belly.

Bo was surprised to find Dr. Dunner in the office. Sitting ramrod straight, he looked more alert than he had this morning.

Dispensing with the formalities, Dunner said, "I received a call from the hospital attorney a little while ago. I thought I made it clear that you were to stay away from Mrs. Adcock."

"Sorry, sir."

"That's not acceptable, Dr. Richards," Vanderworst added. "It's one thing to almost kill the patient with your bonehead move. It's another to start a fight with the patient's husband."

"It wasn't like that. I just wanted to apologize."

Dunner stood up and walked in front of Bo. "I'm going to say it one more time, Dr. Richards. Read my lips: leave Mrs. Adcock alone. Let our lawyers work this out." He continued, "We've agreed that you should stay away from the MRI center for the next month, while you're on probation."

Vanderworst had remained standing. He moved next to Bo and said, "I don't want you reading any of my patients' MRIs or interacting with my patients in any way. All of my patients are private; I make it clear to them from my first consult that no trainee residents will be involved. That's how I've been so successful."

"Do you understand?" Dunner said.

"Yes, sir."

"Stay away from my patients," Dr. Vanderworst repeated. "Or the consequences will be serious."

CHAPTER

32

o arrived at Expectations early, still shaken from the "consequences will be serious" speech, and ordered a pitcher of beer while he waited for his friends. Located three blocks from the hospital, the restaurant attracted nurses, residents, and medical students. The beer was cold, the pizza good, but the location was the reason for its success—an easy walk to decompress after a week of dealing with hard tragedies.

Last year's chief resident arranged a welcoming party here for Bo's group when they first started residency. After the introductions and boring recitation of colleges and medical schools, the residents realized they really liked one another. They were witty, lively, and cynical about the clinical side of medicine. Expectations became their Thursday-night ritual. Everyone was invited—spouses, new significant others, friends, and visiting family. Over the last year, the group helped Bo deal with Cory's death and guided another resident, Skip, through a testy divorce. Two of the residents, Jane and Alex, were now dating.

Walking in off the windy and bustling streets of Denver, leaving behind yuppies in business suits balancing lattes and briefcases, Bo considered Expectations an oasis of sanity. He liked the western motif, right down to the swinging saloon doors. Instead of sawdust or dirt from the old west, cracked peanut shells littered the floor, tossed carelessly by the patrons, encouraged by the owners.

Bo relaxed and listened to the band. He had finished his second mug of beer when Sheri burst through the swinging doors and sat next to him, a trail of strong perfume in her wake. Her dark hair was pulled back in a severe ponytail, her designer jeans pressed so crisply the creases could injure small children, and pain hid behind a false smile.

"You need a beer more than I do," Bo said, pouring her a draft.

"Thanks, Bo. I am a little stressed right now."

"Anything you want to talk about?"

Sheri grabbed her beer. "It's my stupid brother. He's only been out of prison for a couple of weeks and I think he's back on drugs again."

"Sorry."

Sheri shook her head. "He always does something stupid when he's using." She looked at Bo. "Are you close with your brothers?"

"Pretty close. I'm the youngest of three. They're both brilliant and confident. I felt like I was always struggling to keep up with them."

"Yeah, right. You're the smartest guy I know."

"I just try harder."

Bo watched Sheri swallow half her beer. She let out a satisfying belch and put the mug down with a smile.

"Enough about brothers. Anything exciting happen today after I went home?"

"I had a run-in with Mr. Adcock, the husband of my MRI disaster. I was up on the floor visiting my swimming buddy, Raul, and passed Mrs. Adcock's room. She was alone and looked miserable so I went in and apologized for the oxygen tank. She never got a chance to respond. Her husband punched me in the stomach so hard I almost lost consciousness."

"Ouch. How'd you get out of there?"

"Raul. He was walking down the hall, saw what was going on, and saved my ass."

Alex and Jane walked in holding hands, clearly still dating. They were the most unusual couple he'd ever seen, adding credence to the polar-opposites-attract theory. Jane was curvaceous and buxom, big wavy blonde hair, a Dr. Barbie. She was also the smartest person in their residency. Trained at Harvard, she had encyclopedic knowledge, came up with the most obscure diseases, and was usually right. Her mastery of anatomy was remarkable. Alex, on the other hand, was a mousy nerd; Bo kept looking for the pocket protector. His face had the pale hue of too much time spent under fluorescent lighting in the library.

"I hear you're a hero," Jane said to Bo.

Bo looked blankly at Jane until he realized she was talking about the drug mule, not his MRI screwup.

"I got lucky on that one," Bo finally replied and added, "it was the most intense scene in the ER I've ever experienced. She was dead, her heart just fibrillating, when Dr. Nicolai pulled out the leaking condom and brought her back to life. It was—"

Bo's eyes started to well up. His friends waited for him to continue. "—a miracle, a religious experience," he finished.

They sat back in silence, listening to the music and sipping beer, contemplating life's fragility. The pizza came and the conversation drifted to the usual hospital gossip: nurses and doctors cheating on their spouses, power plays in the administration, missed cancer stories. No wonder so many soap operas took place in hospitals.

Bo lost count of the beers. The music sounded a little fuzzy.

He heard the booming laugh before he saw Skip push open the saloon doors. He was sporting a Colorado Rockies shirt and a new girlfriend. It took a minute before Bo realized the girlfriend was Rosie. Without her business suit and perfectly combed hair, he almost didn't recognize the chief MRI tech.

"The Rockies suck," Skip announced to the group. "They should have won tonight."

Skip slapped Bo on the back before heading to the men's room. Bo motioned for Rosie to sit next to him. "How long have you guys been dating?"

"This is our first date. Is Skip always this loud?"

"Only when he's drunk. He's actually a really nice guy."

"Thanks again for the other night, Bo," Rosie said. "I was pretty worried about Vince."

"No problem."

"Skip's calling me over to the pool table. I'll talk to you later."

Sheri watched Rosie leave. "I didn't know Skip and Rosie were dating."

"Just started," Bo answered.

"It's too bad she had to drop out of med school," Alex said. "She's brilliant. She knows more than most of the doctors reading the MRIs."

Bo relaxed to a couple of Beatles songs, and when he opened his eyes, Sheri was tapping him on the shoulder and Rosie stood behind her. "Do you still want that computer help, or are you too drunk?"

"Now?"

"I asked Rosie to come tonight. She's a genius at the hospital system."

Rosie said, "Skip's tied up in a game. He won't even notice I'm gone."

It wasn't until Bo walked outside that he realized he'd had too much to drink. Sheri interlocked arms to steady him, and the three walked down the block and across the empty patient parking lot. They entered the glass atrium, skirted around a sad group of teenagers weeping and consoling each other and texting on their cell phones, passed the closed snack bar and gift shop, and took the stairs down one level to the basement. An arrow pointed to the medical records department, the depository of all patients' charts and billing information.

Sheri produced a key—he really owed her a huge favor—opened a door, and they walked passed carts piled high with charts awaiting doctors' signatures. They entered a chilly, cavernous room divided into rows and rows of shelves stuffed with manila folders.

When were they ever going to get an electronic system?

Rosie sat at the computer. Her keystrokes rattled through the empty room, adding to Bo's mounting anxiety. If they got caught looking at medical records without permission, they could get arrested.

"Let get moving," Rosie said, turning from the computer screen to Bo. "What are you looking for?"

Bo explained about the customs reports, how his name was attached to obviously abnormal X-rays, although the reports had been interpreted as normal. He handed Rosie the list of the drug mules and watched in fascination as her fingers danced over the keys.

He turned to Sheri, who shrugged and said, "See what I mean, Bo? She's a genius."

After several minutes, Rosie let out a string of expletives and slammed the desk. "I knew he was too slick. I can't believe I ever went out with that jerk."

"Who?"

"Vince, of course," Rosie said. "All of these reports were dictated in Vince's office."

CHAPTER

33

Marisol couldn't fall asleep. She wanted to; she was exhausted. She wanted to escape the pain in her belly where the doctors had cut her. She wanted to forget the sound the driver made when she strangled him with her rosary beads and the look on the skinny man's face when she shot him. She wanted to forget it all.

She worried about the police. Would they arrest her now that the doctors had found drugs in her belly? Should she sneak out of the hospital and find the nice priest? She brooded over these thoughts while the sounds of the ICU kept her awake: the constant beeping of her monitors, the clicking of computer keys from the nurses' station, the nonstop ringing of telephones and rushing footsteps. She was so tired. Her belly throbbed and Marisol pressed the button that would deliver the pain medicine from the pump. Her eyes got heavy as sleep began to take her.

Too drunk to drive home, Bo wandered up to the ICU and found an empty call room. He remembered the good times he'd had with Cory when she worked the night shift in the unit—he'd lie awake waiting for her breaks and a chance to snuggle. Tonight, despite the beers, it took a while for Bo to relax. He knew Vince had a drug problem, so there was only one logical explanation for Bo's name being on those customs reports: Vince must have a deal with drug smugglers and was setting Bo up to take the fall.

Marisol's eyes sprung open, her body paralyzed by fear. Her eyes darted around the room, desperate to find the source of her panic. It was the smell. How could she forget? The horrible, unmistakable, piney scent of his cologne seeped into the room. It was El Piojo! He was back to kill her.

She spotted him by the nurses' station, his back turned to her, talking to someone in the same cold, calculated tone he'd used on Marisol when he calmly described ripping the bolitas out of her belly with his knife. He wore the same shiny black suit she saw at the warehouse.

How did he find her?

Marisol had to run or hide. She hadn't even gotten out of bed yet and didn't know if she could stand, much less run past him. Looking around the room in panic, she saw a bathroom. It was her only chance. She ripped off the wires attached to her chest and pulled the tubes out of her arms. She tried to sit up but the pain was too intense. She rolled out of the bed and fell to the floor, stitches stretching and popping, and started crawling to the bathroom.

She didn't know if she could make it. A hot knife ripped through her belly. The room started to go gray, and she stopped so she wouldn't pass out. She had to make it to the bathroom. She didn't want it to end like this.

The machines in her room blared. The alarms woke her up, and Marisol realized she must have blacked out. She continued her slow, agonizing crawl toward the light in the bathroom. She heard excited voices coming from the nurses' station. The smell of cologne was closer, and she tried to hurry. Inch by inch she slid forward. Summoning her last ounce of strength, she pulled the door shut and locked it. Marisol looked down and saw blood dripping out of her stomach. She grabbed a towel and pressed it into the wound, oblivious to the pain, clutching it like she had held Arturo the morning the drug men stormed into her bungalow.

Loud knocking at the door startled Marisol out of semiconsciousness. She heard voices yelling. The door rattled but stayed locked. Marisol cowered in the corner next to the toilet. She was trapped. She heard a metal key clink into the lock, and the door opened. Marisol braced for the worst. She wondered how Sanchez would kill her.

———∞◦❖◦∞———

The alarms woke Bo, and he grabbed his throbbing head. His sticky mouth tasted of stale beer and pepperoni. The room started to spin, and he closed his eyes again. He moaned as he stood up. He cracked open the door, squinted in the bright light, and saw Karen, an ICU nurse and an old friend of Cory's, rushing into one of the ICU rooms. Bo decided he'd better help.

When he got there, Karen turned to him with a mystified look. "Where's the patient?"

The bed was empty, sheets pulled to the ground. A red carpet of blood smeared the floor and led to the bathroom. Bo and Karen ran to the door, found it locked, and pounded on it.

"Mrs. Hernandez, are you all right?"

"Open the door," Bo shouted.

The alarms stopped blaring and the room became deathly quiet: no sounds, no response from the bathroom. A security guard appeared and unlocked the door. Bo saw the body on the floor, wedged between the toilet and the wall, unmoving. Skinny, tan legs protruded from the loose, mustard-colored gown at unnatural angles. Blood stained a towel draped over her abdomen.

"Call Dr. Nicolai," Karen yelled to the nurses' station.

Bo helped the security guard pick up the body and carry it to the bed. Bo pushed sticky hair away from her neck and searched for a carotid pulse. Not feeling a beat he pushed harder, looking at her face for signs of life. That's when it struck him: this was Marisol Hernandez, the Mexican lady from the ER, the drug smuggler.

"She's alive, but barely," Bo said.

———∞◦❖◦∞———

Marisol felt her body being lifted off the bathroom floor. She could no longer fight Sanchez. He had won. She heard a woman's voice. Her mind must not be working right. She was being placed on her bed. She shivered and saw blurry, worried faces looking down at her. She couldn't move. Her hands and feet were tied down. They were about to kill her. She shrieked as she felt a sharp pain in her neck and strong hands holding her down, pressing her against the bed. Marisol tried to resist, but she was too tired.

And then a gentle, warm calmness caressed her. It was so peaceful. Just before sleep finally came, Marisol thought she saw that kind doctor who had prayed with her in the emergency room.

———◦◦○❀○◦◦———

The code team arrived, and Bo stepped back as they efficiently resuscitated the patient. They inserted a large IV into her jugular vein and started fluids. They put the monitoring equipment back on her chest. They pushed drugs until her rhythm stabilized.

Dr. Nicolai rushed in to help the code team. He pulled up the patient's gown, revealing remnants of shredded stitches dangling over the gaping incision. Coiled loops of intestine glistened and slithered out of the wound. Bo felt sick.

The surgical team wheeled in a stretcher and transferred Marisol off the ICU bed. The movement jolted her awake and she screamed, her eyes filled with terror.

Bo tried to reassure her, and she turned to the sound of his voice and her panic eased. Marisol whispered, and Bo leaned closer to listen.

"What's she saying?" Karen asked.

Bo scrunched his face in concentration, trying to remember his Spanish. "I'm not sure. The only words I recognize are 'smelly' and 'louse.'"

"She's probably delusional," Dr. Nicolai said.

"No. I know what it is." They all turned to Karen. "Just before this happened, I was talking to a guy in an ugly black suit, telling him that visiting hours were over long ago. He reeked of terrible cologne."

"Where is he now?" Bo asked.

"I don't know. He was asking about the man in room 6."

CHAPTER

34

A knock on the door startled Vince out of his fitful sleep. His head pounded when he stood up. He shuffled to the door, fighting waves of nausea. He wasn't expecting any visitors; he was supposed to be at work.

Vince had tried to get help last night. After he got thrown out of the bank, he drove to a Narcotics Anonymous meeting at the United Methodist Church in downtown Denver. He sat in the parking lot garnering the courage to attend the meeting—to admit he had a problem. To admit he couldn't beat it on his own. Vince, who knew more medicine than most of the faculty at the university, couldn't fix himself. Vince, the best chief resident the radiology department had ever had, was a loser, a failure. It was tough to admit. A week ago he sat in the same spot in the church parking lot but couldn't get out of his car, too embarrassed to humble himself.

Last night Vince forced himself to walk into the church and sit with the group. He was surprised at the caliber of the members: successful businessmen on their way home from work, a surgeon from Colorado Springs, a United Airlines pilot—impressive people from all walks of life. Vince listened to their heart-wrenching stories, encouraged that he wasn't quite as bad off as some of these people. When the leader asked Vince to stand up, he was ready to tell his story, relieved to get this burden off his chest and move on. Vince cleared his throat and looked at the group.

A flash of blonde hair in the second row distracted him. There was something familiar about it. He looked closer. Shit! A nurse from the hospital. He couldn't have anyone at the hospital know about his problem. Vince lost his courage and started to panic. Feigning sickness he ran to the bathroom, threw cold water over his face, and waited for his hands to stop shaking. Then he hurried out of the church and drove to the first bar he could find.

Now, as the knocking on his condo door continued, he cursed his weakness. He should have stayed at the meeting. He stumbled toward the door and summoned enough energy to open it.

Two mammoth hulks filled the frame, blocking all light. With a grunt, they lifted Vince off his feet and threw him back into the condo. They kicked him in the ribs and stomach, and Vince rolled into a protective ball. They kept kicking.

The room started to dim when Vince heard a familiar voice shout, "That's enough!"

Vince peeked between his hands and saw the angry dealer step between the two monsters.

"Get up."

Vince struggled to stand, still lightheaded and nauseated from last night. He felt a rib crack and bent over in pain. Finally he faced Ramón.

"I want my money now," the dealer demanded.

"I told you I'd have it tomorrow. I'm getting the money today."

"Not good enough." The dealer nodded to one of the savages, and a brutal uppercut ripped into Vince's belly, sending him sprawling to the floor, struggling to breathe.

"We will take a small down payment now"—the dealer pointed to Vince's large-screen TV and computer—"and we'll be back tomorrow for the rest."

Kicking Vince, he added, "And next time the twins won't be so gentle."

Vince watched helplessly, unable to move off the floor, as the men left with his electronics. Fighting a retching sensation, he dragged himself over to his nightstand and grabbed his cell phone. He hesitated before calling. This was his last chance, the only way to get the money.

CHAPTER

35

arisol woke in the middle of the night with a large bandage over her belly and a breathing tube in her mouth. Flickering orange light from the pulsating monitors illuminated the dark room, casting eerie shadows on the ceiling. Marisol tried to recall what had happened, but only fragments, short bursts of painful images, came back to her. She strained to piece the events together, like the jigsaw pattern of cutout material for a dress, but couldn't figure out the correct order. She remembered the nice doctor who'd prayed with her. She remembered being scared, bleeding on the bathroom floor. She remembered the pretty blonde nurse who comforted her on the way to surgery. Marisol wiped a bead of sweat off her oily skin and somehow drifted back to sleep.

She was woken by a group of doctors staring down at her. They wore white coats over blue scrubs, and stethoscopes dangled from their necks like ties. They poked and prodded and spoke words that Marisol couldn't understand. One of them flipped the pages in a large green binder, nodded, and started writing. They smiled professionally and left the room. A new nurse and a man in a white tunic appeared and removed the breathing tube, setting off a coughing spell that sent stabbing pains deep into her chest. The nurse cleaned her with a warm sponge, changed her gown, put her on a stretcher, and wheeled her onto an elevator to a new room.

The room was quiet and peaceful, away from the commotion and noises of the intensive care unit, and Marisol drifted into another deep sleep.

———∞∘❋∘∞———

Later, another nurse came by and changed her bandages and instructed Marisol to go for a short walk; she needed to move her legs to keep blood clots from forming.

Marisol wanted to be a good patient. But more than that, she wanted to get out of here and figure out a way to get back to Mexico.

She eased out of the bed and shuffled to the door. Each step pulled at the stitches and sent a ripping burn through her belly. She stopped at the door and rested, grimacing in pain. She looked down the hall. The nurses' station seemed a long way away. She would go to the next door and turn around. Tomorrow she would go farther. She took another agonizing step and rested. She was almost there.

When Marisol was thirteen, she came home early from school with a dull ache in her lower belly. Her mom thought it was a stomach bug, gave her medicine, and sent her to bed. The pain got better for a while, but during the night Marisol woke up grabbing her belly. It felt like someone was poking a burning, hot stick into her side. Her parents drove her to the medical clinic in town.

Every chair in the one-room building was filled with sick, injured, groaning people. Marisol rolled up in a ball on the floor, stifling her moans. Finally, an attendant carried Marisol to a tiny exam room and placed her on a table covered with starchy, crinkly tan paper. The doctor entered, spoke with her parents, and turned to Marisol with a caring smile. He pushed and kneaded her belly with half-closed eyes until Marisol recoiled in agony when he found the sore spot. He took blood and gave Marisol a shot and she remembered the fuzzy feeling before the room went dark. The next day, she woke up with a different kind of pain, and her parents told her about her dead ovary. It had twisted around itself like a long, tangled phone cord, choking off the blood supply.

Now, years later, standing in a hallway in a hospital in Denver, miles away from that small clinic in Mexico, she still remembered the sick feeling when they told her about the ovary. She still had her right one, they said; she could still have babies. Marisol gritted her teeth and took another hesitant step toward the next room when she saw him.

El Piojo was back! And he was turning toward her.

CHAPTER

36

After a couple cups of strong coffee and a bagel, Vince had enough energy to leave the condo and drive to his fitness club. He had one more month left on his membership, and he needed the "executive workout" today. He hadn't heard that term until recently and laughed when he heard a friend describe a sauna, steam room, shave, and shower without the actual exercise.

He stripped down in the locker room and caught a glimpse of the purplish bruises emerging over his chest. There wasn't much he could do about the broken ribs. He opened the door to the steam room and searched for a seat through the fog. He stretched out on the bench, closed his eyes, and let the drugs and alcohol sweat their way out of his pores.

An hour later, after a liter of Gatorade and a handful of Ibuprofen, Vince began to feel human again. He showered and left the club feeling refreshed. He got in his car and drove west to Evergreen, unsure of his decision for the first time in his life.

Vince had been a guest at the Dunners' home many times during his residency. He first met Susan and Dick at their annual welcome party for new residents. He remembered driving there with a group of nervous first-year residents who were worried about first impressions. Vince had already set himself apart from his coresidents by then. He had solved a couple of tough cases in conference that even the senior residents couldn't figure out.

Vince started the residency way ahead of his peers. He spent the last half of medical school poring over imaging textbooks and hanging out with the radiology residents. During his medical internship he would sneak away from the wards to spend time with the MRI and CT technologists, learning how to position and scan the patients. During this time, Vince discovered he had a gift, a knack for spotting the abnormalities, a "good eye," as the residents said. Just like "finding Waldo" in those kids' books, Vince was faster than anyone else in finding the diseases in a complex background.

Maybe it was his confidence and self-assuredness, but Vince and the Dunners, despite the fifteen-year age difference, became good friends. They invited Vince to dinner at least once a month. Sometimes the evenings were quiet, and Dick would take Vince into his study and show him MRIs of famous athletes, explaining the intricacies of their injuries and describing the career-saving surgeries. On other nights the Dunners had already started drinking when Vince arrived, and a loud, lively evening ensued. Sometimes Vince brought his newest girlfriend, but usually the three of them had more fun alone.

Now, Vince turned in to the Dunners' long driveway and parked around the back near the pool. The large brick and stucco mansion stood apart from the other houses in the cul-de-sac. It sat on a small rise, above the tree line, giving spectacular views of Mount Evans to the west. Only thirty minutes from the hospital, it felt like another world out here. A creek trickled below the house, and National Forest bordered the backyard, adding to the seclusion. Best of all, Colorado's world-class ski resorts were less than an hour away.

Susan came to the back door, drinks in hand, to meet Vince. He had to admit that for a forty-something woman, she looked good. She was tan and slim and her cover-up barely hid the bikini underneath. She handed Vince the drink and led him to the pool deck where she had been sunning.

"I'm so glad you called."

Vince wasn't so sure he wanted to go through with this. But this morning's wake-up call from those thugs reminded him that he didn't have many options. He supported his ribs as he gingerly sat on the chaise lounge and sipped the strong bourbon.

———∘∘○⦅◉⦆○∘——

Last year the Dunners had thrown an extravagant party for Vince after he had been named the new chief resident. It had turned into a wild affair, with drinks flowing freely. Susan, always a heavy drinker, was in rare form that night. She danced and laughed and lit up the room. After the other residents and faculty left, Vince was alone with her. The caterers and bartenders had left hours ago. They relaxed in the cool mountain air. Vince asked about Dick.

"He went to bed early," she said. "He wasn't feeling well tonight."

Vince, usually under complete control, was stinking drunk that night. After all the hard work, the studying, the brutal night shifts, he had reached the pinnacle of the residency. He had the respect of the residents and administration. Better yet, it assured him the best job offers.

"Let's take a dip in the pool," Susan said.

"Sure. Maybe it will help me sober up."

Vince grabbed one of Dick's swim trunks from the pool house and staggered over to the heated water. Susan was swimming laps. Vince sat on the edge of the pool trying to steady himself. Susan emerged between his dangling legs wearing a smile and nothing else. Her breasts floated, swaying and bobbing in the water, seductive shadows in the moonlight.

"You coming in?"

"I'm not sure I should."

"Well I am," Susan replied, grabbing his legs and tugging.

Vince hesitated. It was so tempting. She let go of his legs and floated on her back, revealing her beautiful, uninhibited body. Through the haze of his alcohol buzz, Vince felt guilt. He couldn't betray his friendship with Dick.

"I'm sorry," he said at last.

"You're an amazing guy, Vince. I'll be ready for you anytime."

———•∘∘❧❦∘∘•———

Well, the "anytime" was today, Vince thought as he rested his head on the lounge chair, sipping his bourbon, listening to the nearby creek, ashamed. He noticed Susan standing over him, blocking the sun. Rays of light bent around her shapely figure.

"How about some lunch?" She led Vince into the kitchen and made him a sandwich. They sat together at the kitchen table, Vince eating, Susan drinking. The awkward silence was making this difficult. Her ice cubes clattered as she put her glass down and stroked his arm.

"I meant what I said that night in the pool," Susan said. "I've always been attracted to you."

Vince sat back, chewing, nervous. "Let's have another drink," he finally said. He needed to deaden the guilt.

CHAPTER

37

Marisol cursed and ducked into the room and shut the door.
A teenager sat on his bed reading. He looked at Marisol, surprise in his eyes. Before he could speak, Marisol said, "Please help me. There's a man out there who wants to kill me."

The boy sat up, grabbed his crutches, and hobbled over to Marisol, favoring his left leg. He reminded Marisol of her younger brother.

"That's crazy," he said.

"The man out there by the nurses' station, shiny black suit, slicked-back hair." Marisol paused to catch her breath. "He's looking for me. Please let me hide here for a minute." Marisol felt light-headed. She needed to sit down.

"Whoa! You don't look so good," the boy said. He pushed a chair toward Marisol. "I'll check it out."

Marisol fell into the chair and watched the boy leave. She hoped Sanchez hadn't seen her enter the room. She closed her eyes until the pain subsided and then looked around the room. A stack of greeting cards was piled on the side table. Curious, Marisol inched over to the bed, sat down, and began to read. His name is Raul, she found out, and some of the get-well cards were written in Spanish. He had a lot of friends.

Raul opened the door and pushed a wheelchair into the room.
"I'm sorry," she said, putting the cards back on the table.
"No problem," he smiled. "My name's Raul."
"Are you a swimmer?"

"I'm trying. My coach says I have some natural talent, but I still get beat by the older boys in my age group."

"I like swimming."

"What's going on? I didn't see the man you described out there."

Raul looked kind and easygoing. Marisol liked him and decided she could trust him. Between tears she told Raul the whole story: The financial trouble she and Hector were in; how Hector got involved with a Sureños drug operation that went wrong; how the Sureños forced her to be a drug mule and travel to Denver; how the men tried to kill her after she passed the bolitas. When she finished her tale, she was overcome with relief. It felt comforting to tell someone else.

"Wow. I'm sorry," Raul said with genuine concern. "I'd like to help you, but I don't know what I can do." Then his face started to redden with anger. "I hate the gangs," he blurted out, scaring Marisol with his ferocity. "My big brother was a great athlete. He could run circles around his competitors on the soccer field. He could throw a fastball eighty miles an hour when he was twelve years old. But when he started high school, he started hanging out with some kids in a gang. He liked their fancy watches and designer sneakers. He started to smoke. He came home late. My mother couldn't stop him."

Raul stood up and sat next to Marisol on the bed. "But the police did. We got a call at dinner one night. Now he's serving ten years in prison."

Marisol patted Raul on the shoulder. "I'm sorry."

"I hate the Sureños!" Raul sobbed and turned away from Marisol.

Marisol leaned forward, ignoring the pain in her wound, and hugged Raul. She felt a connection with this young boy. Both their lives had been irrevocably changed by the Mexican gangs, but somehow she was optimistic. The two had formed a bond and maybe, together, they could help each other.

Finally, Raul stood up and wiped his eyes. "Let's get you back to your room. The nurses will be looking for you." Sensing her fear, Raul said, "I'll go with you and make sure that man didn't come back."

Reluctantly, Marisol let Raul help her down from the bed and get into the wheelchair. He looked up and down the hallway before pushing her out of the room. She pointed down the hall, and he wheeled her safely to her room, where a nurse was coming out of the bathroom.

"There you are, Ms. Hernandez," the nurse said. "I was wondering where you went. Let's get you settled in."

Raul excused himself while the nurse helped Marisol. "I'll be back in a little bit. You rest now, okay?" He smiled.

Marisol relaxed for the first time in days.

CHAPTER

38

Susan poured bourbon and Vince followed her back outside. She reached into one of her pockets and pulled out a joint, smiling.

"I have another idea," she said as she lit it up and passed it to Vince.

Vince filled his lungs with the hot smoke. He coughed as he exhaled and Susan laughed. They passed the joint back and forth and finished their drinks. The initial awkwardness faded and they starting joking and laughing uncontrollably.

Vince pulled out the nearly empty bag of cocaine and dangled it in front of Susan. "You want something stronger?"

"Sure. Is that all you have?"

"It's a start," Vince said while making two long white lines on the table.

Susan stood and snorted professionally and Vince knew the stories were true. He had never spoken to Dick about it, but had heard rumors that Susan had a drug problem.

Susan looked up, sniffling, eyes bold, and shook her head. "Wow!" she said and kissed Vince deeply. She tasted like smoke and the sweet scent of bourbon.

Vince pulled her closer so he could feel the fullness of her breasts and continued the long, intimate kiss. She moaned and melted into him, his erection firm against her.

"I want you," she whispered.

"Let's go inside." Vince kissed her once more, grasping her head in his hands, stroking her hair. He pulled away, remembering the leftover coke on the table. He snorted half the line and offered the rest to Susan.

She winked in appreciation and finished it off. "I love sex when I'm high," she said. She grabbed Vince's hand and walked him into the house. She stopped at the doorway and kissed him again, rubbing her hands over his ass. Vince was going to explode. She led him past their bedroom into Dick's study. Vince looked at her inquisitively.

"I want you to take me on Dick's desk. I used to fantasize about this when I saw you two talking in here." She backhanded the papers onto the floor, removed her bikini, and motioned to Vince. "Come over here and fuck me."

Vince didn't hesitate to oblige.

Afterward, as they rested naked, nuzzling on the couch in the study, she asked, "Do you think you could get more of that fantastic coke?"

"Sure. But I'm a little short on money right now."

"Don't worry about that. As long as you promise to come over more often," she stroked Vince's leg. "What do you think you need?"

Here goes, Vince thought. *It's going to work!*

"About $5,000 will get us some great stuff."

"Whew. That's pretty steep."

"I'll make it worth your while," Vince said.

Susan stood up and walked out of the room saying, "I need to go to the safe for that. Stay right there, lover."

A few minutes later, Susan returned and handed Vince a bulging envelope. He tried to restrain his enthusiasm. He had done it! He could get out of debt and turn his life around.

"Before you go," Susan said with a mischievous smile. "I want you one more time."

Vince followed her into the bedroom, surprised by her stamina. This time they were gentle, exploring each other's bodies, stopping at all the right places. Vince brought her to a howling climax and soon she was sleeping.

He slipped out of bed and tiptoed into the study to get his clothes. The bourbon and pot had worn off and the first wave of guilt swept in. How could he do this to Dunner, the man who took Vince under his wing, helped promote him to the chief residency, and recommended him for the southern California job? How could he stoop this low and betray his best friend?

He put his clothes on and shoved the envelope of money into the front pocket. Maybe he could pay Susan back. Vince knelt down, gathered the strewn papers on the floor, and placed them in a neat pile on the desk.

The signature caught his eye: "Bo Richards, MD."

Vince realized he was looking at a radiology report. It was a DIA customs report with Bo's name on it, read as normal. He looked at the next paper in the stack and it was another report with Dr. Richards' name on it. And another. Vince didn't understand. Why would Dick have a stack of normal reports with Bo's name on them? Did this have something to do with the case that Bo missed yesterday?

Glancing at his watch, Vince had to hurry. He turned on Dick's computer and logged on to the university radiology department. He looked at the name on the first report and pulled up the X-ray. Not believing what he saw, he pulled up the next patient, and the next. They were all the same. Obvious cases of bolitas and other smuggled drugs—all interpreted as normal. Vince turned off the computer and rushed out of the house. There was no way Bo could he have missed so many abnormal cases. It wasn't possible. So what was Dunner doing with those reports?

CHAPTER

39

B o was having a quiet Friday in the ER. Vince didn't show up again, of course. Bo thought about making an appointment with the chairman, Dr. Musk, to explain about the unusual custom reports but figured he should take Dr. Wu's advice and let the professor handle it. Besides, Musk wouldn't believe him anyway if Bo told him the reports came from Vince—the shining star of the residency.

The phone rang and Bo picked up. "Reading room, Dr. Richards."

"Dr. Bo?" The voice quivered with fear.

"Raul?"

"Yes. I need help fast."

"I'll be right up."

"No. You'll be too late. Listen. A really bad man just walked into my friend's room. I think he's going to kill her."

Bo sat in shock, listening to his usually calm swimmer friend's panicked voice. He had an idea. "What room is she in?"

"Three twenty-one."

Bo hung up and called the hospital operator. He hated to do this, but Raul sounded serious, and a woman's life might be a stake.

"Code Blue, Room 321," Bo ordered before he jumped out of his chair and ran upstairs.

Bo arrived on the ward at the same time as the code team. He saw a nurse wheeling the crash cart into the room, a respiratory therapist behind her in case of intubation, and finally Dr. Martinez from the ER. He spotted Raul watching from his door, and Bo walked over to him.

"What's happening?"

"It's all my fault," Raul sobbed. "I met this nice lady this morning. She said a gang member was trying to kill her. I thought he was gone."

Bo didn't understand what Raul was talking about. "Let me go down there and see what's going on. I'll be right back."

Bo had never seen Raul this upset. The kid was unflappable, especially in the pool. Bo went to one of the local swim meets last year. Raul had just aged up to the fifteen–eighteen-year-old group. He was the youngest and smallest kid in his heat. Before the race, Raul saw Bo in the stands and shrugged with casual confidence. He won his heat.

Bo caught up with Sal Martinez as he came out of room 321. "Everything all right in there?"

"False alarm. The patient is fine. I don't know what moron called the code." Sal said, annoyed.

Bo stepped around the nurses leaving the room and stopped in amazement.

Marisol! The drug courier! How did Raul get mixed up with her?

Bo's most memorable experience with the drug industry had come during his third year in medical school, during an emergency room rotation. The paramedics wheeled in an emaciated forty-five-year-old man who looked at least sixty-five. Needle tracks covered his arms like a bad tattoo. The man had no idea where he was, thrashed around on the gurney, and had to be restrained so he could be examined. He was so dehydrated the busy ER doc asked Bo to try a central line in his jugular vein, knowing there were no usable arm veins. Bo had performed several of these procedures. He sterilized the neck, looked for the vein with the ultrasound machine, numbed the skin, and pierced the jugular with the first stick. His excitement was short-lived. The addict reared up his head and bit Bo's finger. Later, after he got over the initial pain and put the catheter in the neck, Bo pulled off his sterile gloves and saw blood. His heart sank. His first thought was AIDS.

Bo immediately went to health services and got counseling from the infectious disease doctors. They cleaned up his hand, gave him a tetanus shot, and reassured Bo. They drew blood from the addict. For two long days Bo couldn't concentrate or sleep. He thought of what he would do with his life if he turned HIV-positive. Mostly he was angry.

Bo still remembered where he was standing when he got the call from the medical clinic informing him that his patient didn't have HIV. He and Cory had a special dinner that night, and Bo vowed to be extra vigilant in the future.

Looking at Marisol sitting up in bed with a weak smile, Bo put away his negative thoughts about drug addicts and smiled back.

Raul came in and sighed with relief. "Thanks, Dr. Bo. I didn't know what to do. I thought the guy was going to kill her."

"How about giving me an explanation? How do you guys know each other?"

Marisol remained quiet as Raul recounted their strange meeting this morning. He told Bo the long story of Marisol's adventure from Mexico. Bo felt relieved that his suspicions about her were correct: she was an innocent victim, and she was in danger.

After Raul's explanation, Bo walked over and formerly introduced himself. "I don't know if you remember me, but I was down in the ER when you almost died."

"Of course I remember. You prayed the 'Our Father' with me in Spanish. Well, sort of Spanish, I guess." Marisol laughed. "I didn't think I was going to make it. God saved me so I could go home and see my husband and son again."

"We need to figure out a way for you to do that," Bo agreed.

CHAPTER

40

Before hurrying home for his dinner with Lisa, Bo talked to a friend on the surgical ward and arranged to have Marisol moved to another floor and a false name placed outside the door. He showered and drove to Chez Thuey on Twenty-Eighth Street, one of Boulder's landmark Vietnamese restaurants and Lisa's suggestion for their ... discussion? Or was it a date?

"You've got to try Le's spicy beef and tomato dish," Lisa said as they squeezed around a group waiting for takeout. They ordered separately but shared the enormous servings.

Lisa said, "Tell me why you don't like dogs. I remember how panicked you were when Lucy knocked you over."

"See this scar?" Bo stood up and showed the back of his calf to Lisa. "Those are four teeth marks. I was attacked by a pack of dogs on a bike ride one day in North Carolina." He sat down and told her the story. On a hot, muggy late afternoon in July, Bo veered from his usual course to explore new country roads. A couple of lazy dogs looked at him as he raced down a steep hill, and he didn't think much of it at the time. He rode an out-and-back course through the beautiful countryside, passing row after row of green tobacco plants. Sweaty, tired, and out of water, Bo chugged back up the hill on his way home. He was about a third of the way up the pitch when five dogs appeared in the middle of the road, and he knew they weren't there to cheer him on. Terrified, he looked around: no cars in sight to flag down; no owners in the front yards; just him and the pack of dogs ahead. It was too late to turn around; the dogs would be on him in seconds.

Without a good alternative, Bo continued pedaling up the hill, hoping for the best. He yelled in his best authoritative voice but the dogs only moved closer. They surrounded him, and he got off the saddle and cranked as fast as his tired legs would allow. As he swerved around the largest dog, he felt sharp pain in his calf. He looked back. A mangy mutt had latched on to his leg and wouldn't let go. He didn't want to unclip and lose his momentum, so he kept pounding on the pedals and shouting until the dog finally let go.

Only later did he realize how lucky he was to get away with just a calf injury. If they all had attacked at once, or if he had fallen off the bike, he could have been killed.

"Packs of dogs have killed people, you know," Bo said.

"Those owners should have been arrested."

"Ever since that day, I get a little jumpy around loose dogs. That's why I freaked when your dog, Lucy, knocked me off my feet last week. I didn't know if she was going to attack or not. What really irks me, though, are the dog owners who don't apologize when their animal races up to me with their teeth showing. I back off in terror, and the owner makes me feel like it's my fault."

The dinner crowd thinned out as Bo and Lisa talked. She told him about her undergraduate days at the University of Colorado and her intense training on the track team. After graduation, she took a marketing job with IBM, she said. "But I couldn't stand the endless meetings and the airport travel. I wanted to do something more meaningful and to be outside. And to tell you the truth," she said with a seductive wink, "I had a crush on one of those bicycle cops riding around downtown Boulder."

Bo finished his glass of wine and got up the courage to ask. "Can you tell me more about the accident?"

"You sure you want to hear about it?"

"Let me put it this way. I still haven't packed up Cory's things yet."

Lisa told Bo how she was jogging that day when she came across the accident. "A Honda Civic was upside down in the creek. Cory was lying on a rock, half-conscious. I know CPR but there wasn't much I could do. The ambulances were at the top of the road, so I held her hand as they negotiated the stretcher down the rocks.

"While they carried her to the top, the other car exploded. It must have been leaking gas."

"There was another car?"

"A black SUV. I thought you knew."

"I was at a conference. I got back in time for the funeral. I never even saw her body. Never had a chance to say good-bye."

Bo felt Lisa's hand rest on top of his. He shook his head and said, "Her parents told me it was a drunk driver. A hit and run. Can you find out if they IDd the driver from the other car?"

Lisa pulled out her cell phone and walked outside. She came back in, sullen. "The car was stolen, Bo."

Bo jerked his head in exasperation. "Just my luck," he said. "Wait. The driver might have been banged up. Maybe he went to a local hospital."

Lisa's eyes lit up. "That's a great idea. I don't think the investigating officer checked—he's known for being lazy."

CHAPTER
41

Vince sat in his car and fumed, watching the sun crawl up the eastern horizon. Parked across the street from the Dunner estate, he could see well beyond the Denver metropolitan skyline, all the way to the boring plains of Kansas. After he got home last night, Vince logged on to his home computer and analyzed the customs' cases. He knew Bo couldn't have missed that many abnormal X-rays, and based on the dates and times, Bo couldn't even have been working all those shifts. After sifting through the data, he found something even more disturbing: all the reports were generated from Vince's office. And no one used the chief resident's office except him.

There was only one explanation: Dunner had to be in cahoots with drug smugglers. And he was setting Vince up to take the fall if he got caught. Vince slammed his hand against the steering wheel. He thought Dunner was his friend. They spent countless evenings talking in the vice chairman's study. They skied the moguls at Winter Park together. *How could he do this to me?*

Dunner's Mercedes slithered down the long driveway. "He's going to pay for this."

It had been a long time since Vince solved his problems with violence. In the children's home, Vince stood out. He was smarter than the other kids and was treated differently by the priests, sent to the best schools. He matured late, not filling out his six-foot frame until late in junior year of high school. He was an easy target for the bullies who started shaving in eighth grade, and Vince had to learn to defend himself. He asked to take boxing lessons, which helped when he knew the attack was coming. However, it didn't do much for the nighttime raids after the lights went out.

Dunner stopped at a nearby ATM before driving onto the interstate toward Denver. Vince kept his distance. Traffic on I-70 slowed around an accident and he lost sight of Dunner's car. Vince saw the crushed cars, the glass on the road, and the waiting ambulances and was silently grateful he wasn't on call today.

He spotted the Mercedes again after the accident and followed him to downtown Denver, exiting near Invesco field. Dunner parked and got out, looking around before walking down an alley and into an aging building. Vince waited before driving by. The building looked like it should be condemned. Vince drove around the block and parked near Dunner's car, so he could watch the entrance.

For the next two hours a steady stream of seedy characters entered and exited the building. *What could he possibly be doing in there?*

Finally he came out of the building and headed back down the alley, carrying a small package. Anger replaced the boredom from Vince's wait and he swore as he stormed out of the car. He hid in the shadows until the vice chairman turned toward his car, and then Vince charged him from behind.

Dunner lost his balance and fell, sprawling headfirst to the gutter. A prescription pad fluttered next to him. Before Dunner could turn around, Vince booted him in the head and Dunner grunted before he passed out. Vince turned him over, knelt across his chest, and slammed his fists into Dunner's face. Even later Vince didn't understand the extent of the rage that overwhelmed him. Only when he heard the sharp crack of Dunner's broken sternum did Vince snap out of his furor. He now stood over his old friend, his right boot pushing the breast bone deep and precariously close to Dunner's heart.

Vince stepped back. The horrible site snapped him back into reality and he scanned the street for witnesses. The place was still deserted. Vince reached into the vice chairman's pocket, pulled out his cell phone and dialed 911. He grabbed Dunner's package off the curb and raced back to his car.

CHAPTER

42

Bo woke with more questions than answers and was glad it was Saturday. He only had to work the morning shift in the emergency room and then had the rest of the day off. He wanted to go to the airport to see the drug-screening operation in person and follow up with Lisa about the hit-and-run driver of Cory's accident.

Bo opened the door to the reading room and was surprised to hear someone on the phone. Dr. Musk turned to face him. *This is trouble.* The computer monitors flickered, casting an eerie glow around the chairman's puffy face. But Musk surprised Bo with a smile and an announcement that he was Bo's faculty backup today. Bo tried not to look shocked. He wondered how long it had been since Musk interpreted an X-ray. Didn't he have lackeys for that?

Musk didn't mention the Adcock case and Bo didn't bring it up. The two worked for an hour cleaning up the early morning X-rays. Musk rolled his chair back, groaned as he pushed his portly body out of the seat, and left to catch up with paperwork. Bo took the opportunity to grab another cup of coffee and a bagel.

A trauma activation alert interrupted Bo's snack. He called over to Musk's office before walking to the ER. The chairman appeared a few minutes later, flushed and panting from the short walk. "Three car, high-speed collision on the interstate, death at the scene," the ER secretary informed them.

The paramedics wheeled the victims into the trauma rooms. ER doctors, surgeons, and nurses swarmed around the stretchers, cutting clothes, examining injuries, stabilizing fractures.

"Need help here," one of the nurses yelled, and Bo followed Dr. Sal Martinez into the room of the most critical patient.

Sal examined the patient and looked at the monitors. Through the splattered plastic protective mask, Bo saw a look of concern on the ER doc's face. Sal deftly inserted an endotracheal tube into the airway to assist breathing. He ordered X-rays of the neck and chest and cleared the room for the brief radiation exposure.

Bo noticed Dr. Musk standing quietly behind him and wondered when the last time was the chairman had seen the daily excitement of the emergency room.

When the chest X-ray popped up on the computer screen, Musk moved closer to the monitor, examined the film with interest, and spoke to Sal. "The breathing tube is shifted to the right. And his left bronchus is being pushed down. He has an aortic injury and needs to go to the OR immediately."

Incredulous at the unexpected diagnosis from a plain chest X-ray, Sal asked, "How about a CT first?"

"There's no time. Call the heart surgeon now."

Bo was amazed at the chairman's quick opinion and authority. He knew the statistics: 90 percent of patients with a torn aorta died at the scene or en route to the hospital. Unfortunately, this large artery, which supplies all the blood to the body, is fixed and immobile in the chest, while the heart has room to move. So in a high-speed collision, the heart keeps moving forward, tearing a hole in the artery, and the massive bleeding is usually fatal.

"I hope you're right, Dr. Musk," the ER doc said before turning to the nurse. "Get him to the OR STAT. And tell the cardiovascular surgeon he's on the way."

Bo understood the urgency and didn't question the chairman's judgment. The chest X-ray is a crude, nonspecific tool, and most radiologists would have gotten a CAT scan to confirm the tear before sending the patient to open-heart surgery. But Bo had already seen one patient die in the CAT scan room from this injury and didn't want to see another.

Bo and Musk returned to the reading room to catch up with new barrage of X-rays. Musk was surprisingly helpful. No sooner had they finished the work when the phone rang, and Sal asked Musk to come over to the ER.

"It's too early for feedback on the aortic case," Musk said as the two walked back to the ER.

"I wanted to give you the head's-up," the ER doc said. "Dr. Dunner was just wheeled in. He was brutally attacked this morning."

"Is he okay?" Bo asked.

"A lot of facial and chest injuries. I thought you'd want to know. I've ordered a CAT scan."

"Thanks, Sal," Bo said. "Any idea what happened?"

"Not yet."

Bo didn't recognize the vice chairman when they walked into the CAT scan room. Blood seeped through the gauze that was wrapped around his head like a turban. His shirt was torn and pulled off his left shoulder, revealing a boot-sized bruise over his chest.

Dunner squinted through grotesquely swollen eyes and moaned.

The CT tech informed Bo and Musk that the scan was complete, and the two entered the control room to study the images. Two broken ribs partially collapsed the vice chairman's left lung. The sternum, cracked like a green stick, buckled next to his heart.

"I didn't know Dr. Dunner has a pacemaker," Bo said as he continued to stare at the monitor. "Did you?"

"No," Musk replied as he paged through the images.

After calling Sal with the results, they walked into the scanner room, and Dunner turned his head toward them.

"Theodore?" his voice garbled. Bo had never heard anyone call Musk by his first name.

"I'm here, Dick," Musk said, placing his hand over Dunner's. "Everything's going to be all right. Your sternum and a couple of ribs are busted, but your facial bones are okay. Sal is going to keep you in the hospital overnight, but you should heal up fine. I'll take care of everything."

Dunner nodded and closed his eyes. Bo was surprised by the chairman's concern and compassion. Maybe Dr. Musk was human after all.

CHAPTER

43

After finishing up the emergency room X-rays with Dr. Musk, Bo drove out to Denver International Airport. He wanted to see the drug-screening operation in more detail. Maybe then he could figure out how the smuggling was done. Bo still couldn't believe Vince had anything to do with this. The guy had too much to lose. He was set up with a nice six-figure job in California.

In the computer room the other night with Sheri, they figured out that all the smuggling happened on weekdays. Before heading out to DIA, Bo checked to make sure the weekend technologist was working.

He left his truck in short-term parking, walked over to the international terminal, asked for the customs department, and introduced himself. A little while later a buxom blonde in scrubs bounced over to him and introduced herself as Tracey, the X-ray technologist. Bo explained that he was a resident at the university and that the chairman had asked him to check on quality issues with the customs X-rays. He figured that on a Saturday afternoon, with Dunner in the hospital and Musk home, no one from radiology would ever know he was here. He gave Tracey the number of the emergency room and Sal Martinez's name, along with his hospital ID.

Bo watched her leave and pick up a phone. Satisfied, she returned with a temporary badge and led him through security to the customs offices. Long lines of bored passengers shuffled forward, passports in hand, ready to talk to the agents and move on.

"Busy place," Bo commented.

"A flight just landed," Tracey explained. She took out a key and opened a door that led to a hallway. She pointed out the rooms as they walked. "The first room is for interviews. All suspicious passengers get questioned here by two agents."

In the next room Bo saw a contraption that looked like a bad high school science project: funnels and tubes and pipes. He remembered it from his Internet reading. "Is that the 'drug loo'?"

"Yes." Tracey smiled. "But we like to call it the 'bolitas bowl.'" She walked Bo into the room and pointed out the features. "The suspected smuggler sits on this and defecates. The waste goes through these filters, and any drug-filled condoms get sorted out. It's pretty cool how well it works."

They walked to the next room, which housed the X-ray table. Instantly recognizing the equipment, Bo said, "Now this room looks familiar."

"Yeah. It's your basic X-ray room setup, like you have in the hospital. We use it to take abdomen radiographs if the suspected smuggler refuses to sit on the loo. We also take routine X-rays of the staff for broken bones and such."

"Have you found many smugglers?"

"Every week. The Sureños, the Mexican mafia, are the major drug traffickers in Denver. They send a lot of mules and just need a few to get through to make it profitable."

"Can you show me the procedure for getting the X-rays to the university?"

"Sure. Right this way." Tracey showed Bo the computer station, where she typed in the patient demographics and the procedure for merging that information with the images. "When it's all complete, I press this button, and the digital data gets pushed to the hospital network. Presto."

"What about the reports?"

"When the radiologists read them at the hospital, the typed report automatically gets faxed to us," Tracey said, pointing to the fax machine. "I take the report to the customs official while the suspect waits."

The whole procedure seemed pretty simple and foolproof. Bo couldn't think of a devious way to get around the system. Then he got an idea. "Do you have any old reports I could look at?"

Tracey opened a file cabinet and pulled out a stack of paper. "Here are the faxes from last week." She smiled. "Will that do?"

Bo shuffled through the papers. They all looked like standard reports from the university. Then he noticed an unusual letter/number combination at the bottom of the page, next to the date. Some of the reports had a U1 and some a U2, and he asked Tracey about that.

"I never noticed that before," she said thoughtfully.

"Let's send a test case to the hospital. Do you have a phantom?"

Bo watched while Tracey X-rayed a dummy and typed the data into the computer.

"See that?" Bo pointed. "At the bottom. It says U1."

Tracey nodded. "I see it. I guess it's the default. I don't ever change that."

"Go ahead and send it."

The two waited, and about five minutes later, a "normal" report came back from the hospital, read by one of the second-year residents.

"Try typing in another name and press the U2 button this time."

Tracey did as instructed, and as they waited and chatted for a while, but no report appeared.

"Does it usually take this long?" Bo asked.

When Tracey shook her head, Bo picked up the phone and called the ER radiology resident. After explaining the mock smuggler patient, he waited for the radiologist to find the case.

Bo didn't like what he heard. "What do you mean, it's not there? We sent it from the airport more than ten minutes ago."

Bo thought for a moment. "Okay. Try this. Search by the test patient's name." He waited, listened to the resident, and slammed down the phone.

"That bastard," Bo said and stormed out of the room.

"You're welcome," Tracey mumbled behind him.

But Bo heard her and turned around. "Sorry. Thanks for your help, Tracey."

CHAPTER

44

Vince started the car and headed back to the highway, no destination in mind. He'd never come this close to killing someone. Not even the perverts in the foster home who unsuccessfully tried to molest him. The coke was the problem. Vince remembered sitting in on addiction groups during his psychiatry rotation in medical school. He recalled tragic stories of explosive anger and uncontrolled rage and tearful confessions of unintentionally injuring loved ones. At the time, Vince thought the drugs unmasked underlying anger-management issues. Now he realized he was wrong: the drug changed them into temporary monsters.

What was Dunner doing in that building? It had to be related to drugs—the bag of coke on the seat proved that. He didn't think Dunner saw who attacked him. But the thugs down the alley might have, and if they had any connection to the smugglers, they might be able to track him down.

Vince debated his options. He should probably go to the police and tell them about Dunner's involvement with drug smugglers, but he needed more proof. He would need to have a solid case before taking down an esteemed university professor. Besides, with Bo's name on all the reports, he didn't want Bo to get in trouble. He owed him that, at least.

So it all boiled down to Dick Dunner. And there was only one place to get the incriminating evidence on the vice chairman. His damn study: the book-lined office where Vince spent countless nights learning the subtleties of MRIs with his mentor; the sanctuary where the careers of athletes hung on Dunner's diagnosis of hairline fractures and ligament tears; the same study where the asshole worked to ruin Vince and Bo's lives.

He drove to the Dunners' house, hoping Susan would have been called to the hospital by now. He parked down the block and sneaked through the backyard. He circled the pool, remembering his party with Susan yesterday and her insatiable appetites. He peeked in the back window and saw Susan sitting at the kitchen table, talking to two uniformed police officers.

Vince ducked under the window and ran to the tree line. *That was close!* He trudged back through the woods to his car. He'd have to wait.

CHAPTER

45

Rushing out of the airport, Bo sensed someone following him. A couple of times he twirled around and scanned the crowd, but no one looked suspicious. As he got closer to the short-term parking lot, the feeling grew stronger. He walked faster. He heard footsteps echoing behind him.

He clicked the remote as he approached the truck and hurried to lock himself in. Secure in the vehicle, he surveyed the parking lot. A frustrated young mother was dragging her toddler and suitcase, searching for their lost car. Feeling foolish, Bo backed up and drove to the exit.

That's when he saw the goons.

Two men stood behind a concrete stanchion, watching the exiting cars. They looked right at him as he drove past and pulled into the toll booth. "Hurry," Bo said to the attendant, but it only seemed to slow him down. "I'm in a rush," Bo shouted.

The annoyed attendant turned to examine a small video screen near the cash register.

Bo tapped his fingers on the steering wheel. He saw the men running down the exit ramp. "Come on, come on!" Bo started to panic. He was trapped by the wooden gate.

"I'm waiting for the machine to check your license plate," the attendant explained.

But it was too late. Bo watched the two thugs get into a waiting car. There was no way he could outrun them. In his rear-view mirror, Bo saw a car about to pull in behind him. Refusing to be trapped, he threw the truck in reverse and slammed on the accelerator, clipping the front bumper of the approaching car. Bo spun the wheel while putting the truck in forward and sped back into the parking deck. He drove recklessly up the ramp, scraping against the concrete, and stopped as close as he could get to the airport entrance.

He jumped out of the truck, ran into the airport, and took the elevators to baggage claim. Throngs of people milled about. Bo willed himself to slow down, to blend in with the travelers. He took a couple of deep breaths and followed a large group out the glass doors to the waiting buses. He spotted a rental-car shuttle and hopped in just before the doors closed.

CHAPTER

46

Marisol couldn't get comfortable. She couldn't relax. After Dr. Bo and Raul left, the nurse helped her get back into bed and instructed her to take a nap. Marisol closed her eyes and tried, but sleep wouldn't come. She worried that Sanchez would return to kill her and no one would be around to save her this time. And even if she got out of the hospital alive, she didn't have the money to fly back to Mexico. She might never see her son and husband again.

Then Marisol had a crazy idea. Dr. Bo told her Sanchez was visiting someone in the ICU yesterday. Could it be the skinny man, Miguel, who had picked her up from the airport, the one she shot? Maybe she could reason with him, tell him she wasn't a threat to them, that she wouldn't tell the police. Maybe then the Sureños would leave her alone. That's all she wanted.

When the nurse came in to take her blood pressure, Marisol asked her if the man next to her in the ICU was okay. The nurse made a phone call and told Marisol he had been transferred to the recovery unit upstairs; she couldn't give out his name or room number because of privacy laws. Marisol thanked her and watched her leave. She rested for an hour, trying to regain her strength, and then decided to find the man. She hobbled out of the room, holding a soft pillow over her stomach like the nurse showed her, and looked down the hall.

The nurses' station was empty. Seizing the opportunity, Marisol walked in the opposite direction to the elevators. The doors opened before she pressed the button, and Marisol stepped into the empty elevator. She got off on the fourth floor and stopped to catch her breath.

Marisol began to have second thoughts. She didn't have a plan. What if Sanchez was visiting the man right now? She certainly couldn't outrun him. Ignoring common sense, Marisol shuffled down the hallway, holding her breath as she peeked inside each room.

She found the skinny man in the fourth room.

Miguel looked worse than Marisol remembered. Scraggly, oily, coffee-brown hair soiled the white pillowcase. The angry, flame-shaped scar on his neck blazed from his deathly pale skin. He didn't notice Marisol until she stood directly over him. The recognition in his eyes turned to anger and Marisol stepped back. His nostrils flared as he struggled to sit up and then slumped back to the bed in disgust.

"What are you doing here?" Miguel asked, spit forming on his parched lips.

Marisol didn't know what to say. "I wanted . . ." Marisol hesitated. "I wanted to talk."

"Get the hell out of here, bitch. You tried to kill me."

"I was only trying to escape, señor. I'm sorry." Marisol started to cry.

"You'd better get out of here before Don Mateo comes back. Or you'll be sorry."

Marisol started to leave but changed her mind. She needed to know. "Where were you going to take me that day? I'd done everything the Sureños asked of me. I was supposed to go back home to my family."

"Yeah, well it doesn't work that way with El Piojo. When he finds a cute one like you, he likes to have a little fun first. You're lucky I can't get out of bed, or I'd kill you myself. Now get the hell out of here."

Marisol didn't wait this time. She turned to the door, but before opening it, said, "I'm sorry I shot you. I pray you get better soon."

Marisol walked into the hallway and almost bumped into Raul. His hand was on the door.

"Marisol. Are you crazy?" Raul asked. "That guy is one of the Sureños."

"How did you know I was up here?" Marisol asked, ignoring the question.

"Your nurse said you might be visiting a friend up here. I can't believe you had the nerve to face those guys again."

"I don't know why I came up here." Marisol leaned against Raul for support. "I wanted to see if it was the man from the warehouse, the one I shot the other day. I wanted to apologize."

"Come on. Let's get out of here," Raul said, holding out his right arm.

Marisol latched on and the two hobbled to the elevators. Raul pushed the down button.

Marisol sensed Raul's annoyance in his rigid posture and disturbing silence. She said, "I'm sorry. It was stupid of me to come up here." With a soft ding, the door opened and Marisol and Raul stepped into the compartment.

At the same time, Sanchez bounded out of the stairwell opposite them. As the elevator doors closed, he spotted Marisol, and a deadly smile formed on his lips.

Marisol and Raul were trapped in the elevator! She turned to Raul and said, "What are we going to do?"

"He'll be looking for us on the third floor. We have to hide. Let's go down to the first floor and find Dr. Bo. I know where he works."

As the elevator crept down, Marisol became more and more anxious. When the doors finally opened, Raul looked out and said, "He's not here. Let's go."

He practically dragged Marisol down the hallway to the radiology department, and they slipped into an empty reading room.

Raul locked the door, helped Marisol lie down on a couch, and paged Bo.

"How did you know where to go?" Marisol asked.

"Dr. Bo invited a bunch of swimmers over here one day to show us what he does for a living. It was amazing. We saw broken bones and 3D pictures of the heart. It was cool. I think I want to be a doctor."

—∘∘❧◉❧∘∘—

Bo stood at the rental-car counter and jumped when his beeper went off. The digital text read "Come to your office stat." He rented the cheapest car he could get and rushed to the hospital. The reading room door was locked and he knocked. He was stunned to see Raul stick his head out and double check the hallway before letting Bo in and locking the door.

Marisol rested on the couch, her face pale and tormented.

Bo asked Raul, "Is Sanchez back?"

"It's worse than that," Raul answered.

Bo stared in amazement as Raul described Marisol's inexplicable visit to the man she shot and then being spotted by Sanchez while on the elevator.

"If I didn't know how to get to radiology, El Piojo would have found us, I'm sure."

Why is Sanchez is called The Louse?"

Marisol tried to sit up. "I heard he hates the nickname. But he kind of looks like the bug."

"And he's tough to eliminate," Raul added.

Bo listened and tried to think of a way out of their predicament. He thought about calling the police, but they wouldn't protect Marisol. They'd probably arrest her for smuggling.

Then he had an idea. "Do you know the name of the guy she was visiting?"

"I saw his name on the door. Miguel Jimenez."

Bo logged on to the computer workstation and waited for it to come to life. He searched the hospital database for the name and found Miguel's address.

Raul looked over at him and said, "Well that's not very helpful."

"Why?" Bo asked.

"That's the address of the Limon jail. I know it from mailing letters to my brother."

"Damn. I wanted to get some information on him to give to the police." Bo decided to look at Miguel's X-rays from his admission the other morning. He looked at the image of the abdomen.

"You know what that is?" Bo asked Raul.

"A bullet?"

"Yep. Good job. It landed in the left upper quadrant and probably nicked his spleen. That's why he had the emergency surgery."

"What's that white thing over here?" Raul asked, pointing to the lower margin of the film.

"It looks like a key," Marisol chipped in. "It looks exactly like my house key."

Bo and Raul just stared at her, impressed. Marisol shrugged off the compliment. Bo debated his next step. Obviously Marisol couldn't go back to her room—Sanchez or one of his thugs would come back. He should probably call the police, but then the Sureños would kill her in prison. He only had one good option.

CHAPTER

47

Bo pulled his rental car around to the loading dock and waited for Raul to bring Marisol outside. A few minutes later, a smiling Raul appeared, transporting a large old lady. Covered with blankets and a scarf, even Bo didn't recognize Marisol.

"You like the disguise?" Raul bragged. "I snuck her right past the nurses."

Bo felt guilty taking her out of the hospital without permission, but with Sanchez looking for her, he didn't have much choice. They helped Marisol lie down in the back, and Bo gave her an extra boost of morphine for the ride.

Bo took the back exit out of the hospital, trying to avoid any chance of running into Sanchez. He turned to ask Marisol if she was comfortable, but she was already dozing. She talked in her sleep: low, mumbling words that escalated in volume and pitch; a yelp punctuated by a snort; and then the mumbling again. Bo kept checking the rear-view mirror, satisfied they weren't followed. When they arrived at his condo in Boulder, Bo woke Marisol up, helped her climb the stairs, and guided her into the guest bedroom.

"Thank you," Marisol said. She looked around the room filled with boxes. "Are you moving?"

"No. My girlfriend died. I haven't been able to get rid of her belongings yet."

She pointed to a quilt bulging out of an open box. "What's that?"

"A quilt my girlfriend, Cory, was making. It's made of shirts from my old triathlons."

"Triathlons?"

"It's a competition that involves swimming, biking, and running. I usually race in a couple every year," Bo said before adding, "I'm not that good."

"You look very fit to me."

"Yeah, well so is everyone else in Boulder. I'm really a swimmer. I can beat most of the other athletes in the water, but then I watch them pass me on the bike and run."

"My Hector is a swimmer."

"Hector?"

"My husband." Her eyes clouded with tears. "Hector is a really good soccer player. That's his passion. But he could out-swim most of his friends, and he was a lifeguard for a summer."

"Me too," Bo said. He stood up and grabbed a picture from the bookcase and handed it to Marisol. "That's me from the summer before med school. It was one of the best summer breaks I ever had."

"Thank you for saving me from the Sureños. You are very kind."

He sat next to Marisol as she wiped her eyes and blew her nose with the tissue from the box he handed her. She told him about Hector and Arturo, about their first bungalow and how they fixed it up into a cozy home. She told him how it all changed when Hector lost his job and they couldn't pay their bills. She worked double shifts and Hector worked odd jobs, but their debt kept mounting. She cried as she told him about Hector's trip for the Sureños. He was only supposed to be the driver, but it all went terribly wrong, and Hector almost died on the road that day. She described how the drug lieutenants came the next morning and forced her to swallow the cocaine packets.

"They have Arturo. My beautiful son," she said between sobs. "I didn't have a choice."

"I'll get you back together with your family. I promise, Marisol."

CHAPTER

48

Marisol finally drifted off to sleep, and Bo heard a knock at the door. Lisa stood on the landing with a smile and held up a search warrant.

"You've been busy," Bo said, reading the warrant.

"I read the police report last night after dinner and the cops never looked for the driver of the car that killed Cory. After they realized the vehicle was stolen, they asked a few passersby for descriptions, but that's it."

"There are only two or three hospitals the guy could have gone to. Let's go."

Bo hopped in Lisa's cruiser and said, "Why don't we start in Estes Park? It's a few miles up the canyon from the accident. If we don't have any luck there, we can work our way back to Boulder."

Bo had driven through Estes Park many times on his way to Rocky Mountain National Park. Once, he and Cory spent the weekend at the Stanley Hotel, the inspiration for Stephen King's scary thriller *The Shining*. From the hotel, they biked through town, stopped to admire the thousand-pound bull elks trying to organize their harems, and rode into the national park to climb Trail Ridge Road. Bo still remembered how cold he got on that trip. Cory, better dressed in multiple layers, kept stopping to snap pictures of the expansive vistas and the bighorn sheep precariously perched on rocky cliffs. When they finally pedaled around snow drifts to reach the visitor's center at more than twelve thousand feet, his hands and feet were numb. And then the afternoon winds picked up. Miserable and desperate, Bo convinced a group of college kids to drive them back down to Estes Park.

They passed the small clinic a couple of times before realizing it wasn't just another tourist shop. The director met them, studied the limited search warrant, and checked his computer logs for the day of the accident. Unfortunately, other than a couple of altitude sickness patients, there were no trauma cases.

The next stop was in Lyons, a beautiful town on the banks of the Saint Vrain River, which hosts an annual bluegrass festival each summer. Here the clinic was even smaller and was closed the day of the accident.

It was late afternoon by the time they parked at Boulder Community Hospital. At least this was a major medical center with neurosurgeons and heart surgeons. It was their best chance. They asked to speak to the administrative representative on duty and showed him the warrant. He made a few phone calls before coming back.

"Okay. I can't have you look at any names right now, but I can read you the list of the admitting diagnoses that day and see if there's a match. It's a big list, by the way."

He started to recite a list of bloody noses, urinary tract infections, and chest pains. And then he said, "We might have something here."

Bo perked up.

"At 1800 hours, a white male entered the ER complaining of abdominal pain and a broken ankle. He got a CAT scan, and when the ER doc tried to admit him, he left against medical advice."

"That could be it."

"Do you have a name?"

The administrator clicked buttons on the computer before looking at Bo. "That's weird. He gave a name and we sent him a bill, but the bill came back as unknown person. He must have given a phony ID."

"Can we see the CAT scan? This might be the guy who killed Cory."

The administrator made another phone call and came back. "Yes. I got permission from the hospital CEO. He's happy to help your investigation. If you go to the radiology waiting room, one of our physicians will assist you."

"I hope this is the right guy," Bo said as they walked down the quiet corridors.

Bo paced the waiting room for several minutes, stopping to admire the huge fish tank, before a disheveled, middle-aged man entered and introduced himself as Dr. Findley. Bo noticed the harried look and strained eyes of an overworked radiologist. Findley sat down and listened to Lisa explain the situation: that she was a Boulder police officer investigating a hit and run accident; that the culprit had had a CAT scan at this hospital; that Bo was a radiology resident at the university. After being reassured that he wasn't violating any medical privacy laws, Findley agreed to help and led them back to the reading room.

Bo entered a large room partitioned into four work areas, each complete with a bank of computer monitors. The room would have been completely dark if not for the glow of the monitors and a spotlight behind each workstation. While Findley plunged into the darkness, Bo and Lisa stopped and waited for their eyes to adjust before following.

Dr. Findley searched the computer database for the correct exam. "Here are the images of the patient from that evening."

"Can I see the scout images?"

"There you go," Findley replied.

Bo leaned forward and scrutinized the low-dose X-rays of the entire body that were used to plan the thin section CT slices.

"What's that box attached to his belt?" Lisa asked.

Bo looked at the rectangular object. It was the size of a pager but didn't have the right buttons. Inside, two rows of four metal tubes connected to a switch. "I have no idea," Bo said. "I've never seen anything like it."

"I'll make a copy for you," Findley replied. "Maybe an electronics shop could tell you what it is."

"Thanks. And could you magnify that area over there?" Bo pointed to the driver's pocket.

The enlarged image showed a set of keys in the driver's pocket. One looked oddly familiar. Bo stared at the metal shape before asking Lisa, "There's raised lettering on it. Do you think it could help identify a specific apartment or house?"

Lisa replied, "I doubt it, Bo. I'm sorry."

Bo spun around, swore in frustration, and grabbed his hair with both hands. He needed to find Cory's killer. When he turned back to the computers, he realized they were looking at him. He could read the pity on their faces.

"Come on, Bo. I'll drive you home," Lisa said.

"Wait," Bo shouted, startling Lisa, who reflexively backed away. "Sorry. I didn't mean to yell," Bo said. Looking at Findley, he asked, "Do you have 3D capability here?"

"We have all the fancy bells and whistles."

"Good. Load the CT data into your 3D program, please."

The two watched Dr. Findley turn back to the computer, click a couple of buttons, and then sit back. "This will take a minute to load. What are you looking for?"

"I'm not sure," Bo said. "I've seen some pretty amazing things with this technique. At the university we have a setting called surface rendering, which displays the surface of the patient's body in three dimensions. On some patients it's almost pornographic. Once I could read the lettering on a patient's shirt. It was raised just enough that the surface program picked it up."

Findley added, "One of the CT techs I know calls it a 'package check.' When you put the 3D images up, you can tell how well-endowed the patient is. The detail is amazing."

After a minute, they stared at the 3-dimensional rendering of Cory's killer. It had an alien look. The hairless, red contour of the head, neck, and torso rotated on the monitor.

"There it is," Findley exclaimed. "But I don't know how this is going to help."

"See that! Next to his left eye." Bo pointed to the screen. "Can you magnify it some more."

"I think I know what that is," Lisa said.

"A tattoo?"

"It's a gang tattoo," Lisa explained. "It's the three dots of the Sureños gang, the Mexican mafia."

"A gang member?" Bo asked. "No wonder the guy left the hospital against medical advice. He was probably on drugs."

Lisa nodded. Bo kept watching the rotating image on the screen.

"Stop it there, Dr. Findley. There's something else." Bo pointed to the patient's flank. "Is that another tattoo?"

As Findley zoomed in on the area, they saw an angular slash across the back of the patient.

"Looks like a surgical scar, Dr. Richards," Findley said. "Possibly a thoracotomy."

Bo turned to Findley. "Any evidence of lung surgery on the regular images?"

The Boulder Community Hospital radiologist clicked another part of the screen as the raw data, the actual CT slices through the patient, were displayed. "You're right. I didn't notice that before. He's missing a couple of ribs and his left kidney."

"Now we're getting somewhere."

CHAPTER

49

Bo and Lisa left Boulder Community Hospital and got back in Lisa's cruiser. "That was amazing," she said. "I had no idea you could tell that much about someone from a CAT scan. I'll take the picture of this mechanical device to the station tomorrow and run his description through our database and see what we come up with."

"At least we know what he looks like. That scar in pretty distinctive."

Before she got in the car, Lisa turned to Bo and asked, "What are you doing the rest of the day?"

"I need to go home to check on something. Why? You want to go somewhere?"

"Remember I told you the other day that I'm a terrible swimmer? I'm only good at running, but I like to cross train with swimming so I'm not pounding my joints all the time."

"Are you asking for a lesson?"

Lisa smiled. "I thought you'd never ask."

Lisa waited in her cruiser while Bo ran into his condo to get his swim bag. He peeked into the guest bedroom and found Marisol sleeping comfortably. He changed her IV fluids, searched for an old swim suit and goggles—his regular workout bag was stuck in the truck at the airport—and got back in the car. Lisa drove the half-mile to the

University of Colorado and passed several full parking lots before parking in a private space behind the rec center.

"Benefits of being a cop," she said with a smirk.

Bo liked swimming here. The pool was rarely full, and he was able to use his university credentials to get a discount.

They entered the building and passed the weight room and aerobics facility, both packed with summer students. The deafening noise of cheering parents and whistling coaches assaulted them as they opened the double glass doors to the natatorium.

"That's too bad," Lisa shouted over the din. "A swim meet."

Bo walked over to the lifeguard and talked to him. Returning to Lisa he said, "The guard said we can use the old pool. It's behind these closed doors."

Bo changed into his Speedo in the locker room. He walked past the cheering parents—he loved summer league swim meets—and through old wooden doors into the quiet auxiliary pool. Bo took a scuba certification class in this pool last year but had never swum laps in it. Built in the 1930s, the original pool was definitely showing its age. The tiles were cracked, the lighting was terrible, and the air was stale. But the place was empty except for a lonely lifeguard who now took the stand when Bo entered.

Bo was stretching his triceps when Lisa walked into the pool room. She had a towel wrapped around her waist and a swim cap stretched over her bunched up hair. She smiled demurely as she unwrapped the towel and walked over to Bo.

"Ready to go?" he asked.

"Sure. Just don't laugh at my bad form, okay?"

"I'm sure you'll be great. Why don't we both do a 200 yard warm-up and we'll regroup and start some drills?"

Without answering, Lisa jumped in, pushed off the wall, and started swimming. Bo watched her form for a couple of laps before he braced himself for the chilly water. It only took one lap for his body to get accustomed to the shock, but he hated that first lap.

"You look pretty good," Bo said when Lisa finished her warm-up. "The first thing I want you to work on is keeping your elbows high on your recovery, when your arm is finished with the stroke and is moving back up over your head. One of the most common mistakes is to drop your elbow too low and you don't get the full extension before the next stroke. So as you recover, let your fingertips drag through the water. That will keep your elbows high."

Bo was impressed at how easily she picked up the technique. He got out on the deck and watched Lisa for a few laps before jumping in next to her.

"You've got that down. I'm going to give you one more tip before we start the main set. I want you to think about body rotation this time. Watch a professional baseball player swing a bat or Tiger Woods hit a tee-shot. They use their hips and core for power, not just their arms. It's the same thing in swimming. Arms and hips work together to propel you forward. When your right arm is stretched out in front of your head, your hips should be facing to the left, not flat in the water. If your left hip could actually be poking just above the surface, that's even better. Then, as your right arm pulls through the water, rotate your hips and trunk to the right so your hips face the other way. Your head stays straight, but your hips rotate to create power. It takes a little while to get the hang of it, but if you can master that you will be steps ahead of the average swimmer."

"I never heard of that before. Let me try it once. You watch me, okay?"

Bo watched. Her hips rotated, but she picked up her head too much and started zigzagging around the lane.

"Here. Let me show you. Just lay flat in the water." Bo stood to her side, gently grabbed her hips, and rotated them to the right so she was facing him. "Just let your hips start the motion like this and the rest will follow. And don't pick up your head too much. Keep your eyes on the bottom of the pool."

Lisa turned with his guidance, and he found himself looking directly into her sparkling hazel eyes. Bo stopped, stunned. For the first time since he'd met her, he realized how beautiful she was. He'd been so wrapped up in trying to find Cory's killer, he never noticed.

Now as he held her light body in his arms, she looked so innocent, her lips so inviting, that Bo almost bent over and kissed her.

But then she turned her head away as her hips rotated to the opposite side. Bo let go and she pushed off the wall and swam down the lane.

He gave Lisa an easy set and started doing his own intervals with increasing speed and decreasing rest until he was totally spent.

After the workout and shower, Bo met Lisa at her cruiser.

"Thanks a lot," she said, bouncing with energy. "That really helped. I've never felt so smooth in the water."

"Swimming is 90 percent technique."

"I wish I had yours."

Outside Bo's condo, they lingered in the cruiser, neither wanting to say good-bye, making small talk.

Bo touched her hand. It felt so smooth. He rubbed the soft hairs on her wrist. Lisa looked up at him and moved closer. She was inches away from kissing him. But Bo pulled back at the last moment. It didn't seem right. Not while they were looking for Cory's killer.

He hugged her and said he'd call later.

Bo returned to the condo to find Marisol awake in bed. He prepared soup and crackers and talked to her while she ate.

She saw a picture of Cory on the dresser and asked if that was his girlfriend. Marisol listened while Bo described meeting Cory in medical school, overcoming his initial shyness around her, and their first date at the rock quarry.

Marisol opened up to Bo, telling him more about her harrowing trip from Cabo San Lucas to Denver. She talked about growing up poor but proud in Mexico. Her parents both worked two jobs so they could afford to send their kids to Catholic school. Sundays were special in the Hernandez house. After church, they would visit friends and family and share in a big potluck lunch. It was the only day Marisol's father relaxed and laughed.

After she was done eating, Bo cleaned up and helped her into the bathroom. When she came out he said, "I know a police officer. A really nice lady."

Marisol shot her head up in panic. "No police."

"I think she could help you get back to Mexico."

Marisol's hands shook. "No police. They'll kill my baby. Please, Dr. Bo."

"Okay. Okay. We'll find another way."

CHAPTER

50

Vince spent a lonely Saturday night in his car parked down the street from the Dunner residence. Luckily he had the bag of coke he took from Dunner to keep him company. He woke up when he heard Susan's car backing out of the driveway. She must be going to visit Dick.

Vince waited a few minutes before sneaking around the back of the house and letting himself into the unlocked kitchen door. He headed for Dunner's study. The customs reports with Bo's electronic signature remained in a neat pile on the desk. Vince sat in Dunner's high-backed leather chair and read the reports again. All were identical, computer-generated normal exams, with Bo Richards' name on them. The code at the bottom of the report indicated the room where the film was interpreted.

Vince swore when he saw the chief resident's office number—his own office—on the report. "That bastard."

Next, Vince logged out of the hospital network and started to search Dunner's personal computer files, hoping to check bank records. He'd already seen a list of passwords foolishly taped to the side of the computer. As Internet Explorer loaded, a loud thud shook the house. He jerked his head up, looked around, and strained to listen. A disturbing quiet filled the house. Then a splintering sound ripped from the back door, and Vince jumped out of the chair, backed up against a built-in bookcase, and held his breath. He heard footsteps. Heavy footsteps. And they were getting closer. Vince twitched his head in panic, eyes darting from the floor to the wall, from the desk to the ceiling, desperate for a place to hide. He had to hurry.

Finally he spotted a small closet he'd never noticed before and ducked inside seconds before the intruder entered the room. Vince wiggled behind a golf bag, coaxing his body into the tight space.

Too late, Vince remembered he had left the computer on. The man would realize someone was here. The footsteps stopped at the desk. Drawers opened and slammed shut. Papers rustled. The man yelled out and Vince stifled a scream. The intruder was talking to an accomplice. At least two of them were in the room now. The closet door opened with an eerie squeak and Vince hugged the golf bag for dear life, pushing his face into the hard leather, hoping they couldn't hear his heart pounding in his chest.

CHAPTER

51

Marisol woke to the smell of fresh coffee. She looked around the dark room, disoriented at first, until she remembered where she was. She slept better last night than any night since leaving Mexico. She sat up, her wound still sore, and swung her legs over the bed to stand. She grabbed the IV bag and shuffled into the kitchen, drawn to the odor of strong coffee.

Dr. Bo was sitting at the kitchen table reading when Marisol walked in. He stood up when he saw her and helped her sit down. She placed the nearly empty IV bag on the table and eased into the chair, pressing her hand against her belly as she sat.

"Coffee?" Dr. Bo asked.

"Please."

She watched the doctor pour the mug and bring it to the table. He was taller than Hector, and much thinner. But he looked strong, his muscles compact and wiry.

She grabbed the mug with two hands and brought it to her lips. She inhaled the aroma with closed eyes, savoring the sweet flavor, before taking a sip. She smiled.

"I guess you like coffee," he said.

"I haven't had a cup in a long time. I work at a resort in Cabo, cleaning rooms. They have excellent coffee there, and the workers are allowed to drink it in the kitchen. I guess I've gotten addicted to the flavor."

"Help yourself while you're here," Bo said before asking, "How is it you speak such good English, by the way?"

"A group of Americans stayed at our church one year, helping build houses. I spent a lot of time with them. A few months ago, the resort started training me to be a concierge."

They sat in silence while Marisol finished her coffee. Her stomach started to feel queasy, and she leaned forward and rested her head on the table. The sick feeling faded and she sat back and looked at the concern on Dr. Bo's face.

"I'm okay," Marisol said, "just drank it too fast."

"Let's take a seat in the living room." Bo guided her to a couch. That's when he noticed the quilt, the one Cory had been working on when she died. He'd packed it away after several weeks when he couldn't bear to look at it anymore. It was draped over the arm of the sofa.

"Did you take this out of the box?" Bo felt the anger rising.

"I saw the beautiful stitch work. I work at a sewing factory."

"You had no right. This is very personal to me." Bo balled his fists. "This was Cory's last project. You shouldn't have touched it."

He noticed the fear in Marisol's eyes as she cowered on the couch. "I'm very sorry, Dr. Bo."

"Give that to me." Bo reached for the quilt and a needle pricked his thumb. "Fuck!" he shouted and sucked the blood off his finger. And then the tears came. The quilt, made from his old triathlon shirts, brought back a flood of memories. Bo dropped to the floor, hugged the quilt, smelled Cory's lingering scent, and bawled. He saw the torn shirt from his first triathlon in Charlotte, North Carolina. Cory had suggested it during his easy fourth year of medical school. Bo bought his first road bike, a clunker by today's standards, and starting riding the rolling hills of Durham, Chapel Hill, and Hillsborough. When he got to the starting line in Charlotte, he had no idea what to expect. He swam a zigzag, convoluted course, couldn't find his bike in the transition area, and cramped up during the run. But he never had so much fun in his life. And Cory was there to cheer him on.

Bo felt Marisol's arms wrap around his back and he leaned into her. "I'm sorry," he said between sobs. "I shouldn't have yelled."

Finally, Bo pulled himself together and stood up. "I've got to get to work."

"I'll put it back," Marisol said.

"No. I have a better idea. Would you like to finish if for me? Then I can display it in Cory's memory."

Bo went into the guest bedroom and brought out the box with the remainder of the shirts. He took them out and looked at the fronts, remembering each event. At the bottom of the box, a white paper stood out. He picked up an unopened envelope. *Great. Probably a bill from the hospital.*

He read the bill with growing concern. It was from the University Hospital. And it was for Cory's autopsy.

CHAPTER

52

A least an hour passed after the house quieted before Vince was brave enough to leave the safety of the closet. He uncoiled his stiff body from around the golf bag and crawled into the study. Papers, broken picture frames, and books covered the floor. He dodged the mess, walked into the foyer, and explored the remainder of the first floor, peeking into each room to assure the men were gone. More strewn books and albums littered the floor. In the kitchen, the back door hung askew on one hinge.

Vince returned to the study and sat in front of the computer. From his shirt pocket he removed the list of account numbers and passwords he found before the interruption. Vince saw a Wells Fargo password and opened up Dunner's bank account information. He was surprised at the meager balance. This was the vice chairman of a major university, after all. He looked more closely at recent transactions and noticed a pattern of big cash deposits followed by similar withdrawals. He'd seen enough. He printed the statements and stuffed them in his back pocket.

Vince stood up to leave when he heard movement at the back door. He hugged the wall, assuming the smugglers were back, afraid to leave the study when a scream startled him. He peered into the kitchen and saw Susan standing wide-eyed in shock, surveying the mess.

Vince walked into the kitchen. "Susan, it's me, Vince."

She shrieked and reeled back in surprise before recognizing him. "What the hell is going on, Vince?"

Vince realized he couldn't tell her about the real purpose of his visit. Improvising, he moved closer and hugged her. "I came over to surprise you."

She relaxed in his arms and Vince continued. "I was waiting for you in the study. I thought we'd reenact those desktop maneuvers from the other day." He winked. "The next thing I knew, some men were prowling around the house. I hid in the closet behind Dick's golf bag. At one point they almost spotted me. When I didn't hear them anymore, I came out and saw this mess."

Susan looked worried. "You think I should call the police?"

"That depends. Do you know what they were looking for?"

"No. It must have something to do with what happened to Dick yesterday."

Trying to act surprised, Vince replied, "What are you talking about?"

"Dick got attacked yesterday morning in downtown Denver. He's been admitted to the university hospital. I came back to get him some clothes."

"That's terrible. Is he okay?"

She nodded.

"Did they catch the guys?"

"I don't think so. I spoke to the cops and they don't have many leads." Susan started to cry. "Do you think the same men came here?"

"Let's sit down and have a beer. You look like you need it."

They sat in the kitchen and drank in silence as the afternoon breeze rustled through the busted door. Susan drained the beer and closed her eyes. Vince saw her face contorted in pain and felt guilty; he had deceived Susan. He had come here Friday to use any means necessary to exact money from her. He used her to pay off his drug debt. And then he pummeled her husband, sending him to a hospital bed. She didn't deserve that.

Susan finally spoke. "What did the men look like?"

"I didn't see them, but they spoke Spanish."

"Dick has been acting weird recently. The last couple of nights he's locked himself in the study."

Screwing me over, Vince thought. "Can I ask you something personal?"

"After the other day, I think it's a little late for that, Vince."

Vince blushed. "I guess. I don't know how to say this, but how expensive is your cocaine habit?"

Susan stood up and tipped the chair over. "You're right," Susan fumed. "You don't know how to ask. I don't have a problem."

"I didn't say you did. But I had the feeling the men here today were working for drug dealers. Could Dick be involved with something illegal?"

Susan's face flushed. "If you're going to insult Dick, then get out." Susan pointed to the door.

"I'm sorry," Vince said and started to leave.

"Wait." Susan's eyes widened. "Did the men go in the study?"

"That's where they started."

Susan rushed down the hall into the study. Vince followed. Baffled, he watched her climb up a bookcase and push books around. She returned to the floor and said, "Dick's prescription pads are missing."

Susan leaned against Dick's desk. Shaking her head, she said, "It's all my fault." A tear ran down her face, smearing her makeup.

Vince walked over to her and stroked her shoulders and neck.

"If he wasn't downtown buying me drugs, this would have never happened." She moaned as the tears flowed.

Vince wrapped his arms around her quivering body.

"I don't know what I'm going to do." She rested her chin on his shoulder. "I don't want to go back to rehab."

Vince, always stoic and steady, was suddenly overwhelmed with sorrow. This once proud and confident woman now trembled, vulnerable in his arms. She must have sensed his sadness, sensed the emotional connection. She turned toward him, eyes hopeless and yet somehow optimistic, and kissed him.

He tasted her salty tears and the briny beer and her loneliness. He pulled her tighter and kissed her harder, his tongue exploring, probing. They kissed as if this would be their last time together and neither wanted it to end. This was nothing like yesterday's drunken sex. This was true passion, unencumbered by drugs.

Vince walked away in disgust. He didn't know what to think.

"What's wrong?" Susan said.

"It's not right, Susan."

"I don't know what happened just now, but I've never experienced anything like it before. Stay, Vince."

"I need to go. I need to set things right." Vince headed for the back door.

He shuffled back to his BMW, confused about his feelings. He felt something special in that kiss. But Susan was old enough to be his mother. He opened the door to the car and saw Dunner's package of cocaine on the front seat. He knew it would be great shared with Susan. Cursing himself, he returned to the Dunner house. Susan must have sensed his approach. He held up the coke. She smiled and let him in.

CHAPTER

53

B o arrived at the hospital for the Sunday-morning readout with a lot of questions. Cory's parents never told him about the autopsy. Wouldn't they have authorized it? Maybe it was standard in all suspicious deaths.

Bo relieved his sleepy-eyed co-resident Skip from his night shift.

"How's it going with Rosie?" Bo asked.

"It's over. She has a chip on her shoulder from not getting into medical school."

After Skip left, Bo worked for a couple of hours. When the pace slowed, he stopped by the ER and checked in with Sam Carter. He found Sam relaxed in a recliner in the ER physicians' office, watching *Sports Center* and eating a donut.

"Where are all the patients?" Bo asked.

"Don't worry. They'll be here after church."

Bo told Sam he was off duty in an hour but had an errand to run in the basement and to page him if anything came up.

Sam raised his eyebrows. "Is the 'errand' cute?"

Bo took the stairs down to the subbasement and found the morgue. As he expected, the place was empty. Three silver metal tables shined in the fluorescent lighting, ready for the next set of bodies. Bo hadn't stepped into an autopsy room since his third year of medical school, but ten years later, he remembered every detail of his first and, thankfully, only case. It was hard to forget. The deceased was so fat, the assistant had made him hold up her huge belly in order to make the midline incision. And as he hoisted the fat, a half-eaten Oreo cookie fell out. Bo gagged, but the coroner took it in stride. He'd seen everything.

Bo hurried through the autopsy room and opened the unlocked door to the offices and file room. He guessed the ominous tables were enough to scare any potential thieves. He searched a file cabinet, found the case number for Cory's autopsy, and pulled her file.

He sat and took a breath. He'd already broken down once today. He closed his eyes, said a prayer, and opened the chart.

The technical words helped Bo keep his emotions in check. The report described her physical appearance, height and weight. He rushed through the descriptions of her organs. When he got to the inspection of the chest, he almost dropped the file. *Circular wound in the left axillary line, consistent with treatment of a pneumothorax.* Bo didn't know Cory had suffered a collapsed lung, and Lisa never told him the paramedics had treated her for that. Maybe it happened in the ambulance.

He kept reading. *Examination of the internal thoracic cavity reveals the brass bore of a ballpoint pen.*

A pen in Cory's chest? Bo wondered if she'd tried to relieve her own collapsed lung.

Bo finished the report, which attributed her death to cerebral hemorrhage from trauma. On the last pages, copies of the X-rays were attached. Bo took out each one and examined them. He saw the deformity of the broken ankle she'd suffered from a mountain bike fall a couple of years ago. He hesitated as he pulled out the chest X-ray. But like the report said, along the left side of the ribs was part of a pen. Bo knew a collapsed lung could be treated by removing the insides of a pen and creating a channel between the lung and the outside air, relieving the built-up pressure inside the chest cavity. But whose pen? Surely not the paramedics'. They have medical equipment for that. And it was unlikely to have been Cory, who was probably in no shape to start cutting into her own chest.

His beeper jarred him back to reality.

"Bo. Sam Carter in the ER. I've got a patient that's not doing well. Mr. Lyerly had back surgery a couple of days ago, and now he's lost control of his bladder function. Something bad is going on. He just got back from MRI. Can you take a look at it?"

"Is Sheri on duty yet?"

"No. She's running late."

"I'll be right there," Bo said as he replaced the files.

Bo met Sam in the ER. He was looking at the MRI on his computer.

"I don't know how you guys read these things."

Bo studied the images and compared them to the MRI before surgery. The large disc had been removed; that was the good news. Unfortunately, a massive fluid collection now occupied the back muscles along the course of the surgery. Tiny air bubbles in the fluid indicated an infection. It was so large that it squeezed through the surgical tract and was now pressing on the man's spinal cord. If it got any bigger, he'd be paralyzed.

"It's bad, Sam," Bo said as he pointed out the massive fluid buildup, "like a huge ball of pus waiting to pop."

Dr. Carter walked over to the ER control area and asked the secretary to page Dr. Vanderworst again.

"It's Vanderworst's patient?"

"He's not been responding to our pages," Carter said.

"Doesn't he have backup?"

"That guy doesn't let anyone touch his patients. Everyone else is incompetent—haven't you heard?"

"Unfortunately, yes."

"Dr. Carter," the ER nurse interrupted, waving her hand over her nose. "Mr. Lyerly has just lost control of his bowels."

Carter turned to Bo. "Shit. If we don't drain that fluid right now, it'll only get worse. He might never regain the use of his bladder or bowels. Not to mention permanent paralysis."

"After I screwed up with that oxygen tank in MRI this week, Vanderworst warned me to stay away from his patients. There must be someone on call, a resident or somebody."

"Not for this."

"Doc!" The patient wailed from his room.

Bo and Sam walked in. The nurse removed the sheets and the room smelled like feces and Lysol.

"I can't feel my right thigh."

Carter explained that the man had an infection and it was pushing on his spinal cord. "It needs to be drained, but we can't get a hold of Dr. Vanderworst."

"I never liked that arrogant little guy anyway. Can someone else help me?"

Bo looked at Mr. Lyerly. He was about forty, with neatly trimmed and combed hair. A business suit and polished shoes were arranged on the side table. But his chalky white face and mouth set in a grimace told Bo the man was scared. Bo would have been too.

"Please. Can you help me?" the man asked Bo.

Bo knew he had the skills to drain the fluid. He'd performed this procedure as a surgical resident several times. And now, with ultrasound and X-ray available to him as a radiologist, it would be pretty straightforward to guide a drainage catheter into the collection. *Stay away from my patients.* Isn't that what Vanderworst said? *Or the consequences will be serious.*

"I can help you, sir. It's just that Dr. Vanderworst is picky about other doctors operating on his patients."

"I don't want to end up in a wheelchair the rest of my life," the man said, his eyes widened in fear. "If you think you can do it, go for it. I've got a wife and two kids who deserve a healthy father." He started to cry.

Bo felt awful for the man. His own eyes started to well up in sympathy and he turned to Dr. Carter. "Any word from Vanderworst?"

Carter shook his head. "There's no one else who can do this, Bo."

"Screw it. I'll help him."

Bo wheeled in the ultrasound machine while the nurses turned the patient on his side and cleaned up the sheets again. The room reeked of stool. Bo scrubbed the man's back with Betadine and numbed up the skin. He squirted sterile ultrasound jelly over the skin and scanned around for the fluid collection. It wasn't as obvious as on the MRI, and Bo started to sweat. If he screwed this up and missed the pocket of fluid, he could make the situation worse.

Bo backed away and took a deep breath.

"Are you all right?" Carter asked.

"Yeah. I just need to check the MRI one more time," Bo said and walked over to the monitors. He counted the spinal levels and measured the depth of the collection from the skin and returned to the patient.

He placed the ultrasound probe on the back again and scrutinized the area. There was one area, slightly darker than the surrounding tissues, that probably represented the fluid. Probably. But what if Bo was wrong?

"How's is going, Doc?" The patient moaned.

"I'm almost there," Bo replied. He punctured the skin with the needle and watched it advance to the darker area on the ultrasound screen. Just before the needle entered the collection, he heard movement behind him.

"What the hell are you doing with my patient, Dr. Richards?"

Shit. Vanderworst!

Bo didn't turn around. The needle was half an inch from the man's spinal cord, and Bo was not going to screw this up.

"I'm talking to you," the neurosurgeon said, tapping Bo's hand. "I need you to back away."

Bo had no choice but to take out the needle and step aside. The neurosurgeon put on sterile gloves and resumed the procedure. Vanderworst scanned the area with the ultrasound and again inserted the needle. Bo watched in dismay when he saw that the needle was heading the wrong way. He looked down at the surgeon's hands and noticed he held the ultrasound probe backward. He was headed away from infected fluid, directly toward the spinal cord.

Bo had to stop him. "Sir, could I make a suggestion?"

"I thought I told you to back off."

The patient interrupted. "My penis just went numb."

Vanderworst advanced his needle and pulled back. No fluid came out. Bo saw sweat start to drip down the side of the surgeon's face.

"Hurry, Doc."

After several unsuccessful tries, an exasperated Vanderworst threw the needle on the tray and turned to Bo in disgust. "I need to take him back to the operating room to drain this."

"Now it's my foot. I can't feel my foot."

Bo looked at the obnoxious neurosurgeon. He knew he could do this. He just needed the chance. "Let me give it one try, sir. At least while they're getting the OR ready."

"Be my guest. Better you paralyze him than me."

Bo saw a group of nurses had moved closer to watch. He grabbed the ultrasound probe and the needle and approached the patient's back. As he advanced the needle toward the pocket of pus, he blocked out the stares and concentrated on the fluid. On his first try, he knew he should have been close, but when he pulled back on the plunger, nothing came out.

"See?" Vanderworst chided, "It's not so easy. It's probably too thick for the needle size."

Bo looked back at the ultrasound machine and realized the settings were wrong. He turned the knob and adjusted the resolution, and there it was! The pocket of fluid was right there, just a little to the left of his needle. Bo pulled back and redirected the needle. "Steady now," Bo whispered to himself.

Vanderworst leaned closer.

The needle entered the collection, and fluid shot out of the hub, spraying Vanderworst's designer shirt with the nastiest-smelling brown liquid that Bo had ever encountered.

"Ugh," Vanderworst said, backing away.

Now that the needle was in the collection, it was a simple matter to feed a plastic drainage catheter into the area. Bo hooked it up to a collection bag and sutured it to the skin. Finished, Bo walked around the bed to talk to the patient.

He was smiling. "I've already got sensation back in my groin, and I can feel my toes again. Thank you."

Bo washed up and walked out of the room, relieved that the procedure went so well, but worried about the consequences.

Vanderworst stood at the nurses' station. He had changed into a scrub shirt and his arms were crossed. He stared at Bo, about to explode.

"Dr. Richards," a nurse behind Vanderworst said, holding out a phone. "Phone call."

"Bo, it's Lisa. We got a hit on the driver. Can you come over to the police station?"

CHAPTER

54

Bo entered the police station and asked the receptionist for Officer Folletti. He wandered around the foyer, stopping to look at the plaques commemorating officers lost in the line of duty. On his only other trip here, a policewoman fingerprinted Bo when he first moved to Colorado as part of a background check for his medical license. He remembered the careful manner the officer held his hand and pressed each finger against the glass, rolling his thumb more than once until she got it right.

Lisa met him in the foyer and led him into the squad room. Numerous partitions divided the large room into small cubicles, each equipped with an identical industrial desk.

"I've asked the local DEA agent to join us," she said. "Have a seat in my office."

While Lisa went off to get the agent, Bo looked around her work area. The cubicle was sterile, devoid of any personal effects: no "best cop" coffee cup, no barrettes or favorite hats, no calendar with doodling in the margins, no awards or trophies. The lone picture on the wall behind the desk gave any indication that this was Lisa's space. Bo studied the framed photograph. It showed Lisa standing next to a smiling gray-haired man, both dressed in full police regalia.

"My father never wanted me to be a cop," Lisa said following Bo's eyes. "But he was sure proud the day I graduated from the academy. Come on. Agent Slattery is waiting."

Bo followed Lisa down the hall into a conference room where she introduced him to the DEA agent. Sam Slattery looked like an ex-offensive lineman who never lost the muscle. His standard-issue blue blazer strained under the bulges, and his tight collar choked off ropy, purple neck veins. Bo wondered how he squeezed into a Kevlar vest.

Slattery eased his massive frame into the conference room chair and said, "Let's get down to business."

Lisa started. "I showed the electronic device on the driver's belt to our technical people. Turns out it's an old-style garage door opener."

Slattery continued. "Back in the 1970s, the typical opener had eight on/off switches. That's sixty-four thousand unique combinations, and it worked really well. The chances of opening up your neighbor's garage were pretty slim. Unfortunately, thieves figured out a way to capture the signal and use it later for robberies. Nowadays the devices are much more sophisticated; it's almost impossible to steal the codes."

"Best of all," Lisa added, "the X-ray shows the position of the eight switches, and our techies are programming a duplicate door opener for us. It might come in handy."

"We hope the smugglers are like everyone else and don't go to the trouble to change the code on their door openers," Slattery said.

"That's good. But what about the driver himself. Could you ID him?"

"I was just getting there," Slattery said. The chair creaked as he continued. "Using your astute observations on his CAT scan, we ran the tattoo and the scar on his back through the FBI's computer files. You probably don't know this, but every criminal who's booked or imprisoned gets photographed, and all tattoos and distinguishing body marks are entered into a database called N-DEx. It's a big help to local police, especially if witnesses only see the tattoo but not the face of the perpetrator. Anyway, we got a hit on the guy this morning. He's a gang member with the Sureños who just got out of prison. We have his last known address under surveillance, Bo."

"Do you have any idea why your girlfriend would be run off the road by a gang member?" Lisa asked.

"No." But Bo didn't believe it when he said it. Could there be some relationship with the smuggling at the hospital? Didn't Raul tell him the Sureños were responsible for the drug trafficking around Denver?

"Bo?" Lisa asked again. "Do you know anything else?"

"I did find something interesting today that might help: Cory had an autopsy. The coroner found part of a pen in her chest. She must have had a collapsed lung, and she either tried to save herself or someone else was there that day."

"I never saw anyone."

"Well, I'm going back to the scene to try and find the rest of the pen. Maybe it will shed some light on her accident."

CHAPTER

55

Vince woke up in the late afternoon, hung over, and found Susan stark naked, covers tossed to the side, snoring beside him. He swung his legs over the side of the bed and grabbed his head with both hands, pushing his skull as if he could squeeze out his stupidity. Every day this week had started out with a promise to stop snorting and ended in a haze of drugs and unprotected sex.

He wanted to leave before. He knew his attraction to Susan was wrong. The Dunners were like the parents he never had. A psychiatrist would have a field day with Vince: sleeping with his surrogate mother and beating up his only father figure.

As the late afternoon sun peeked around the lodge pole pines, Vince tiptoed into the bathroom. "Today will be different," he said out loud. Vince showered quickly and sneaked back into the bedroom to retrieve his clothes.

Susan opened her crusty eyes. "Where are you going, lover?"

Vince cringed. "I'll call you later."

"No you won't."

"Look, Susan," Vince said, sitting on the edge of the bed and covering her with the top sheet. "We can't do this. Whatever's going on between you and Dick, please work it out."

Susan remained silent and closed her eyes in pain as Vince stroked her hair. "I've got to stop the coke. It's ruining my life," he said before realizing she had fallen back to sleep.

Twenty minutes later Vince found the chairman's palatial faux mansion on the south side of Denver. He hadn't been here since last spring, when Musk hosted a party for the new chief resident. In a lavish affair, surrounded by neoclassical fountains, a professionally manicured landscape, and stunning views of the Rockies, the chairman praised Vince's intellect and wished him success.

So much had changed over the past year, Vince thought as he walked up the flagstone path to the house. He rang the bell and turned around to admire the view while he waited. The house and surroundings were modeled after an Italian villa. The architect had cornered Vince during the party, boring him with the details of the construction.

Once, during a summer before college, he worked with a catering company, putting up tents for swanky parties like this. Vince would arrive the day before the event and help erect the huge tents, driving in stakes, arranging tables and chairs. It was good, hard work and he liked it, for the most part. One day he drove rebar into one of the pipes of the sprinkler system, causing a geyser and soaking the lawn and incurring the wrath of the owner. Vince still remembered the look on the rich guy's puffy, red face while he shouted obscenities at the caterer.

After several minutes and one more ring, the massive door swung open, and Musk stood before Vince in a bathrobe. The few remaining hairs on his head were pointing to the east, and Vince wondered how many follicles it took to have a "bad hair" day.

Vince moved his sight to Musk's unhappy, unshaven face before saying, "I'm sorry to bother you on a Sunday, Dr. Musk. It's an emergency."

Musk looked at Vince with a long pause before saying, "Come on in. Just make it quick, all right?"

Vince heard a voice call from the hall. "Who is it, darling?"

"I'll be right there." Musk shrugged at Vince.

Vince had heard all the stories. In the two years since his divorce, the chairman somehow—obviously not with his looks—charmed many females into his villa.

"Make it quick, Vince."

Vince launched into a short summary of the customs X-rays: how a mule was recently admitted after a cocaine packet rupture; how Bo Richards' name was on the mule's X-ray report from DIA even though he didn't interpret it; how he found multiple reports with a phony electronic signature on them in Dr. Dunner's study, all of them drug mules.

Musk listened without interruption before saying, "So you're telling me my vice chairman, a man I've known and trusted for the last ten years, is helping drug smugglers."

"Yes."

"Sounds a little far-fetched. How could he possibly do something like that? It's not like he can sit around and read all the customs X-rays—he's a busy man, Vince."

"I have some ideas"

"Well, you keep those ideas to yourself, Dr. Flickinger." Musk's ruddy face turned a darker shade. "If the press ever got hold of this, I can see the headline now: University Hospital Helps Drug Smugglers. I'm already in a lot of trouble over the oxygen tank in the MRI scanner."

"But, sir—" Vince started to say.

"I'll look into this. Now I've got business to attend to."

And that was all Vince could do: hope the chairman would honor his commitment. He shook Musk's hand and walked to the foyer.

As he opened the door to leave he heard a sultry voice say, "Teddy, Candi has something sweet for you."

Vince rolled his eyes and walked to his car.

—◦◦◦⫸◉⫷◦◦◦—

Vince drove to the BMW dealer and turned it in for cash. He'd need the money to start his rehab. Yes. Today he was finally going to go. Just like he meant to a year ago. He hoped this time it wouldn't end so badly. But Vince had one more stop to make, and he wasn't looking forward to it. He needed to come clean with Bo once and for all.

CHAPTER

56

"I don't think it's here, Bo," Lisa said. They'd been searching the scene of Cory's accident for more than an hour, turning over every rock, picking up every tree branch. So far they'd found everything except a pen: beer caps, used condoms, and power bar wrappers. Deep inside Bo felt that pen was crucial to finding out why Cory died. Frustrated, he heaved a boulder over his head and slammed it down, fragments ricocheting onto his legs.

"Okay, Bo. I think you've had enough."

"I guess you're right. Slattery is searching for the driver. Maybe that will help solve this."

"How about a run to get your mind off the pen?"

Bo shrugged. "There's not much else we can do around here."

"What about going up to Brainard Lake for a trail run? I'll even leave my gun at home." She winked.

"The air's pretty thin up there, you know."

"I'll be fine. The question is, can you keep up?"

Back in Boulder, Lisa stopped by her place to change while Bo checked on Marisol. She was sleeping on the couch, the triathlon quilt spread over her.

Lisa came by in her car wearing a "Sea Level is for Sissies" shirt, courtesy of last year's Bolder Boulder 10K run, a Memorial Day classic for fifty thousand or so runners, joggers, and walkers.

"How high are we going?" Bo asked.

"I thought we'd go up to Lake Isabelle; about eleven thousand feet. Since it's only two miles from the trailhead, I like to start at the gatehouse and run the paved road around Brainard Lake. That adds a couple of miles, so the whole thing is eight miles roundtrip. You game?"

"Sure."

Bo sat back and enjoyed the scenic drive up Left Hand Canyon Road. He watched the bikers struggling up the last mile into the hippie town of Ward, some zigzagging across the road and a few walking the steep pitch. After passing the one-stop-sign town, they entered the Brainard Recreational Area in the Indian Peaks, part of the National Wilderness Preservations System. Bo snow-shoed here last winter and was curious to see the park in the summer.

Lisa parked and was tying her running shoes when Bo leaned against a Ponderosa pine to stretch his tight calves. He pressed into the warm cinnamon-red bark and inhaled the sweet vanilla scent.

Lisa stepped out of the car with a water bottle and a couple of Power Bars. She had removed her Bolder Boulder T-shirt and looked stunning in her running outfit, another one of those skirt/shorts that Bo found so appealing, and a matching sports bra. She leaned over and touched her palms to the ground, accentuating her wiry muscles. As she twisted her auburn hair into a ponytail and pulled it through the back of her CU baseball cap, she caught Bo staring and smiled.

"Ready to go?" Lisa asked.

"Waiting on you."

"You won't be waiting long," she said with a smirk and took off.

Bo followed close behind, but his lungs weren't ready for the quick pace and he slowed down to catch his breath. He let Lisa run ahead, and by the time he rounded Brainard Lake, she was out of sight. Through the willows, Bo spotted two fly-fishermen casting in unison, their graceful arcing motions more art than sport.

Lisa waited underneath the wooden sign at the Long Lake trailhead watching a yellow-bellied marmot dart into the woods. She pointed out the course on the map and they started up the trail. After Long Lake, the ascent steepened and Bo leaned forward and shortened his steps. The trail widened and Lisa ran next to him, apparently not bothered by the altitude.

"That's a weird tree," Bo pointed.

"It's called a banner tree," Lisa said. "The wind is so fierce up here the leaves only grow on the leeward side."

After a steep, rocky pitch, they rounded a corner and Lake Isabelle sat below them, sapphire-blue water surrounded by radiant wildflowers and framed by the thirteen thousand-foot peaks of the Navajo, Apache, and Shoshoni mountains. Patches of fluffy snow interrupted the granite-gray mountainside.

"This should be a postcard. Look at the reflection of the mountains in the water." Bo stood in awe.

"Spectacular," Lisa agreed. "And if you look up the valley you can see Isabelle Glacier about two miles up."

"Popular name."

Lisa smiled. "An engineer in Boulder named both the lake and the glacier after his wife."

Bo followed Lisa around the grassy edge of the lake to a small waterfall. They sat on a large, flat boulder, warmed from the afternoon sun, and sipped from their water bottles. Bo leaned back, arms under his head, eyes closed, and listened to the pleasing rush of the stream. He started to drift off to sleep when he heard a loud splash. Confused, he sat up and saw Lisa breast stroking in the lake below. Sweaty and hot himself, Bo took off his running shoes and jumped in. The fifty-degree water immediately took his breath away and he panicked for an instant until he realized he could stand.

Lisa laughed. "Thought I was going to have to rescue my cute swim coach," she said.

Bo smiled and tried to grab her, but she was too fast, and he slipped on the smooth rocky bottom. By the time Bo got out of the lake, Lisa was already stretched out on the boulder, goose bumps dotting her tan legs. When he sat next to her, she touched his hand and an electric sensation raced through his body. She turned to face him and her hazel eyes sparkled in the afternoon sun. Like yesterday in the pool, Bo had a sudden urge to kiss her, but guilt crept in and he backed off.

Lisa must have sensed the change in Bo. She sat up and started putting her running shoes back on.

Bo hopped down from the rock and stood below her. He placed his hands on her ankles and said, "I'm sorry. It just doesn't feel right."

"I understand," she said.

The descent was much easier. Bo carefully watched the rocks, trying to avoid twisting his ankle, and they were back at the car in less than an hour.

As they started back to Boulder, Bo had an idea and turned to Lisa. "There was one place we didn't look for the pen. Would you mind driving back there?"

CHAPTER

57

Marisol woke up when the front door swung open and smacked against the wall with a thud. Hugo, the bald man from the warehouse, stomped in with a vicious sneer. Marisol tried to stand up and run, but Hugo grabbed her hair, jerking her neck back, and tossed her back to the couch.

Marisol winced when she landed on her stitches. She turned on her back, bringing her knees to her chest, ready to kick Hugo if he got any closer. He moved a chair in front of her and pulled an enormous knife out of his coat. Marisol avoided his deadly stare, instead looking at his bald head, completely white except for a red-blue stain above his right ear. The birthmark appeared to change colors as he barked at her.

"Who have you told about us?"

Marisol was too frightened to speak. The thug leaned closer. His breath reminded her of the hot dumpster behind the hotel.

"No one," Marisol finally whispered.

"I don't believe you," Hugo said, stabbing her calf in a movement so quick Marisol never saw it happen. She looked down to see blood oozing out of the wound a second before the excruciating pain registered. She clutched her leg and pleaded, "What do you want from me?"

"The truth." Another stab.

Marisol grabbed Cory's triathlon quilt, clutching it like a child's security blanket, when she felt the embroidery scissors. Could she defend herself against this animal? She palmed the scissors and sat back, waiting for the right moment.

Hugo was not satisfied with her answers. He wanted to know if she told anyone about the smuggling operation. Marisol refused to tell him about Dr. Bo or Raul. With each denial, the bald man grew madder and madder. Once he stabbed her in the foot, piercing the webbing next to her big toe.

Leaning forward, with revolting breath, his jagged birthmark inches from her face, he spoke through clenched teeth. "If you don't tell me now, I'm going to kill you."

He grabbed Marisol's long, dark hair, and she knew this was the moment.

Now!

She thrust the embroidery scissors into Hugo's neck, aiming for his bulging jugular. The scissors plunged through the skin until Marisol felt bone and let go. The attacker dropped his knife in shock, grabbed the scissors with two hands, and struggled to pull them out. Warm, pulsing blood sprayed over Marisol's face as she stood up and started running. She ignored the burning pain in her calf and hobbled on her good foot through the back hall to a door that led to a deck.

She fumbled with the doorknob, her bloody hands slipping off the release, when she heard the bald man grunt. She didn't bother to look. He was so close. The door opened and she took one step outside when the killer grabbed the back of her shirt. The thin material ripped as she struggled and fell back inside.

Marisol shrieked. Hugo towered over her, unfazed by the blood oozing from his neck wound, an enraged animal closing in for the kill. With a snarl, he held the bloody scissors over her face. Refusing to give up, Marisol let out one last kick and he glanced down at his leg in irritation.

He looked back at Marisol, pure evil in his eyes. "Wha …?" he blurted as his expression changed to confusion. He let out an inhuman growl before dropping to his knees and collapsing on top of Marisol.

Marisol yelled, trapped underneath the weight of the disgusting assassin. She tried to take a deep breath but couldn't. She pushed the man but he didn't budge. She started to suffocate. Warm blood dripped from his neck and soaked her shirt.

Get off me!

And then, miraculously, the bald man rolled off. For a moment, Marisol thought he'd come back to life, but that's when she saw a tall blond man dragging him away. A knife stuck out of the killer's back, buried to the handle.

Marisol stood and looked at the man, speechless. Who was this man?

The tall stranger spoke first. "My name's Vince. And what are you doing in Bo's condo?"

Before Marisol could answer, she saw movement out of the corner of her eye. The animal was up, moving fast, and hurled himself against Vince. They both fell hard to the floor. The blond man freed himself, jumped up, and positioned himself between the grunting thug and Marisol.

Groaning, the bald man picked himself up off the floor, pulled the knife out of his back, and wiped the blood off his own weapon.

He started walking toward Vince.

"The door. Quick," Vince urged.

Marisol ran down the stairs onto the deck. Vince followed, walking backward to keep an eye on the bald man. But he tripped over the door jam and fell down the deck stairs.

Marisol heard the unmistakable crack of a bone.

The thug sneered, looking down at the two on the deck below, and took his first step down the steps. Marisol ran to help Vince, but it was too late. The thug was on the deck, poised to attack, when suddenly he dropped to his knees, his eyes rolled back, and he slumped over.

Marisol saw Vince crawl over and feel for the Hugo's pulse and nodded, satisfied, before standing up with a grimace.

"I don't know how he lived so long," Vince said. "I stabbed him right in the heart. He should have died immediately."

CHAPTER

58

Lisa sped down the canyon as the late-afternoon sun disappeared. When they arrived at the accident scene, the embankment looked ominous; faint slabs of granite emerged out of dark shadows.

"It's too late, Bo," Lisa said from the top of the road.

Ignoring her, Bo said, "Maybe this unknown person with the pen climbed up to check on the other driver. It's worth a shot. Where did the other car end up? The black SUV that knocked Cory's off the road and burned up?"

Lisa looked around and pointed. "There, I think."

Bo hiked down the slope, grabbing the cold rocks for balance, wishing he had a flashlight. He found a large boulder with a blackened, charred top. He kicked a few loose stones away and the pen cap rolled into view.

"I found it," Bo said.

"Don't touch anything," Lisa yelled from above and started working her way down the rocks.

"Amazing," she said when she joined him. She pulled on a latex glove and picked up the pen cap and rolled it over in her fingers. "I wonder who VF is?"

"No fucking way," Bo said when he heard the initials.

"What?"

"I knew it. I knew that jerk was hitting on Cory."

Lisa stared at Bo.

He explained, "There's only one guy I know arrogant enough to have an engraved pen: Vince Flickinger."

"Who's that?"

"He's my chief resident at the hospital, a good-looking, blond-haired, surfer-type from southern California. The guy's a genius when it comes to radiology. But he's also a self-centered and egotistical jerk. He's a real ladies' man, a smooth talker who's scored with more medical students and interns than anyone I know—that's why I can't believe Cory would have anything to do with the guy."

"Maybe there's an innocent explanation."

"Why else would they be together when I was on business trip?"

"Do you know of any connection between Dr. Flickinger and the Mexican mafia?"

Bo started to tell Lisa about the drug-smuggling films but stopped himself. He couldn't tell her about Marisol. He'd promised.

"Bo?"

"I think Vince is addicted to drugs. I had to rescue him from an overdose the other night. Maybe that's the connection."

CHAPTER

59

"Where are we going?" Marisol asked, stopping on Bo's front steps as Vince tried to drag her out of the condo.

"I'll explain in the car. We have to hurry."

"What about Dr. Bo?"

"We'll call him later. Come on."

Not seeing a better alternative, Marisol acquiesced and got into the front seat. Vince got in the driver's seat and started up the car. She knew it wasn't his car. She had watched him reach into the bald man's pockets and remove the keys and a cell phone.

Marisol didn't know if she could trust Vince. But he saved her life and said he was a friend of Dr. Bo's. He had helped her wash the killer's blood off her hands and gathered up the medical supplies.

The car merged onto a highway, and Vince turned to Marisol and asked, "Aren't you the drug smuggler, the one who almost died of a ruptured cocaine packet the other day?"

"Yes. Dr. Bo saved me."

"What are you doing in his condo?"

Marisol explained about her attempted murder in the hospital and how Dr. Bo offered her a safe place to recuperate.

"So how did they find you?"

"I don't know. Maybe someone followed us from the hospital."

Vince shook his head. "A lot of strange stuff has been happening. And it all started when you came into the hospital."

"I'm sorry." Marisol started to cry.

Vince pulled the car over to the side of the highway. He opened the glove box, took out a tissue, and wiped her tears.

"I didn't mean it was your fault," Vince said apologetically. "It's just that everywhere I turn, someone from the Mexican mafia pops up."

"I am not one of them," Marisol shouted at Vince. "I hate the Sureños." She lowered her voice to a whisper and told her story.

Vince leaned back against the driver's side door and listened. When she was finished, Vince picked up her hand and said, "You're a very brave woman." He pulled back onto the highway.

Marisol saw the signs to Denver, closed her eyes, and tried to rest, but images of Hugo and the birthmark on his bald head kept flashing through her mind. She could still see the vicious sneer of the killer reflected on the blade of the knife. She'd almost died tonight. If Vince hadn't shown up, Dr. Bo would have found her dead in his condo. Worst of all, her family would never know what happened. She had no passport or any other identification; she'd be buried alone, without a funeral Mass, thousands of miles from her worrying loved ones.

Marisol felt the car stop and opened her eyes. She looked around disoriented and said, "Where are we?"

"The last place anyone will look for you. The hospital."

CHAPTER

60

When Lisa dropped Bo off at his condo, she said "I know you're upset. Would you like some company?"

"I'd rather be alone. Let me know if Slattery found the hit-and-run driver."

"You're not going to do anything stupid about Vince, are you?"

"Not tonight." Bo was thinking about Vince's pen when the pungent odor snapped him out of his fugue state. He had worked in enough emergency rooms to recognize the familiar scent of blood and feces. Fully alert now, he left the door open in case he needed to run and listened for movement.

He called out for Marisol. Nothing.

Could the Sureños have found Marisol and killed her? Bo rushed into the guest bedroom but only found an unmade bed and discarded IV bags. He left the room and turned on the living room lights. Smeared blood covered the floor by the couch and trailed into the utility room.

Bo stopped and contemplated his next step. What if the intruders were still here? He suddenly felt vulnerable. Bo retreated to the front closet and grabbed an old bike pump. Holding the makeshift weapon in front of him, he entered the dark room and flipped the switch.

The path of blood tracked toward the back door. Bo walked around the mess, hoping Marisol wasn't dead on the deck, and turned on the outdoor lighting. A big man with an ugly port-wine stain on his bald head lay sprawled on the wood, face down, clutching a huge knife. Bo walked down the steps and checked the dead man's pulse. The fetid smell gagged Bo and he backed away, pulling his feet out of the coagulated blood with a sickening sucking sound.

Bo removed his shoes before walking into the kitchen. He pulled Lisa Folletti's business card out of this pocket and dialed her mobile number. She answered on the first ring.

"Lisa," he said, looking toward the utility room. "It's Bo."

"I was hoping you'd call," she said in a sexy voice.

"Could you come back over?" He stared at birthmark on the dead man's body.

"Should I bring a bottle of wine?"

"Wine?" Bo realized he wasn't making himself clear. "I need police help, Lisa." He waited a few beats before adding, "There's a dead body in my condo."

As instructed by Lisa, Bo waited outside. She arrived fifteen minutes later, accompanied by a uniformed male who introduced himself as Officer Ed Fogarty. Bo led the officers through the utility room to the top of the deck stairs.

He watched Lisa approach the body and feel for a carotid pulse with her gloved fingers. She stood up, snapped off the gloves, and turned to Fogarty. "Call the homicide detectives and medical examiner. I'll talk to Dr. Richards."

Bo and Lisa convened in the kitchen while Fogarty secured the scene and made his calls.

Lisa began, "Tell me what happened."

"There's not much to tell. After you dropped me off, I walked in and found a dead body on my deck."

"Do you know who he is?"

"Never seen him before."

"The man is clearly a Mexican gang member."

"How do you know?"

"The three dots in a row with two lines underneath them. That's the Aztec symbol for thirteen."

"Thirteen?"

"The Mexican mafia uses the number thirteen, since M is the thirteenth letter of the alphabet."

Bo wondered how Marisol could have killed someone so powerful.

Lisa interrupted his thoughts. "You need to tell me what's going on. This is serious. This is the second time a Mexican mafia thug has been associated with you."

"It's a long story."

"I've got the time. Go on."

"I brought someone home the other night. She was a drug smuggler."

Bo saw Lisa take an exaggerated swallow. "You're having a relationship with a drug smuggler?"

"No. No. It's not like that. It's not romantic."

"Then what is it? You've put me in a compromising position, Bo."

"Let me start over. The lady's name is Marisol Hernandez. She was a drug mule for the Sureños. After she delivered the cocaine, they were supposed to send her back home, but they changed their mind. She thinks they were going to force her into prostitution. Marisol was able to escape and hide in a nearby church. The next day she collapsed, and a priest brought her to the university hospital. That's where I met her."

Lisa squinted and her face reddened. "A drug smuggler? A criminal was here?"

"Listen to me. She's really a nice person who was forced to swallow cocaine packets to save her family back in Mexico. The Sureños threatened her husband and son. I first met her in the emergency room when one of the cocaine-filled condoms ruptured, almost killing her. She needed emergency surgery to save her life."

"How did she end up here?"

"A couple of days after surgery, a guy named Sanchez, the boss of the Mexican mafia, came to the hospital to kill her." Bo saw Lisa's eyes widen at the mention of the name. "You know him?"

"Of course. He goes by El Piojo, and he's pure evil."

"Yeah, that's him. It was by blind luck and coincidence that Marisol escaped unharmed. I knew they would come back and try again, so I sneaked her out of the hospital yesterday and put her in my guest room."

"Where is she now?"

"I don't know. She's not here."

"Great. Just great. My boyfriend is harboring a fugitive. That's going to look real good at the station."

Bo didn't like the sarcasm. "Boyfriend? Let's not get too carried away. We had a couple of workouts and you helped me with Cory's investigation."

Lisa slapped him and walked away from the kitchen table.

The condo was now filled with crime scene investigators, detectives, and the medical examiner. Flashes of light from the police photographer added to the eerie scene. Bo watched the investigators place the body in a black bag, zip it shut, and haul the corpse onto a stretcher. Lisa and the detectives conferred in the living room. Bo couldn't hear what they were saying but could sense the tension.

Lisa turned from the group with an exasperated look and walked back into the kitchen with her partner. "I need to take you down to the police station. The other detectives want to question you."

"Oh come on, Lisa," Bo said. "You know I didn't kill that guy. I was with you all day."

"I know," she said coldly. "*Investigating.*"

Fogarty spoke. "We have to do this by the book. You admitted to harboring a criminal, and that clearly has something to do with the dead gang member on your deck."

"Do I need a lawyer, Officer Folletti?"

"It wouldn't hurt," she said, avoiding his stare.

CHAPTER

61

Vince helped Marisol out of the car, and they hobbled through a side door of the hospital. Riding the elevator to the fourth floor, Marisol doubled over in pain, and Vince helped her stay on her feet.

"My belly hurts."

Vince understood. She had just gotten out of surgery and had been through a lot the past couple of days. Most patients would be resting in bed. When the elevator doors opened, Vince spotted an empty wheelchair and helped Marisol sit. He pushed her down a dark corridor, past a vacated nurses' station, using the handles of the wheelchair to lessen the weight off his throbbing ankle. The obstetrics ward had recently moved to a new unit and the old labor and delivery rooms were temporarily vacant. They were supposed to be converted to a new psychiatry ward, a cute OB nurse told Vince after seducing him a couple of weeks ago. Vince could still picture the nurse, feet up in stirrups, inviting him for an "examination."

Skipping the exam room, Vince wheeled Marisol into a large single room with a private shower. He placed the medical supplies he took from Bo's condo on the bedside table, along with the cell phone he'd removed from the killer's pocket. He returned to the hall to get linens off the laundry cart parked near the elevators. After making Marisol's bed and settling her in, he rested on a reclining chair, leaned back, and propped up his horribly swollen ankle.

Vince looked at Marisol resting peacefully on the bed. She was a tough woman, he thought. After all she had been through—swallowing the cocaine, two surgeries, escaping from Sanchez—she still had the courage to stand up to that ugly, bald-headed thug. Vince shuddered as he remembered stabbing the guy in the back, aiming for his heart. He had never killed anyone before, but if he hadn't found the knife next to the couch and acted quickly, the man would surely have killed Marisol.

After Marisol drifted off to sleep, Vince set out to attend to his ankle. He recalled passing an old X-ray room on this floor. Trying not to disturb Marisol, he got out of the chair and hobbled down the hall. He spotted the radiation sign, entered the musty room, and turned on the generator and film processor, remembering the days before the department converted to digital X-rays. He found a dusty box of film in the dark room and slipped one inside an empty cassette. Guessing the exposure technique, Vince stretched the trigger cord around the protective shield, climbed on the X-ray table, and pressed the button. He ran the film through the developer and hoped for the best. Ninety seconds later the X-ray rolled out of the processor and Vince held it up to the hall light. It wasn't pretty, but it was good enough to confirm a fracture. Damn! No wonder his ankle hurt so much.

Vince wandered over to the supply room to see if he could find anything useful. He really needed a walking boot but doubted the labor and delivery floor would have one in stock. As luck would have it, he found a couple of packages of fiberglass casting material and cotton padding. Pregnant women break bones too. After wetting the fiberglass material, Vince sat down, wrapped the purple ankle with the cotton, and proceeded to make the ugliest ankle cast he'd ever seen. It had wrinkles and lumps and looked like a knobby tree stump, but it would have to do until he had time for professional help.

A shrill cry echoed down the hall. Vince jerked his head up and listened. How could anyone have found them up here?

He limped on the still-soggy cast, following the panicked shrieking to Marisol's room. Vince hesitated at the closed door, afraid of the unknown terror within.

The screaming stopped.

Vince pulled the handle and peeked inside.

Marisol sat on the edge of the bed, eyes wide with fright, holding a cell phone at arm's length. She stared petrified at the ringing unit, whimpering, "No. No."

Vince grabbed the phone from Marisol. A picture of the caller stared back at him.

"That"—Marisol stopped to calm her shaking hands—"that is El Piojo."

CHAPTER

62

Vince stared at Sanchez's picture on the cell phone he had stolen from the bald man. He resisted the overwhelming urge to call him back and shout at him. Sanchez had been the one who sent the thug to torture Marisol, the thug Vince had to kill and now live with that memory for the rest of his life. Sanchez must be the one working with Dunner to get the mules through customs. Vince wanted to reach through the phone and strangle the bastard.

Frustrated, he slammed the phone on the bed and stormed away, roaring in anger. He bumped into Marisol's wheelchair, sending it sliding across the floor, and yanked a picture off the wall and slammed it on the ground.

He turned back and saw Marisol cowering in the corner of her bed, knees up defensively, warily looking at him. Crusted blood covered her ankles and feet.

"Sorry. My temper gets a little out of control."

Marisol seemed to relax after his apology. Vince cleaned and dressed her knife wounds. He restarted her IV, injected antibiotics into the liquid solution, and gave her a sedative.

Marisol thanked him before drifting off to sleep.

Vince returned to the lounge chair and pushed it back as far as it would recline. He closed his eyes and tried to relax. He needed to concentrate and think this through. Should he call Sanchez and convince the drug lord that he wasn't a threat to their business? No, not after killing the bald guy. Should he go to the police? But Vince didn't have any real proof of the conspiracy, and it wouldn't take long for cops to realize that the phony X-ray reports had come from his office. Worst of all, his fingerprints were on the knife that had killed the bald man. The cops might arrest him.

Vince fidgeted in the chair, a gnawing urgency growing deep inside. He pictured the bulging bag of cocaine he had shared with Susan this afternoon. Should he call her? It might help him concentrate and figure a way out of this predicament. One more night wouldn't hurt. Tomorrow he would get Marisol to safety and then go to rehab. Vince straightened the chair and prepared to leave the room.

He walked into the dark hallway and stopped when he heard the voices. He flattened his body against the wall. Despite the blackness, he was sure they could spot his blond hair against the olive wallpaper. Vince strained to listen. Nothing. Just the hum of the X-ray generator he had powered up earlier. And then he heard whispers. They were right behind him!

Vince whirled in panic. Marisol stood at the doorway with a puzzled look on her face.

"They're here. Get back in the room," he urged in a hushed voice.

"Who?"

"Don't you hear them? They're getting closer."

Vince watched Marisol drop her head, close her eyes, and listen. He could still hear the whispering; bits of Spanish filtered down the eerie hallway. Surely Marisol must hear them. She looked up, bewildered, and started backing away from him.

"I don't hear anything. You're scaring me," she said, retreating into the room.

Vince stood in the hallway, confused. Could he be imaging the whole thing? He hobbled back to his chair and sat down. At least the terror had temporarily stopped his craving for the cocaine. But it hadn't quelled his anger. He picked up the bald man's cell phone, pressed redial, and watched Sanchez's face fill the screen.

"Hugo?" a smooth voice answered.

"He's dead," Vince replied. "And you will be too, asshole, if you don't back off."

CHAPTER

63

B o ducked under the yellow crime-scene tape and walked down
the steps past a small crowd of curious onlookers. He recognized
a few neighbors and gave an embarrassed shrug. Lisa opened
the back door of her police cruiser and motioned for Bo to get in.
He slid in, and his knees bumped into the hard partition. The locks
thumped closed. Bo turned toward the sound and slammed his fist
into the door.

Bo saw Lisa's ice-cold reflection in the rear-view mirror.

"We'll be at the station in a minute," she said, her voice muffled
by the protective barrier. Whatever relationship had been building
with Lisa, he knew he ruined it. But she made him so mad when
she accused him of harboring a fugitive. If she could meet Marisol,
she would understand.

Bo pulled out his cell phone and called Sheri.

"A dead body?" Sheri exclaimed.

"Can you help me or not?" Bo asked, annoyed.

"Sorry. I'm just shocked. I'll call my brother's lawyer and come
pick you up."

Lisa pulled the car into an empty space in front of the police
department. She led Bo inside, into a small room, barren except
for a table and three chairs. Bo had seen enough cop shows to
know that this was the interrogation room. About thirty minutes
later a middle-aged man in a rumpled suit and a battered brown
briefcase entered and sat next to Bo. He introduced himself as Sam
Meadows, criminal attorney. His breath smelled like mouthwash

and his long-past five o'clock shadow interrupted a keloid on the first of his two chins. His right hand covered the scar as he pensively stroked the stubble.

"Thanks for coming. I'm Bo Richards."

Meadows listened while Bo described his unusual discovery of a dead body in his condo. Bo told him about Marisol, how they met, and how she came to be staying with him. The dead man looked like a gang member, and, Bo speculated, the most likely explanation is that Marisol killed him in self-defense and ran away.

Meadows offered legal advice before the detectives came in to question Bo. The lawyer said he would sit by him and stop him if he started to get into trouble.

A detective Bo recognized from earlier entered the room, carrying a notebook and cup of burnt coffee. He handed Bo and Meadows his card.

"I just need a statement from you, Dr. Richards," the detective said. "And then you can leave. I've already spoken to Officer Folletti, who's given you an alibi for the dead gang member."

Bo answered a barrage of questions, including his relationship with Marisol Hernandez and her involvement with the Sureños gang.

It was after 1:00 a.m. when Bo was released from the police station. After thanking Meadows, Bo found Sheri snoozing in the waiting room. He touched her shoulder and she jumped awake, startled.

"Sorry to wake you. We can go," Bo said. They trudged out of the station into the cool night and got in Sheri's Prius.

Sheri sped through the empty streets, and in minutes they were on the Boulder Turnpike heading to her apartment in Denver. "You can stay with me tonight," she said. "For that matter, you can stay with me every night." She winked in a feeble attempt at humor. "Just kidding. One of the officers said your condo will be ready either tomorrow or Tuesday."

"Can I ask you something personal, Sheri? And you need to tell me if it's the truth."

"Of course."

"Was Vince having an affair with Cory?"

"I'm not sure, but I did see them together a couple of times. Very close together."

CHAPTER

64

"Dr. Vince. Wake up."

Woozy, Vince opened his eyes. Marisol shook the reclining chair and handed him a ringing cell phone. He flipped it open and struggled to get up. His whole body was sore. The ankle still throbbed, his head ached, and now his neck was stiff from sleeping upright in the chair beside Marisol.

"Dr. Flickinger," he managed to say.

"Vince, where are you?" It sounded like Musk, but of course the chairman didn't bother to introduce himself.

"In the hospital, sir."

"Well, get over to my office. I have someone here who wants to talk to you."

Vince stumbled to the bathroom and attempted to make himself presentable. He changed into new scrubs—at least the extralong pants hid his terrible-looking cast. He used a disposable razor and toothbrush he found in the cabinet. After combing his hair, he had to admit he looked okay. Not his usual debonair self, but acceptable.

Who was in Musk's office? The Denver police? Could they have already traced his fingerprints off the knife he left sticking out of the bald man? Maybe Dunner woke up and realized it was Vince who had beat him up.

Vince couldn't think of any good possibilities, so he took the elevator to the basement; he was one of the few people in the hospital who knew about Musk's "back door." Vince decided he would eavesdrop through the rear door first—just in case trouble waited for him.

Walking down the orange-colored hall, he tested his knobby cast and realized it supported his ankle pretty well. As long as he didn't put all his weight on it, it didn't hurt that much. He turned down a remote corridor toward the sounds of dishes clanking, cardboard boxes being ripped open, and a faucet left running. When he got closer, he saw steam billowing out of the dishwasher room. Breakfast was definitely in full swing. He eyed a patient food cart waiting for delivery, lifted one of the plastic covers, and helped himself to someone's croissant and orange juice. He'd need his strength to face Musk.

Vince stopped to get oriented in the basement corridors and smiled as he remembered the day he'd discovered the back stairs to Musk's office. He'd been chasing a cute pathology resident around the morgue one night on call last year when she playfully darted out of the room and opened a door Vince had never seen before. He followed her up to the landing, trapped her against a locked door, and proceeded to get a private anatomy lesson. Afterward he noticed the sign on the door. A few months ago, Musk's secretary confided to Vince that the chairman sometimes needed a quick escape route— particularly during his nasty divorce.

Vince listened to laughter and polite chuckling. It didn't sound like the police. He knocked and waited for the chairman to let him in.

"Unusual entrance, Dr. Flickinger," the chairman said.

"I was down in the morgue getting follow-up on an interesting case when you called. You made it sound important so I rushed up the back stairs."

Musk let him into the office, and Vince relaxed when he saw Dr. Hammond sipping coffee.

The senior partner from southern California stood and shook Vince's hand. "Good to see you again, Dr. Flickinger. I'm sorry your sinus troubles interfered with our dinner conversation last week."

"Thanks for understanding."

"What happened to your ankle, Vince?" Musk asked.

"I slipped hiking yesterday," Vince responded, trying to think of something athletic to impress the RASC partner.

Vince accepted coffee and the three sat down around the chairman's conference table. Vince couldn't believe his good luck. The RASC radiologist apparently bought his lame story about a sinus infection. And by the way Musk beamed, it looked like Hammond was here to offer Vince the job.

Hammond began, "I was just congratulating Dr. Musk on his excellent residency training program. The last partner we hired—a chief resident, about seven years ago—is superb. And the chairman tells me you're the best resident he's ever had."

After all the trouble he'd been through the last few days, Vince loved hearing these words. He really wanted this job. He'd always dreamed of returning to southern California. And this time he'd have enough money to enjoy it, not just the few dollars the priests doled out for good behavior.

Dr. Hammond reached into his briefcase. A knock at the door disturbed the expectant silence in the chairman's office. Musk stood and cracked open the door to his anteroom.

Vince could hear Emily's strained voice.

"Police?" Vince heard Musk say. "What's this about?"

Vince never heard the reply. He was already hobbling down the stairs.

CHAPTER

65

The jingling of silverware and the smell of fresh coffee woke Bo from his restless sleep. He looked around the living room, squinting at pictures of a young Sheri playing at the beach, an older Sheri graduating from high school, and a formal portrait of her family.

Sheri walked into the living room dressed for work. "Sorry about the noise. I'm kind of compulsive about keeping the place neat. Stay as long as you want. There's coffee on the burner, and my car keys are in the kitchen."

"Thanks for letting me sleep here." Bo sat up and pointed to the bookcase. "By the way, who's the hunk in that picture with you—the guy with the wavy bleach-blond hair? Your boyfriend?"

Sheri laughed. "No. That's me and my brother, Jack, at the Outer Banks. My folks rented a place in Kitty Hawk every year. Those were great times."

Sheri's smile faded as she told Bo about her troubled brother. "We were inseparable growing up. Best friends, really. We watched each other's soccer games, spent the summer surfing and fishing together at the beach. Jack even made sure my dates treated me right. That's why this is so tough now." She stopped and looked at Bo. "You sure you want to hear this?"

Bo nodded.

Sheri continued. "He started getting into trouble in high school, cheating on tests. He stole a car once and drove it to Wrightsville beach for the day. School bored him and his grades dropped, but he managed to graduate and get into the University of North Carolina in Wilmington. It's a step down from the main UNC campus in Chapel Hill, but still a pretty good school. He started out as a computer programmer and switched to education. He planned on becoming a high school teacher. He wanted to take a year off first so he came out to Colorado to ski, working as a part-time waiter to pay the bills. Anyway, he got involved with some bad people, doing drugs and getting drunk every night. Eventually he started forging bad checks to cover his debt, got caught, and ended up in jail. He's out now. He's the reason I decided to do my residency here—so I could visit him on weekends."

"Where is he now?"

"I haven't seen him in a day or two. I think he's back using drugs again," Sheri said as she picked up her purse and lunch. "Are you going to work today, Bo?"

"No. Could you tell Vince I won't be in today? I don't think I could face him anyway, and I have to follow up with the detectives.

"I'm really sorry I had to tell you about Cory."

CHAPTER

66

After Vince left, Marisol decided it was a good time to take a walk around the empty corridors. She swung her legs off the side of the bed, noticed dry splotches of cherry red splattered on her ankles, and whipped her head away in disgust. She needed to clean up.

She went into the bathroom, locked the door, and turned on the shower. Trying to keep her bandage dry, Marisol turned her back to the stream. She leaned back and let the steamy water run over her head. She found a small bottle of shampoo on the floor and washed her hair. She sat on the plastic white seat in the corner, held on to the metal rails, and scrubbed Hugo's blood off her feet and ankles.

She stepped out of the shower feeling fresh, alive, and human again. And for the first time since she left Mexico, she forgot about the misery she'd endured and allowed herself to smile and dream. She'd find a way out of here. She'd be home soon.

The cell phone on the bed stand was ringing when Marisol opened the bathroom door. She flipped it open and heard a voice she would never forget: the voice of evil, El Piojo.

"Leave me alone. I delivered the drugs. I did everything you asked me to do."

"Marisol," Sanchez said with his slick Mexican accent. "I had a lot more in store for you, lovely lady. But you had to ruin it by killing my men." Sanchez paused and Marisol thought she heard a baby crying in the background. "But we can chat about that later. Right now I have a surprise for you."

Marisol listened to shouting and shuffling noises. And then a voice she thought she would never hear again came on the phone. "Marisol," he said, and with that one word her body went limp. She tried to open her mouth but no words came out. "I love you. Don't listen to him," he said before the phone was pulled away and she heard a grunt.

El Piojo was back on the phone. "Well, well. It seems that Hector swallowed more bolitas than you. And I think he's lonely. He's missing his wife." Pausing again for effect, Sanchez added, "And Arturo—cute baby, by the way—is definitely missing his mother. If he cries any more, I'm going to have to cut his tongue out."

Vince bolted down the basement corridors as fast as his makeshift cast would allow, and hopped on the little-used blue elevator. He didn't think anyone followed him, and he needed to get to the safety of the old delivery ward so he could think. When the elevator doors opened he scanned the area and found the ward empty.

He knocked before entering Marisol's room. When he opened the door, he didn't see Marisol in the dark room and called her name. No answer. He searched the bathroom and was about to call her again when he heard soft sniffling. Marisol was hiding behind the bed, balled up and mumbling prayers.

"Marisol." Vince nudged her. "It's Vince."

Marisol stopped praying, looked up at Vince, and vomited explosively.

CHAPTER

67

Bo called Lisa from the road and asked if he could meet her and agent Slattery this morning. For the third time in as many days, Bo walked through the doors of the Boulder Police Station. He hoped this was the last.

They met in the same room. Lisa looked like she hadn't slept much last night.

Lisa asked, "What's going on, Bo?"

Bo sat down. "There's something important I didn't tell you about last night."

"Like harboring a fugitive."

"Come on, Lisa. She was the victim, not the problem."

Slattery interrupted. "I don't know what's going on between you guys, but let's keep it professional. First, Lisa. Tell Dr. Richards about the knife."

Lisa folded her hands. "The fingerprints on the knife that killed the guy in your condo didn't match yours."

Bo smirked.

"So with that and my own alibi, you aren't a suspect in the murder of the gang member."

"But," Slattery said, "we still have possible charges pending against you for harboring the drug mule."

"Perhaps the information I have will help you drop those charges," Bo said.

"What did you want to tell us?" Slattery asked.

"I know this isn't going to sound good. Especially after last night. But I didn't tell the whole story."

"Go on."

Bo told them the details about the X-reports from customs, how his name appeared on the film performed on Marisol two days before she came to the ER. "I started looking into it, and it turns out there's a whole series of drug mules with obvious abnormalities on X-ray being allowed through customs because the X-rays were reported as normal.

"The trouble," he continued, "is that my signature is on all the reports."

"What?" Lisa and Slattery said in unison.

"But I know I didn't read them. I wasn't even working some of those days."

"Why didn't you tell us this before?"

"Marisol made me promise not to go to the police. She was worried about the repercussions to her family. And last night, with a dead body in my condo, it didn't seem like the right time to tell you I'm involved—even unwittingly—in a drug-smuggling conspiracy."

Slattery sat back. The back of the chair creaked under his enormous bulk. "So you're telling us someone at the hospital— not you, of course—is helping the Mexican mafia smuggle drugs through customs at DIA."

"And I think I know who. A friend of mine traced the reports to a specific computer at the hospital."

"Dr. Vince Flickinger?" Lisa asked.

"How did you know?"

"Because his fingerprints are on the knife that killed the gang member in your condo."

Slattery shook his head in disbelief. "Let me get this straight. This Vince Flickinger arranged a bunch of phony X-ray reports so drug mules could pass through DIA. And he killed a member of the Mexican mafia in your condo."

"Don't forget we found his pen at the scene of my girlfriend's accident a year ago, an accident we think was caused by the Mexican mafia guy you found in the database."

"Have you found Dr. Flickinger?" Slattery asked.

"A unit went over to the hospital today, but he escaped into the basement and hasn't been found yet," Lisa said.

"Damn!" Bo slammed his hand against the table. "What about the hit and run driver?"

"Not yet, Bo."

Bo stood up to leave, but Lisa motioned him to sit. "There's something else I need to tell you. It's about Cory."

Bo waited while Lisa sifted through a police folder. "Here it is. About twelve years ago, on May 10, 1998, Cory Dodson was arrested for possession of heroin."

CHAPTER

68

Vince dragged Marisol's shivering, inert body away from the vomit on the floor and hoisted her up onto the bed. He wrapped a blanket around her shoulders and then cleaned up the mess. He changed into an extra pair of scrubs in the bathroom. Marisol remained motionless, zombielike; only her watchful, panicked eyes followed him around the room.

Vince knew enough psychiatry to recognize that she was in shock. He tried speaking to her in a calm, reassuring voice, but she didn't respond. He offered her a glass of water—it always worked in the movies—but she stared through the glass as if in a trance. Exasperated, Vince sat next to her and waited.

After several long minutes, Marisol pulled the cell phone out of her pocket and showed it to Vince. "He called," she said in a hushed whisper.

Vince took the cell and reviewed the recent calls. "Sanchez?"

Marisol nodded. "It's worse. He has my husband, Hector, and my baby, Arturo, here in Denver. He told me Hector was a drug mule."

"What does he want from you?"

"He wants me to come back to him," she sobbed. "Or he'll kill Arturo."

"You're not going to go, are you? He'll kill you for sure."

"I need to save my family."

Vince stood up and paced the room. He couldn't believe Marisol would go back. It was suicide. Maybe she should go to the police and tell them about the drug warehouse, and they could raid the place. But if the Sureños had already moved Hector and Arturo, they'd be dead.

"I need the key," Marisol said.

Vince looked confused. "What key?"

"The skinny man. The one I shot outside the warehouse. I looked at his X-ray with Dr. Bo."

"Do you know his name?"

"Miguel Jimenez."

"What day did you shoot him?"

Marisol sat still, thinking, and finally said, "I think Tuesday."

Vince hoped that the IT department was as slow to turn off the computers as they were to fix them. He helped Marisol stand up and they sneaked down the hall to the empty nurses' station. Vince powered up an old computer and smiled when it connected to the radiology network. He searched the database for emergency CAT scans and found the case. He saw the bullet in the spleen and a key in the guy's pocket.

"That's the guy I shot," Marisol said. "Is there any way to get a copy of his key?"

"We might be able to make one," Vince said. He removed his own condo key and measured its length. Then he magnified the computer image until it was the same size and printed it.

"I spent a lot of time with juvenile delinquents where I grew up. They taught me how to make a key from a Coke can, believe it or not. If you unfold a Coke can and trace the key with a pen, you can cut out a flimsy key that actually works. I'm going to do better than that, though."

"Do you have any scissors? I work in a sewing factory. I'm good with patterns."

Vince handed Marisol a pair of scissors from the desk and watched her deftly cut the pattern. Minutes later Vince sneaked down to the maintenance shop in search of Tony, the manager. They had become friends after Tony had a serious pneumonia last year and Vince had to drain the fluid that had built up in his chest. Tony didn't ask many questions when Vince handed him the cutout key. He placed it in the machine, and minutes later Vince walked away with two perfect copies.

CHAPTER

69

Bo flew out of the police station, ignoring Lisa's pleas to talk. He didn't believe her. The Cory he knew wouldn't even smoke pot. He remembered lying in bed with her, stroking her smooth arms, never wanting to let go. She didn't have any needle tracks. Lisa had to be wrong. Maybe it was another Cory Dodson.

Without thinking about where he was going, Bo ended up at the Boulder Reservoir. He couldn't go home—his condo was still a crime scene. Bo pulled up to the guardhouse and paid the toll. He'd been here many times to swim and run and had even competed in the Boulder Peak triathlon last July, starting the swim in the reservoir. He parked, slipped on his bathing suit, and walked over to the beach. A couple of toddlers frolicked at the water's edge while their mothers chatted in beach chairs. Bo waved to the lifeguard before wading into the cool water. At this time of year, the temperature didn't get above sixty-five degrees, and Bo fought off the shivers. He usually wore a wet suit for the triathlons, but today he didn't care. He just wanted to forget everything for a while. Maybe the cops would arrest Vince soon so he could ask the jerk some questions.

The area was roped off, protecting swimmers from the boaters, and a dock floated about fifty yards from shore. He stroked to the wooden platform, pulled himself up the stairs, and stretched his arm and back muscles before jumping back in. He swam along the length of the beach for about thirty minutes, trying to do an easy mile. Bo worked on his sighting for a couple of lengths. He had a lot of trouble trying to swim straight in open water. When Bo did his first triathlon here last year, he zigged and zagged all over the course. He figured he swam an extra two hundred yards, costing him about two precious minutes. The trick to proper sighting was to glance ahead during the arm recovery: take a breath, look ahead, and then put your head back in the water for a few strokes. If Bo lifted his head too high, he felt his hips sink and cause too much drag. He worked on it for a while until it felt more natural.

When Bo was a junior in college he got a job as a lifeguard at the Jersey shore. He remembered his father calling him up one afternoon, during final exams at Rutgers, telling him to get down to the shore for a lifeguard tryout on Saturday. There was one opening that summer for a coveted position. Bo hadn't been swimming much at that point, mostly concentrating on his studies. When he got to the beach that Saturday morning, he found seven other competitors vying for the spot. A couple of "muscle beach" types who looked like they belonged on *Baywatch* were flexing their biceps. Bo felt out of place, scrawny, and pale after a long semester.

The course started on the beach with a hundred-yard swim to a buoy, a left turn, and a quarter-mile swim along the coastline until another left turn around a jetty and back to shore. When the whistle blew, the muscle-bound guys charged headstrong into the water, smacking into the three-to-four-foot swells, and got knocked backward. Bo got off to a slower start but timed the waves, going under the swells before they crested. As the others struggled and fought the waves, Bo found himself in the lead at the first buoy. About halfway along the quarter-mile straightaway, a couple of swimmers caught him, and by the time he reached the jetty, Bo was in third place. Never a sprinter, built for more long-distance, endurance events, Bo knew he was in trouble.

But he knew the ocean well. Growing up he had spent nearly every Saturday at the shore with his parents and brothers, riding waves and goofing around in the water. Bo saw one of the lead swimmers turn toward shore too early and get caught up in the rough water rebounding off the jetty rocks. He had to stop and swim back out.

Bo had one more swimmer to pass to get the job. Unfortunately, the leader was two body lengths ahead and only twenty yards from the shoreline. Bo realized the only way to beat this guy was to use the power of the waves to accelerate past him.

He had been timing the swells as he approached the beach. It was low tide, and the conditions were perfect for body surfing. With ten yards to go, the lead swimmer made the classic mistake of standing up too early to run in the last few yards. Bo knew there was a steep drop-off at the water's edge and running would be impossible. The other swimmer discovered this too late when he tried to stand and his feet didn't touch the bottom. He had to restart his stroke with no forward momentum.

Just then, Bo felt the water pull him backward into a large cresting wave.

Out of shape, arms burning, struggling for oxygen, he remembered all those Saturday races with his brothers. Using his last ounce of energy, he took three powerful strokes and kicked as hard as he could. His body rose as the wave sucked him into the sweet spot. For a split second, which Bo will never forget, he was stretched out, suspended above the water, motionless. Ahead, the lead swimmer struggled to restart his stroke; on the beach, blurry figures jumped and cheered; and in the water, his own gasp for air resonated in the quiet before the crash. And then the powerful surge torpedoed Bo forward. He stretched his arms out like superman, held his breath, and waited until the sand scraped his knees. He pushed up, staggered in the receding water, and crossed the finish line steps ahead of the frustrated second-place swimmer.

Bo got the job!

The whistles alerted Bo that his swim was over. The Boulder reservoir guards were off their stands now and waving him in. They had cleaned up the beach and were ready to go home, and Bo apologized for keeping them waiting.

"It's all good, dude," one of the guards said. "But someone really wants you. Your cell phone keeps ringing," he said, pointing to Bo's towel.

Bo walked over to his gear and picked up the cell. There was a text message from Dr. Musk's assistant: "Emergency meeting, 6:00 p.m., Dr. Musk's office." Bo glanced down at his watch. He had less than an hour to get there.

CHAPTER

70

Marisol stood on the corner of a deserted street in downtown Denver waiting to be picked up by the Sureños. Vince dropped her off and then called Sanchez to tell him where to get her. She was starting to like Vince. He definitely had a temper, but deep down Marisol thought he had a good heart and wanted the best for her.

Marisol concentrated on being strong for Arturo and Hector. She didn't know what Sanchez had in store for her—she knew it wasn't going to be pleasant—but she had to remain focused for Arturo's sake. She was even resigned to being killed if it meant she could save her precious baby.

A car screeched to a stop in front of her and a door opened. Miguel waved her in with a snarl. As she took her seat next to him in the back of the car, Marisol thought he looked even skinnier, if that was possible. He stared at her, his eyes intense, as if imaging all the terrible things he would do to her later.

"I'm sorry I shot you," Marisol said and turned away from his murderous stare.

The car entered the freeway, and Marisol, more familiar with directions now, realized she was heading toward Boulder. She kept her eyes on the signs, trying to remember every detail of the trip, just in case. But the fact that the Sureños didn't blindfold her was a somber indication that she would never escape, never come out of this alive.

The car stopped in a residential neighborhood, and the skinny man led her into a two-story brick house. Kids were playing in the yard next door, kicking a soccer ball around on the grass, oblivious to the trauma Marisol was about to endure. She took a deep breath and entered the house.

CHAPTER

71

o arrived at the hospital just in time for the meeting with Dr. Musk. The door to the private office was open, and Musk was talking to Dr. Vanderworst. *This can't be good,* Bo thought. He knocked once and walked into the antechamber.

Musk met Bo at the doorway and said, "Dr. Richards, come in."

Dr. Vanderworst sat on Musk's couch, wearing an expensive blue suit, leaning forward so his feet touched the floor. Through the open coat, a small paunch interrupted the straight contours of the creased white shirt.

"I'll get right to the point, Dr. Richards," Musk said, squeezing into his office chair. "Last week you ruined our magnet and almost killed a patient with an oxygen tank. Then you proceeded to get into a fight with the injured patient's husband. And now it's come to my attention that you sneaked a drug felon out of the hospital and took her to your home."

Musk stopped to catch his breath. Vanderworst nodded in assent.

"This is not appropriate behavior for one of our residents. Dr. Vanderworst and I have discussed the matter with the hospital CEO."

Musk stood. "I'm going to have to let you go, Bo. Clear out your locker tonight."

It was close to midnight when the lights in the MRI center finally went out. Bo sat in Sheri's car thinking, stewing, and then began planning.

For the first hour, he felt sorry for himself. He loved radiology. He'd never get into another program now. He thought of the long nights studying in the Rutgers library, the football and basketball games he'd missed to get into medical school. He thought of his time at Duke, studying hard to learn anatomy and physiology, the late nights on call. He couldn't imagine not being a doctor—it's all he ever wanted to be.

But then he got angry. Something wasn't right. If the police told Musk about Marisol, wouldn't the chairman also know that Vince was a suspect in a murder? Why didn't Musk give Bo a chance to explain his actions? Why not wait until he was charged with a crime before firing him? It didn't make sense. One thing was certain: if Bo ever wanted to clear his name and get his job back, he needed proof of the smuggling conspiracy.

Bo slipped back into the hospital, down the stairs to the basement, and navigated the winding corridors to the MRI center. He needed a computer station and figured the center would be closed now and no one would bother him. He nodded to a janitor pushing a waxing machine down the hall.

Bo entered the MRI reception area and fumbled for the light switch. Only the eerie glow of the EXIT sign and a spiraling yellow screen saver flickered off the peach walls. He crossed the room, opened the next door, and stepped up into the empty control area. Feeling foolish, he announced "Hello?" into the echoing, dark void and jumped as the door closed with the sucking noise of an air lock.

The chilly, dimly lit room reminded him of the cellar in his childhood house: the dank, subterranean storage area had been the perfect place for Bo to play hide-and-seek with his brothers. The creaky plywood steps and the two-by-four railing that wouldn't pass code today had descended into utter darkness. After a brave journey across the cold cement floor, dodging boxes that resembled monsters, the string attached to the bare lightbulb dangled just out of his brothers' reach. Navigating by the day-glow Styrofoam planets orbiting in the corner, Bo had always found the best spot to hide: no one had ever looked next to the growling furnace.

Shaking off his fear, Bo surveyed the MRI control room. The long, rectangular space housed two computer desks, each controlling a separate multimillion-dollar MRI unit. Here the technologists typed in the complex scanning parameters. In front of each computer a large, magnetically shielded window allowed the technologist to observe the patient. Bo leaned forward and peered through the glass. Yellow construction tape covered a silver ventilation duct, a sad reminder of Bo's disaster with Mrs. Adcock. For the hundredth time, Bo cursed his stupidity. At least the faulty ventilation system was being fixed—the only good thing to come out of this.

Bo quickly found the cases of the fake customs reports. He knew about the code at the bottom and the way to identify the source computer. He'd make some copies and show this to the police. If Musk or Vanderworst were behind this with Vince, he'd take them all down. Bo found the information and popped a blank CD into the computer and pressed the copy button.

Nothing.

He pressed the button again. A warning flashed across his screen: "You no longer have access. Please see the administrator." Damn. Bo looked at his watch: 12:01. Musk must have cancelled his privileges at midnight.

He wondered if hospital security would be alerted that he was accessing the computers and started to worry. He broke into a cold sweat. He'd better get out of there. Bo turned the computers off and raced into the reception area, glad to find it empty. He peered out into the lobby, and panic set in. Flashlights shined through the glass; security was outside the front door. The only way out was through the corridor that led to the main hospital. Bo rushed across the lavish atrium. But halfway across he saw the corridor doors open and another security guard stepped into the foyer.

Bo skidded to a stop. He was trapped.

He looked around, desperate for a place to hide. But where?

He moved behind a large plant and scanned the atrium. He was hidden until they turned the lights on. He saw a Starbucks cart—too small. Should he make a run for it? And then he saw the water feature: a wishing pond with a two-foot waterfall. It was his only chance. Bo crawled across the smooth, tile floor, and without stopping, slid headfirst into the pool with a splashless entry. The shock of the cold water stunned him, and he suppressed the urge to grunt in pain.

He could see the flashlights. They were close. He used his hands to crawl forward to the waterfall. He passed underneath it, turned around, and leaned against the faux rock structure. He had to cock his head to the side to breathe in the cramped space. He saw the blurry security guards reflected through the downpour as they left the lobby toward the MRI scanner. He was safe for now. But he was already shivering.

He was in for a long night.

CHAPTER

72

The night in the Sureños house was worse than Marisol anticipated. After humiliating her by stripping off her clothes, performing an aggressive body search, and throwing her in the shower, they made her sit in the living room while a group of young thugs smoked and played poker. Covered only by a threadbare towel that didn't hide all of her nakedness, Marisol cowered on the couch trying not to make eye contact. She kept her head down and prayed. She tried to concentrate on her husband, drawing strength from his memory. Hector wasn't a muscular man, but he was athletic and the years of soccer and swimming gave him surprising power. Marisol had only seen him lose his temper once in their five years of marriage, and that was to defend Marisol from unwanted advances in a bar one night. If only he were here by her side now, they might have a chance against these drug dealers.

Marisol noticed that from time to time, one of the men would rise from the table and go into a bedroom on the first floor. Each visit was followed by muffled screams that tore at Marisol's heart. She was so helpless.

The game must have ended when the four gang members stood up, laughing and playfully pushing each other. She made the mistake of looking into the kitchen as the four looked at her, and she knew what they were thinking. The largest man sauntered over and asked her insincerely how she was feeling. When she didn't reply he slapped her face and yelled at her. Then he yanked the towel away from her and forced her up. The other three stared at her, and she could tell they were getting aroused. Apparently the fresh scar across her belly didn't scare them like she'd hoped it would. Whistles followed Marisol as the first man pushed her into another bedroom and threw her on the bed.

The rest of the night was a blurry series of dirty men, reeking of alcohol and cigarettes, taking turns with her. Marisol stayed silent, didn't fight them, and kept her thoughts on Arturo. She'd get him back one day, take him to the beach, and build sand castles with him. She didn't know how many men visited her—she lost track after the first couple—and she didn't care.

When the humiliation was finally over, she dozed in fear, sore and sticky. She hoped this would end soon. At least she had the key. She noticed when they locked her in the room in the early morning hours that the key was the same. She carefully checked her surgical wound and planned her revenge.

CHAPTER

73

After several hours in the wishing pond, Bo couldn't feel his toes and fingers anymore. He decided he'd better get out here or die of hypothermia. He ducked under the waterfall and crawled out of the pool. He shook the water off and bounced up and down to try to warm up.

When he turned around to leave, Vince Flickinger stood before him, offering Bo a towel.

Bo almost fell back into the pool. "You?"

Bo collected himself from the shock and then the anger took over. This was the asshole who had purposefully misread Marisol Hernandez's X-ray, letting her slip through customs to die on the streets of downtown Denver. This was the asshole who used his medical degree to conspire with drug smugglers. Worst of all, this was the asshole who had killed his girlfriend.

"Get the fuck away from me, Vince. I swear I'll kill you."

Vince backed away. "I'm not the jerk you think I am. Let me explain."

Bo wasn't listening. He charged Vince and landed a vicious uppercut to his soft belly, knocking him to the floor, gasping for breath. He started to pounce on the writhing chief resident when reality set in. What was he doing?

Still shaking with fury, Bo forced himself to sit and calm down. He looked at Vince, who remained on the floor, rubbing his stomach. "All right. Explain."

"I guess I deserved that." Vince grunted and began to tell Bo what happened over the last couple of days. He started with his cocaine addiction, how it happened so easily after a party one night, how he couldn't stop. He told Bo about the anger and paranoia and his debt. He even told Bo about Susan Dunner and their drug-fueled relationship.

"Tell me about Cory. Were you guys having an affair?"

Vince looked incredulous. "Is that what you think?"

"I found your pen at the accident scene, Vince. I know you were with her that day."

"Last year, I wanted to stop the cocaine. It was ruining my life. But I couldn't. I finally went to a Narcotics Anonymous meeting. I was determined to kick the addiction. At one of the meetings I ran into Cory."

So it was true. Cory was an addict. How could Bo not know?

"Cory told me she was going to tell you about her problem. It was a long time ago—high school I think. She'd been clean for twelve years. She wanted to tell you about her past but was afraid of your reaction—she knew how opposed you are to recreational drugs, with your triathlon training and all."

"I found a private rehab facility that catered to physicians. Cory didn't want to take me to rehab that day Bo." Vince started crying. "But I pleaded until she finally gave in." Sobbing, his words stuttering, "I killed her, Bo. I'm so sorry."

"What happened on the road that day, Vince?"

"We were winding our way up the canyon toward Estes Park when this black Cadillac SUV rammed into us. Cory tried to avoid the ravine, but the guy was determined and kept crashing into us." Vince closed his eyes and dropped his head into his hands. "It was terrible, Bo. There was nothing we could do."

Vince looked up from the floor with tear-streaked eyes. "I tried to save her. I really did. I pulled her out of the car. She had a tension pneumothorax that I treated with my pen. But I couldn't do anything about her head except call 911. When I heard the sirens, I panicked and left. I didn't want to explain to the police why I was in the car."

"But why did they try to kill you? Did you double cross the Sureños?"

Vince stared at Bo, baffled. "I don't know why we were run off the road. I figured it was because I owed a lot of money to my dealer."

Bo punched Vince in the chest. "Tell me the truth, Vince. I deserve it after what you did to Cory."

"I am."

"I know the driver of the car that forced you off the road was a member of the Mexican mafia. And I know you're working with them to fake the customs X-ray reports."

"You think I'm involved with those reports?"

"They came from your office."

"It's Dick Dunner, Bo. He's the one behind this. I don't know if you remember, but Dick set up the operation between DIA customs and the university."

"Maybe Dunner is the reason I got fired tonight."

"What?"

"Yeah. Musk and Vanderworst fired me earlier tonight because I helped a drug smuggler escape from the hospital. But if you're right about Dr. Dunner, he must have persuaded them to fire me."

Vince sat, and Bo noticed a strange-looking cast extend out of his scrub pants.

"You need to turn yourself in, Vince. I met an agent from the DEA. He's a good guy. Name's Slattery. We should tell him about Dunner."

"You tell him. I'm not sure I can trust the cops right now."

Bo heard a door open and footsteps approach. Vince motioned for Bo to follow and led him back to the MRI control room. "We'll be safe here for a minute." He handed Bo a cell phone. "Give this to Slattery. I took it off that thug who tried to kill me and Marisol."

"Marisol's alive?"

"She was before this guy named Sanchez called and she agreed to meet up with him."

"The Sureños boss?" Bo asked in shock. "He'll slaughter her."

"That's what I told her. But he has her husband and baby here in Denver, and he threatened to kill them. Marisol made me take her back to them."

Bo felt sick at the thought of Marisol returning to that monster.

"I also made a copy of the phony customs reports for you," Vince said, holding up a CD. "It's the only proof we have. I'll bet Dunner will erase the computer records now that he knows we're on to him."

The MRI door swung open and Dr. Vanderworst walked in. He did a double take when he saw Bo and then turned to Vince, astonished.

"Vince?" the surgeon said. "You want to tell me what's going on?"

"It's a long story," Vince said, walking closer to him. Bo kept his distance behind Vince.

"You, Dr. Richards. I thought we took care of you last night. I'm calling security."

Vince slugged Vanderworst in the jaw and the neurosurgeon fell onto his back.

"Let's go!" Vince said and rushed out the door.

Bo followed across the lobby, past the frigid wishing pond, and out the front door. As he turned toward the parking lot, a white painter's van raced up in front of them, almost hitting Vince. The side door slid open and three guys jumped out.

"Run, Bo!" Vince shouted as he took off running through the parking lot. Vince was pretty fast for a guy in a cast.

But Bo was faster. He raced through the lot, dodging cars until he got to the frontage road that ran around the hospital. Then he accelerated into an all-out sprint, not looking back until he didn't hear any huffing and puffing behind him. The chasers had given up, and Bo saw them stopped, bent over, trying to catch their breath. He ran behind a hedgerow and peered around to find Vince.

Bo's heart sank. Vince lay spread-eagle on the asphalt, two thugs standing over him. His broken ankle must have slowed him down. Bo watched them pick Vince up, throw him in the back of the van, and slam the door. Then he saw one of the men bend over and pick up the computer disc that must have fallen out of Vince's pocket. Bo watched the man examine the CD—the proof of the drug smuggling conspiracy, the last chance for Bo to get his residency spot back—before cracking it into pieces and dropping Bo's dreams and aspirations on the dark pavement.

CHAPTER

74

The van careened out of the parking lot, throwing Vince against the side panel. He braced himself for the next turn, grasping the ridges on the hard floor. Through the divider, he heard the muffled sounds of the Mexicans urging their driver to hurry. When the van turned on to the highway, Vince sat up and assessed the situation. It wasn't good. He'd reinjured his ankle during the chase and it throbbed with shooting pains. His head was bleeding from the fall in the parking lot. And the three armed gang members in front were not happy. He could hear them arguing about failing to capture Bo.

How had it gone so wrong?

The van slowed. Vince heard a short horn blast and through the side window saw a large metal door roll open. Not usually a religious person, despite the best efforts of the priests in the orphanage, he now prayed for strength. The back doors swung open, and the gang members surrounded him and dragged him out into a large, empty warehouse. They pushed him forward at gunpoint and walked him toward a staircase. The eerie quiet in the cavernous room was magnified by the echo of their creaky footsteps as Vince ascended to certain death. For at the top of the stairs, waiting with a vicious smile, El Piojo waited with his razor-sharp knife.

The thugs strapped him to a chair. Without a word, Sanchez thrust the knife into Vince's left shoulder, and the chief resident blacked out.

CHAPTER

75

B o paid the taxi driver and knocked on Lisa Folletti's apartment door. She had written her address on one of her police cards. Lisa opened the door with a surprised expression. She was covered in a scarlet kimono; her feet were bare, and her wet hair was pulled back.

"Lisa, they've got him," Bo blurted. "They've got Vince."

Lisa scanned the street and opened the door wider. "Come in. Tell me what happened."

"Okay, but we've got to hurry," Bo said, closing the door. "Vince Flickinger and I were leaving the hospital when a van pulled up. We both ran, but Vince has a broken ankle and they caught him. I ran to the nearest hotel and took a taxi here."

"Who took Vince, Bo? Slow down. You're not making any sense."

Bo took a couple of deep breaths. "I got fired tonight, for some bogus reason, but I think the real reason is that someone knows we're close to figuring out how the Sureños smuggle their drugs through customs."

"Yeah—Vince."

"It's not Vince. After I got fired I was doing some research to clear my name and I ran into him. After nearly knocking him out, he told me Cory was driving him to rehab when her car was run off the road—they weren't having an affair like I thought. He admitted helping her at the scene and then leaving when the ambulances came. He thinks Dr. Dunner, the vice chairman, is behind the smuggling operation at DIA."

"Sit down and tell me everything that happened," Lisa said. "But first I'm going to call Sam Slattery."

Bo sat on the couch and watched Lisa walk away. The sheer kimono left nothing to the imagination. He heard her speaking on the phone, and then she returned to the living room and sat next to him. Bo repeated the story, with Lisa interrupting for details.

"As we left the hospital," Bo finished, "this white van pulled up and some men jumped out and grabbed Vince."

She asked about the van—if he remembered any distinctive markings—and whether he'd ever seen the men before. Unfortunately, Bo couldn't remember much about either. Then he remembered the cell phone in his back pocket and told Lisa Vince had taken it from the bald man he had killed in Bo's condo.

Lisa eyes brightened as Bo handed her the phone. "This is very helpful. We can hopefully search the phone records and get a trail off the calls."

Bo leaned back on the couch and tried to calm down.

Lisa touched his hand.

"I've never been that close to dying before. And I feel so bad for Vince."

Lisa intertwined her fingers with Bo's and looked into his eyes. "I'm sorry I yelled at you the other day about hiding Marisol. I know you were doing it for the right reasons. But I wish you would have told me."

"I wanted to."

"I thought this was more than an investigation, Bo. You really hurt me."

"I was upset too. I didn't mean it. You're the best thing that's happened to me in the past year."

She leaned over and hugged him.

Bo pulled away and looked at Lisa. He saw relief in her eyes. He didn't know if it was tonight's near-death experience or the stress of getting fired, but when he saw the profound understanding in that look, his heart skipped. He pulled Lisa toward him and hugged her so tightly he felt her nipples harden through the thin cover-up. This time he didn't hold back. Everything told him this was the right moment, that he should trust his emotions. He kissed her neck and tasted her sweet body lotion.

Lisa moaned her approval and turned her head to face him. They paused for a moment, eyes and lips hungry, passion building in that brief hesitation before giving in to their mutual desire. The kiss, the one Bo wanted in the pool when her body floated so close to his, the one he wanted at the top of Lake Isabelle surrounded by glaciers and budding flowers, was exquisite, timeless, beyond Bo's wildest imagination. Her lovely mouth matched his perfectly and tasted like farm-picked strawberries as their bodies became one.

The doorbell rang and startled Lisa and Bo off the couch.

CHAPTER

76

Vince woke up with ice cold water dripping off his head and Sanchez sitting in front of him.

"That," El Piojo said, pointing to Vince's shoulder, "was for killing Hugo." Impeccably dressed in a designer suit, Sanchez leaned back in his chair, arms resting in his lap, his shiny Cole Hahn black loafers crossed. He picked up the knife spotted with Vince's blood and stabbed it into the other shoulder.

Vince screamed and started to pass out again, but someone slapped him awake.

"Now that I've got your attention," Sanchez continued, "I need some answers."

Sanchez asked Vince about Bo: What did Bo know about the smuggling operation? Had he talked to the police? How did he know Marisol? What were Bo and Vince doing tonight?

Vince answered his questions. He told Sanchez that Bo saved Marisol's life in the emergency room and they had made a connection. When Marisol felt threatened, Bo agreed to let her recuperate in his condo. That was all. Bo hadn't gone to the police. And Bo didn't know anything about the smuggling, Vince lied.

When the questions were answered, Vince looked away from Sanchez, too frightened to hold his stare.

Sanchez nodded as he mulled over Vince's explanations, and for a moment Vince relaxed. Maybe his answers had satisfied the thug. Maybe they'd let him go.

But then Sanchez leaned in and grabbed Vince's shirt, pulling him so close Vince felt the killer's frigid breath waft across his cheek. When he looked into Sanchez's vacuous wolf-eyes, Vince's body shivered uncontrollably in fear and his bladder emptied on the floor.

Sanchez sensed the acrid urine and laughed. "You're not so tough now, are you?" he mocked. "Threatening me on Hugo's cell phone."

Without further warning Sanchez plunged the knife into Vince's chest, missing his heart by inches, and twisted the blade.

Vince doubled over in excruciating pain. "You bastard," he managed to say.

Worse than the shock of watching Sanchez's knife tear into his chest, and worse than the excruciating burning pain under his ribs was the screeching hiss of Vince's imminent death. With each labored breath, Vince felt his lung collapsing, precious oxygen sizzling out of the wound like a punctured balloon. The room started to spin and turn black. The end was near.

Angered by the futility of his situation, Vince felt a sudden burst of energy and roared at Sanchez. "You and Dunner will pay for this, you bastard. Just wait."

Vince's head slumped to his chest and he stared at the floor, waiting for death to overtake him. He heard footsteps and saw shoes approaching Sanchez. They looked vaguely familiar. With tremendous effort, Vince raised his head, following the shoes up to the protuberant belly, the hollow chest, the double chin to the ruddy face of his esteemed chairman, Theodore Musk.

Sanchez and Musk? He must be hallucinating. Vince tried to blink the otherworldly scene away, but they remained, as odd a couple as he'd ever dreamed.

Just before he passed out he heard Sanchez turn to Musk and ask, "Who's Dunner?"

CHAPTER

77

Lisa ran into the bedroom to put on a bathrobe while Bo let Sam Slattery in and led him into the kitchen. Lisa brewed coffee and the three discussed the new developments. Slattery was still skeptical that Vince was innocent. He suggested that Vince might be weaseling out of his predicament with the Sureños now that he knew the cops were after him.

Bo had trouble concentrating while Slattery talked police business with Lisa. He watched Lisa's soft lips moving, not hearing what she was saying, hoping the DEA agent would leave them alone soon. That kiss on the couch was the most erotic experience Bo had ever had.

Slattery finally stood up, and Lisa showed him to the door. She handed him the Sureños's cell phone and scheduled a meeting for the morning.

After locking the door, Lisa turned and leaned against it. "I thought he'd never leave."

Bo took a couple of steps toward her and wrapped his arms around her. "I didn't hear half of what he said. I couldn't stop thinking about that kiss."

"And I thought that old expression about seeing stars was bullshit. How wrong I was," Lisa said, pulling Bo closer.

The second kiss was slower, deeper, and even more erotic.

Lisa purred with delight and, without a word, took Bo's hand and led him into the bedroom.

CHAPTER

78

The night with Lisa was amazing. No awkward nervousness. No uncomfortable moments. It was pure delight. They woke up in each others' arms and had to rush to their meeting with Agent Slattery.

Slattery took a seat across from Bo and Lisa in the conference room at the Boulder Police Station. He wore gym shorts and a tight Under Armour top that accentuated his bulging muscles. "Excuse my appearance, but I've been busy since last night."

"Was the cell phone helpful?" Lisa asked.

"Not so far. Lots of calls to Limon prison, but that's no surprise."

"I don't know if this will help, but I have a connection to the Limon prison," Bo said.

Lisa rolled her eyes.

"Wait. Before you think I associate with the criminal element, it's through one of my swimmer friends, Raul. His brother is in the Sureños gang and locked up in Limon. You should talk to him."

Slattery wrote down the name and address. "I want to thank you for the tip on Dr. Dunner. We followed him this morning to a clinic in downtown Denver. It's preliminary, but we think he's involved with writing prescriptions for medical marijuana."

Bo nodded, thinking. "Did you find a connection to the customs X-rays yet?"

"Not yet. But we'll subpoena his bank statements. It won't be long." Slattery added, "I need to go, Dr. Richards. Look, keep a low profile for the next couple of days. The men who took Dr. Flickinger might have recognized you. Why don't you stay at a friend's house, or a hotel? I'll call you later."

CHAPTER

79

Marisol woke to sounds of feet stomping outside her room. She heard a key turn in the lock and braced herself for more agony. The door opened and a man was thrown into her dark, windowless prison. He grunted when he hit the floor, and with that one sound, Marisol knew it was Hector. She jumped out of bed and hugged him. After so long and so much anguish, Hector was back in her life. She didn't want to let him go. Tears streamed down her face as she stroked and kissed his rough, unshaven face.

"Where's Arturo?"

"Sanchez has him in the other room," he whispered. "I'm sorry, Marisol. I'm so sorry I got you into this mess. It's all my fault. If—"

Marisol placed her fingers over his mouth. "Stop, Hector. It's okay. I know you were only doing what you thought was best for our family. I love you so much."

Hector tried to smile but his bruised and swollen lips wouldn't turn up. Marisol leaned forward and kissed him gently. When she pulled away, he told Marisol that Sanchez was making him go back to Cabo.

"He's planning a big smuggling operation later this week. He wants me to fly back and get some of my friends to be mules. He says Arturo will stay with you while I'm down there. If I don't cooperate he'll kill Arturo in front of you."

Marisol winced. Before she could reply the door opened and El Piojo loomed in front of them. The light from the living room shined around his shoulders, casting a threatening shadow on the floor.

"My little Marisol." Sanchez smiled as he took a couple of steps into the room. "So nice to have you back with us. Did you enjoy the party last night? Did you tell Hector all about it?"

"Fuck you," Hector said.

"Later." Sanchez sneered. "After she gets cleaned up, I'll teach you a thing or two about fucking. I'll even let you watch." Sanchez closed and locked the door, and Marisol heard his footsteps retreat.

Hector looked at her and started to cry. "What did they do to you, my love?"

"I'm all right, Hector. I only thought of you and Arturo and what we need to do to get out of this mess." Marisol told him about the plan. She had a way to get out of here. If she could get Arturo and escape, Hector could stay in Cabo.

Hector shook his head. "I need to do this trip. If I don't come back, they'll track us down and kill us. Believe me."

CHAPTER

80

Lisa kissed Bo in the parking lot. "Thanks for last night," she said before getting in her cruiser. "I've got to get going. Someone IDd the painter's van that took Dr. Flickinger."

"Be careful."

"I'm more worried about you." Lisa hugged him again and drove away.

What an amazing turn of events, Bo thought. Only a week ago he was praying for Cory, thinking she'd died because of a drunk driver. Now he knew she was an ex-addict, was helping another addict she really didn't like, and had somehow gotten in the way of the Mexican mafia. Bo still didn't understand the connection between her death and the mafia, but maybe it would clearer when Dunner was arrested.

And only a week ago he never thought he'd love another woman. Cory had been everything to him. She was smart and funny and witty. He could always count on her, whether it was an encouraging smile at the transition area during one of his grueling triathlons, or a back rub when Bo tensed up watching Duke basketball almost lose to a fifteen seed in the NCAA tournament. She was always there. Bo didn't know where his relationship with Lisa was going, but somehow he thought Cory would approve. But he needed to say good-bye to Cory one last time.

He took the bus from the police station and walked a couple of blocks to his condo. Not seeing any suspicious cars, he walked through the backyard and sneaked in the back door. Blood covered the floor. Bo danced around the stickiness and donned his biking clothes. He took his mountain bike off the rack and stopped to wipe the dust off Cory's matching bike. They had ridden the trails together so many times, he felt this was a fitting way to pay tribute to her. Bo pumped up the tires, opened the side door, and looked both ways. Satisfied that the Sureñoses weren't outside, he headed up Highway 36.

A few miles down the road, a Toyota Prius passed him, two canoes strapped to the roof. The boats were so large they almost dragged the ground. Bo shook his head in dismay. *Only in Boulder ...* and his thoughts drifted back to his second date with Cory.

They'd rented the canoe on a whim—luckily the outdoor shop didn't ask any questions about their qualifications—and they strapped the two-man boat onto Bo's pickup and headed to the launch site about an hour north of Durham. It was a typical hot and humid afternoon in the South, perfect for the cool water. The Haw River trickled that day, easing Bo's fears about negotiating rapids. They worked well together, paddling in sync, mastering quick turns. It was fun. An hour into the trip, the river widened and the current picked up. Bo and Cory were talking and flirting—they didn't see the bridge until it was too late.

Cory saw the trouble first and yelled: the canoe was headed sideways into a bridge support. Bo dug the paddle into the water, trying to straighten the boat, but there wasn't enough time. The canoe rammed the concrete pillar and let out an agonizing moan, wood creaking as it buckled around the stanchion. The impact launched Cory and Bo into the water. Cory didn't panic—she even assumed the "lawn chair" position, floating on her back to avoid getting a foot entrapped on the rocky bottom.

Bo swam to the paddles and food and grabbed Cory, and together they kicked to shore. They sloshed up to a large rock to dry off, laughing at their stupidity. It was one of those rare moments: the gentle trickle of the river, the sun filtering through the trees, when they both looked at each other and realized this was something special. She could be the one, he realized. Bo slid over and kissed her. About twenty minutes later the battered boat bobbed down the river and Bo pulled it to shore and straightened it out. The canoe actually floated. Cory bailed out the leaking boat while Bo paddled back to the car.

Bo saw the SUV in his helmet mirror as it accelerated toward him. He'd noticed the car a few minutes ago and wondered why it didn't pass him. Lost in his memories about Cory, he forgot about the car. Now, as it raced up next to him, Bo got worried. He had nowhere to go but down, and the river was about fifty yards below on a steep drop off.

The passenger window opened. A gun appeared.

That was all Bo needed to see. He ducked as he hopped the curb and plummeted down the side of the hill. A big boulder blocked his path, and he pulled up on the handlebars to jump it just in time. His tires skidded on the slick surface and he fought to keep control. The rock ended with a four-foot drop, and Bo let the front shocks absorb the impact.

The pitch of the hill steepened and he was about to topple over, but at the last second he remembered a lesson from a mountain biking trip to Moab, Utah, and hung his butt over the back of the seat. The bike didn't flip—but he didn't see the tree stump until it was too late. It caught the front tire and flipped the bike.

Bo braced for the impact with the next boulder. The last thing he heard was the awful sound of his helmet cracking against the rock.

CHAPTER

81

The lock clicked and the door swung open, startling Marisol and Hector out of an embrace that neither wanted to end. In the few minutes they had alone after Sanchez left, Hector caressed Marisol's bruised and battered body, kissing the surgical wound where the doctors cut the leaking bolitas out of her small intestine, consoling her with sweet whispers of better times: Sunday dinners after church, dancing around bonfires at the beach, wiping the light-blue splatters off Hector's cheeks while he painted Arturo's room. And for a little while anyway, Marisol relaxed and drifted to more peaceful times, forgetting last night's violence and humiliation.

Just as quickly as it opened, the door slammed shut and the lock engaged.

"Mama," Marisol heard the soft voice and jumped out of the bed. "Mama," Arturo said again.

She had never heard more beautiful words. The sounds of her son. Sounds that had kept her going as the men brutalized her. Sounds she didn't think she'd ever hear again. She stopped and sat on the floor as her little man stumbled toward her.

Arturo was walking! Little steps in fits and starts. Two quick steps, stopping to catch his balance, and then forward in a pitter-patter controlled fall toward Marisol.

"Oh, baby. Look at you!" Marisol cried. "When did you start walking?"

"Two days ago," Hector said. He had risen from the bed and was sitting next to her on the floor. "He's so proud of himself."

Marisol picked Arturo up and hugged him, squeezing him so hard she thought she might smother him. She inhaled his scent, the lemony shampoo, the comforting sweet baby smell on clothes she had washed only last week. She felt Hector's strong arms engulf them, mother and son protected by their loving father. And locked in a room in a house in Colorado, far away from the beaches of Mexico, an eternity from their mundane life in Cabo, they were a family again. Marisol cradled Arturo in her arms as Hector smiled with bruised, swollen lips.

The family moment was short-lived. The door opened again and two men Marisol recognized from last night entered. They sneered at Marisol, forced Hector up, and pushed him out of the room. Hector struggled free from the men and turned and looked at Marisol with sad and desperate eyes.

The door slammed shut, and stifling darkness swallowed Marisol and her son.

CHAPTER

82

Intense, burning cold woke Bo. Icy water trickled through his hair. He hung upside down, still clipped into his pedals, suspended by a fallen tree, the river gurgling in his ear. He picked his head out of the cold water and looked around, struggling to remember what had happened.

He fought a wave of nausea and assessed the situation. Rapids swirled underneath him.

Then his bike dropped into the river.

His head crashed onto a rock below the surface and everything started to go dark again. He inhaled the frigid water and started choking. He poked his head out of river and fought the urge to panic. He'd floated into the center now, the bike still attached to his feet. He pulled and pulled at the pedals before his sluggish mind realized his mistake and he twisted his feet free.

He heard rapids ahead.

The river deepened and the swift current pulled him downstream. Bo scanned ahead, eyes desperate for something, anything to stop him. Ten yards ahead he spotted a fallen tree. It leaned over a boulder, dead brown limbs dangling into the water. With frozen fingertips he paddled closer. This was his last chance.

Now! He reached up and grabbed the biggest branch, refusing to let go as the splintered bark tore into his palm and the river relentlessly pulled. His strength fading fast, Bo yanked on the limb, swinging his body toward the rock. The limb snapped, but his momentum carried him into the eddy behind the boulder. The fatal current swept by, inches away.

Bo trudged through the calmer water and collapsed at the riverbank.

He didn't know how long he was lying there before he heard the twigs crack by his side. Two men painted in tattoos stood over him. He tried to pull himself up and run when a violent shock ripped through his back and sent him sprawling back to the ground.

Bo tried to stand but his muscles twitched in spasm and wouldn't work. He was paralyzed and helpless. He could only shudder as he saw one of the men raise a baseball bat high in the air. He closed his eyes, waiting for the wood to strike his head, and everything went black.

CHAPTER

83

Bo opened his eyes but couldn't see. Darkness surrounded him. He raised his head and bumped into something hard, sending shooting pains down his neck. He tried to rub his bruised head but realized his hands were bound behind his back. His legs were tied. He screamed for help but the quick reverberations told his muddled brain he was in a small space.

He was trapped!

He kicked from side to side, trying to estimate the size of his confinement, and fought the mounting claustrophobia—he didn't even like sitting in church when the pews were full, crushed between the parishioners. He had to get control of himself or he'd never get out of this. That's when he felt movement and realized he was in the trunk of a car. Bo remembered those movies where the kidnapped guy counted lights and bridges and turns, figuring out where the bad guys were headed. But he had no idea how long he had been unconscious. He had no idea where they were going.

He heard loud music thumping from the backseat and the muffled sounds of men talking, but he couldn't catch what they were saying. The car came to a sudden stop, and Bo rolled forward, bumping into something soft. He thought it might be clothes or blankets when he heard a soft moan.

A moan?

Bo rolled toward the sound and felt something wet and sticky on his right cheek. For the first time he noticed the unmistakable rusty smell of fresh blood.

"Who is it?" Bo asked the bleeding form.

"Bo?" the voice creaked back.

"Oh my God. Vince. You're alive."

Bo heard the car doors open and men walk away. He braced for the worst, waiting for the trunk to open and another taser blast, but nothing happened.

"What happened, Vince?"

Vince didn't respond.

Bo tried to nudge him with his shoulder. "Vince!" he yelled again.

"It's not Dunner," Vince said more clearly and then sighed.

Bo tried to kick him awake. "What are you talking about?"

Vince was mumbling words Bo couldn't understand. He heard "Dunner" a couple of times and then Vince's voice trailed off.

Bo turned onto his back and waited. It was just a matter of time before the Sureños returned and killed them both. While he waited, Bo thought about ways to defend himself. He learned how to subdue a distraught, drowning swimmer during his lifeguard training back at the Jersey shore. He had never used it though, and it probably wouldn't work on land anyway. He could outrun and out-swim nearly anyone, but not with his arms and legs tied up.

He heard the car doors slam again and woke up; amazingly, he must have dozed off. The car started moving and Latin music blasted through the trunk. After what Bo guessed was about thirty minutes, the car stopped and doors opened. Bo felt his heart pounding as he heard the men walk around to the back, and the trunk popped open. He stopped breathing. His eyes squinted from the sudden light.

Two men pulled him out of the trunk.

"Taser him again, Marco," the taller guy said.

Wait. Bo knew the taller guy. Where had he seen him? His mind couldn't think straight.

Marco fired and Bo grunted as his body seized. The larger man picked him up and threw him over his shoulder. Bo couldn't turn his head to see where they were going. A door opened and Bo smelled a familiar scent—chlorine.

A pool? Why would they take him to a pool? Bo tried to think, but his mind was sluggish. He felt like he had an ice pick through his brain and was certain he had a skull fracture. The big man dropped him, and Bo hit the pool deck hard. Intense pain blasted through his left hip. He remained motionless and listened to the two men arguing about who was going to drown him. They were going to make it look like an accident.

But something wasn't right. They were arguing in Spanish, but the taller guy Marco had called Torrero had a strange accent that Bo couldn't place.

Think!

"Time to go swimming, Dr. Richards," Torrero said, removing his shirt. When he bent over to take his shoes off, Bo saw the scar, the one he saw on the 3D images in the hospital. It was unmistakable.

This was the thug who had killed Cory.

Torrero picked Bo up, and for the first time Bo looked around at his surroundings.

He was in the natatorium at the University of Colorado. Night reflected off the glass windows. Bo had swum in this pool many times, and he and Lisa had been here the other day, swimming in the old pool that adjoined it. When was that? He tried to remember but his thoughts kept jumping.

Bo fought through the pain to assess the dire situation. The only advantage he had was that he was a better swimmer than either of these guys. He could probably hold his breath longer too. At the end of each swim practice Bo would work on his breathing—or not breathing, actually. He would do ten separate fifty-yard swims, taking one fewer breath each time. He would start with ten breaths for the two lengths and end up trying for no breaths, although the best he'd ever done was one.

If they were going to make it look like an accidental drowning, Torrero would have to get in and hold him under. That might afford an opportunity, but not much, especially with his sore hip. He had a nagging feeling that there was something special about this pool, but his muddled mind couldn't quite remember. The two taser blasts and the baseball bat to the head didn't help his thinking too much.

Bo didn't have much time to figure this out. He looked around the pool deck but didn't see anything he could use as a weapon. His hands were bound anyway. Without warning, the taller guy pushed Bo into the pool. The cold water jolted him alert. Survival instincts kicked in. He dolphin kicked to the surface and took a big breath.

Bo had to think fast. What did he know about Torrero? What about the CAT he saw at Boulder Community Hospital? The scar. His ribs. That was it! He was missing three ribs from previous chest surgery.

It was his only advantage and Bo had to use it.

Torrero stepped down the ladder into the pool.

There was no way Bo was going down easily. He forgot about his throbbing head and hip; this was the fucker who killed Cory! Bo bobbed to the surface to catch his breath. It was difficult to stay afloat with his arms and legs bound. Torrero approached. Bo waited for the right moment.

Come one. Take one more step, asshole.

His feet were bound at the ankles, but he could still bend at the waist. Just as the thug stretched out his hand to grab him, Bo performed a perfect flip turn. He balled up his body, head tucked against his chest, hips and knees bent—Michael Phelps would be proud—and Bam! Bo's feet exploded and caught the killer along the left side of the chest. Bo knew he nailed it when he didn't feel the ribs. His feet punched through the scar and exploded into lung. Bo surfaced to see the panic in Torrero's eyes as his lung collapsed.

Bo turned toward Marco standing on the side of the pool. He was shouting something to his partner. *He can't swim!*

Bo took an expansive breath and pushed off the bottom of the pool and dolphin kicked underwater away from the two men. As he swam underneath the lane ropes, he finally remembered what was nagging him.

The new natatorium shared the same water as the original 1930s pool that he and Lisa swam in the other day. Although separated by the tiled pool deck and wooden doors on the surface, they were connected by a short tunnel underneath so they could use the same filtration system. A grate along the east wall of the new pool blocked access to the tunnel.

Bo remembered reading about it recently. The Virginia Graeme Baker Pool and Spa Safety Act required reconfiguring pool filters after an unfortunate accident involving a young swimmer who got sucked into the grate by the strong pull of the filtration system. Because of the unique configuration at the CU natatorium, compliance with the federal law was going to be very expensive.

Bo surfaced once in the middle of the pool, grabbed a needed breath, and dived under again heading toward the east wall. He kicked as hard as he could until he got to the first lane and found the grate. He kicked it hard and felt it move. Bo surfaced to get another breath and saw that Marco had pulled Torrero out of the pool and was now running around toward Bo. A gun was drawn. This was his last chance. If he couldn't get through the grate, he'd be a sitting duck.

Bo inhaled and sank to the grate along the wall. He turned his back to the wall so his hands could grab the metal edge. He pulled with all his strength and felt it budge slightly. He concentrated on Cory and the last few agonizing moments of her life! The anger energized Bo, and the grate moved a little more. He was running out of breath now and sensed that Marco was rounding the east side of the pool. He turned to face the wall, wedged his feet into the space between the tile and the grate, and pushed as hard as he could.

It bent open!

Bo peered up through five feet of water and saw Marco standing over him, gun drawn. With his chest burning and lungs about to explode, Bo maneuvered his body into the opening as bullets ricocheted off the grate. He needed to breathe. But he had twenty feet of dark tunnel in front of him. The urge to gasp for air was overwhelming.

With a sudden burst of adrenaline, Bo dolphin-kicked down the tunnel until his head bumped in the grate to the old pool. With his last remaining ounce of energy, Bo flip-turned and kicked the grate as hard as he could. It opened, and he sped to the surface, gasping for air. He floated on his back as his chest heaved, and he felt consciousness start to slip away. He flopped onto the pool deck, found the fire alarm, and pulled it down with his chin before collapsing in a heap.

CHAPTER

84

Violent thumping and splintering wood woke Bo. Echoing voices pierced the fog of his semi-consciousness.

"He's over there," he heard a man say, relieved it didn't sound like the Sureños thugs.

"Call an ambulance."

"Get those restraints off him."

Someone lifted Bo off the pool deck, and suddenly he was floating, drifting; the water warm and comforting; peaceful and secure like in his mother's womb. Bo relaxed and let darkness overtake him, welcoming the deep sleep he so desperately needed. But wait! He wasn't drifting anymore; he was circling the middle of the pool. He was spinning, the water now whirling, pulling Bo into smaller and smaller circles. Bo turned onto his stomach and tried to swim away, but his arms didn't budge. Powerless, his body spiraled faster and faster. Through burning eyes he could see the drain at the bottom of the pool, the grate open, gaping and malevolent. "Noooooo!" he screamed as bubbles gurgled from his mouth unheard and he was inexorably drawn into the vortex.

"Bo. Bo, relax. Relax." Strong hands held his arms and legs.

Bo opened his eyes. A concerned face looked down at him, surrounded by blinding lights.

"It's Sal Martinez. You've been transferred to the ED at university hospital."

"Sal?"

"You've got to relax, Bo. We're going to take good care of you."

He woke up to the electronic voice of the CT scanner telling him to hold his breath. "What?" he tried to move but his head was strapped into the head holder, and a hard cervical collar prevented Bo from turning.

The CT whirred.

His head was killing him.

He felt himself sliding onto the hard backboard and then taken to the exam room. He was only faintly aware of techs and doctors coming in and out, blurry images, and muffled voices. He looked up again and saw a fuzzy figure. Bo thought he was seeing double.

"Bo, it's Skip."

"Skip?"

"Yeah. Your co-resident, buddy. I've been looking at your scans. You've got a skull fracture and a nasty little bleed in your head. Neurosurgery is on their way over here. Just hang in there, man."

"Hip?" was all Bo could utter.

"Your hip hurts?"

"Can't move it," Bo said and everything went black.

"Bo. Bo." He felt himself being shaken. He managed to open his eyes.

"It's Dr. Vanderworst."

"No," Bo mumbled.

"Well, you're stuck with me." Bo thought he saw a smirk. "I've just looked at your CAT scan and you have a subdural hematoma pressing on your brain. I'm going to have to drain it to relieve the pressure. It will be a piece of cake. The anesthesiologist is here to put you to sleep. And don't worry. I'm your doctor now. I'll take good care of you. I owe you one from the other day."

Bo felt a stinging sensation in his arm and a metallic feeling in his mouth. He had a strange feeling that Dr. Dunner was standing in the corner. He tried to speak when an overwhelming sense of peace settled over him.

CHAPTER

85

Marisol couldn't remember how many miserable days and sleepless nights had passed since Hector left; they all ran together. She met two other women who slept in the adjoining bedroom, connected to Marisol's through a shared bathroom; Ruby and Esther shared similar stories. Both were poor and living in the slums of Mexico. Promises were made and broken. And like Marisol, after they delivered the cocaine packages, the Sureños brought them here and forced them into slavery. Other women had come and gone, Esther said, but she didn't know what happened to them after they left the house.

Marisol quizzed the women about upcoming drug shipments but was met with blank stares. Ruby, a short, stocky bleached blonde was in the worst shape. She refused to talk and sat on the bed looking at, but not really watching, the television. She stopped showering days ago, her hair now greasy and sticky.

Esther had been held captive for two weeks. She knew the names and schedules of the men living here. Only eighteen, she had a sixth sense about the captors and could tell when a bad night was in store. She showered two or three times a day, applying makeup after each vigorous cleaning. Esther loved playing with Arturo and watched him when the men visited Marisol.

At night, Marisol would sit by the locked door and listen to the men talk in the kitchen. Smells of greasy food wafted into her room and turned Marisol's stomach sour. Beer can flip tops clicked open, followed by belches and crushing noises. Occasionally she'd hear a snippet of conversation. Last night the men talked about a doctor Sanchez had "taken care of." She prayed it wasn't Dr. Bo.

Marisol heard someone approaching and backed away from the door, hoping the man would be visiting Esther tonight. She stared at the door knob, praying for a break from their lusty appetites, but the knob turned and her stomach lurched. A different man entered this time. He glared at Marisol for a long time, studying her face and intimidating her with his silence. His three-dot Sureños insignia looked more like a scar than a tattoo, and Marisol tried not to stare.

The man asked her a series of questions. Who helped her and who hid her in the hospital? How did she know Dr. Richards? What did Dr. Richards know about the smuggling operation? And then about the boy in the hospital: Who was he and how did she know him?

Marisol answered the questions as best she could, trying to protect Dr. Bo and Raul. Dr. Bo saved her in the hospital, she said. He didn't know anything about the Sureños. And the boy wandered into her hospital room one day, she explained. She didn't know his name. She was forced to tell him about Dr. Vince, though. She had to tell the truth about Vince and hoped he would forgive her.

The interrogator stood up, satisfied with Marisol's answers, and walked to the door. Marisol took a chance and asked about Hector, hoping she wouldn't infuriate him.

"Do you know if Hector is okay?" she pleaded.

The scarred man stopped and looked back at Marisol. "You just enjoy the nightlife here. I hear you're real popular with the men."

"Please. When will I see him?"

"After Friday, I doubt you'll even care." He laughed and watched Marisol cry.

But when the door closed, a devious grin replaced the tears on Marisol's face. For now she knew when to escape. Her plan was going to work!

CHAPTER

86

Click. Click. Click.

Bzzzzzzzzzzzzzzzzzzzzzzzz.

Bzzzzzzzzzzzzzzzzzzzzzzzz.

Click. Click. Click.

The buzzing woke Bo up. His head throbbed. He couldn't move his arms and legs, and a shadowy gray ceiling loomed inches from his face.

Where am I?

The brain-stabbing buzzing stopped and his body moved. A door clicked open and Bo heard footsteps. He tried to turn his head, but his body was strapped down, his head stuck in place.

I'm in an MRI machine, he finally realized.

A shadow approached from his left. A man in a white coat stood over Bo. Dr. Musk? Bo blinked a couple of times—he must be dreaming—but the pudgy chairman remained.

"Dr. Musk. What's going on?"

"You had a subdural hematoma evacuated a couple of hours ago. And now your doctors can't figure out if your left hip is broken. The X-rays were inconclusive. So they ordered an MRI."

"Why are you here?"

"To keep an eye on my nosy resident." He sneered.

Bo looked around. *Where's the MRI tech?* Why was he alone?

"Don't worry. I sent Rosie off for coffee."

Something's wrong, Bo thought.

Musk held an empty syringe in front of Bo's face. "Now just relax and let me give you some medicine." Musk pushed the plunger down. Intense pain rushed through Bo's head and his vision blurred.

"How's that feel, huh?" Snickering and snorting with excitement, Musk refilled the syringe with air.

Bo realized the chairman was injecting air into the drainage catheter in his head, the catheter that was supposed to evacuate any remaining blood from around his brain. The next injection would kill him, squeezing his brain against his skull. By the time the code team arrived, Bo would be dead and the air absorbed—the perfect crime.

"Doesn't feel too good does it?"

Through the blinding pain, Bo managed to say, "Why?"

"Because this is much bigger than you can imagine. Because you got too close. Because you wouldn't back off when I fired you."

Musk heard a noise and turned to check the control room. Bo tilted his torso and wiggled his right arm out from underneath the Velcro restraints. But before he could get the other arm out, Musk reconnected the syringe.

He pushed the plunger down.

Bo had a split second to save his life. He whipped his free hand up to his head. He fumbled around the soft gauze dressing until he felt the catheter tubing. Yes! He pinched it with his fingers.

Musk swore and tried to swat Bo's hand away. But there was no way Bo was letting go. Cursing, Musk used his free hand to smack Bo on the craniotomy site.

The room went black.

"Give me that syringe," Bo heard a male voice demand.

Bo opened his eyes and let the room come back into focus.

"Are you out of your mind?"

Bo looked over to see Dr. Dunner push Musk aside and grab the air-filled syringe. *Dick Dunner? What's he doing here?*

Bo worked on removing the restraints while he heard Dunner grappling with Musk. He felt the loose end of the Velcro but couldn't pull it off his legs; his muscles didn't seem to be working right. Then he then realized he was pushing, not pulling. Finally he reversed the direction and the strap came off. He slid out of the MRI gantry and sat up. The room started spinning, and he thought he would black out again. He remembered the drainage catheter, the one Musk had injected with air. He looked down and saw the hub turned off, keeping the injected air and new blood trapped between his skull and brain. Bo turned the hub back to the open position. Fresh blood oozed down the tubing into the drainage bag, and Bo started to feel better. He took a couple of deep breaths and stared in amazement at the scene below.

The doctors were rolling on the floor, each swinging wildly at each other. Dunner had the advantage over the much smaller chairman and soon had him pinned to the ground. With one vicious punch, Dunner knocked Musk unconscious.

Dunner looked over at Bo. His face was ashen. Dunner clutched his chest and slumped lifeless to the floor.

Holy shit! He's got a pacemaker, Bo remembered from reading his chest X-ray the other day. He would die if Bo didn't get him out of the magnetic field and restart his heart. Bo lowered his feet to the floor and his legs buckled. He crawled over to the blue-faced Dunner and felt his pulseless wrist.

He had to call a code. He knew he didn't have enough strength to carry or drag Dunner out of the room. Bo grabbed the IV pole next to him and slowly, too slowly, pulled himself erect. Fighting the excruciating pain in his hip, he took agonizing steps toward the door. He could picture the red phone on the wall. Hurry!

There it is. Bo grasped the lever and pulled it down with him as he collapsed to the ground.

CHAPTER

87

Bo drifted in and out of consciousness. Blurred images of familiar faces appeared at his bedside: Skip and Rosie, Lisa, Cory. Cory? His drugged mind couldn't separate dreams from reality. Visitors' lips moved, but he couldn't figure out what they were saying. All he knew was that he was in the hospital, he was still alive, and his head was on fire. Every time he woke up, a nurse came by and injected his IV and he faded back to sleep.

Now Dr. Vanderworst stood over his bed, talking to residents, joking. The neurosurgeon pointed to Bo's head while the white coats smiled and nodded. What was so amusing? Bo tried to talk but couldn't form the words.

A fuzzy image of Sheri appeared one day, a concerned look on her face.

"Do I look that bad?" Bo managed to ask.

"Yes," she answered. "But at least you're alive."

When he opened his eyes again she was gone.

He felt like he was lost at sea in a fog. Every now and then someone emerged from the mist to change his gown or adjust an EKG lead and then disappear, and Bo would drift back to sleep. Bits and pieces, flashes of remembrances flowed in and out of his wounded brain: a gun pointed at him from an SUV; the pain of a taser blast; a long, dark tunnel of water.

Slowly the haze lifted, and Bo noticed Dr. Vanderworst standing next to him holding a bloody catheter. Bo started to form a question when the surgeon said, "You gave us a pretty good scare there, Dr.

Richards. If it weren't for my brilliant surgical skills, you might have been an overeducated vegetable for the rest of your miserable life."

Bo pointed at the catheter.

"Yes. I've just taken out the drainage catheter. The bleeding has stopped and your intracranial pressure has finally normalized. You probably didn't lose too many IQ points. But then again, you're just a radiologist, not a brain surgeon." Vanderworst chuckled.

"Thanks," Bo managed to say through his parched lips.

"I also owe you an apology. But that can wait. A DEA agent wanted to talk to you as soon as you woke up. He's been outside on and off for the past couple of days."

"What day is it?"

"Thursday night. You've been unconscious for about forty-eight hours."

Bo started to shake his head in dismay but it hurt too much to move. He watched Dr. Vanderworst let Slattery in and whisper a warning to the agent. The agent tiptoed into the room as if the very sound of his footsteps could send Bo into a coma.

"Dr. Richards," Slattery whispered. "I'm so glad you're going to pull through."

"Me too."

"I wanted to fill you in on what's been going on and see if you had any information that might help us, okay?"

Bo blinked his assent.

"First of all, we found Dr. Flickinger. Unfortunately he had expired in the trunk."

"I think the Sureños tortured him. The Mexicans threw me in the trunk with Vince, but he was too far gone at that point."

"Did he say anything at all?"

"He mumbled, 'It's not Dunner,' I think."

"Huh." Slattery stopped and looked down, thinking. "We probably will never know. Dunner died in the scanner after he tried to kill you."

Bo didn't think he heard Slattery right. "What?"

"Dr. Musk saved your life. He found a syringe full of air next to Dunner's body," Slattery said. "Maybe you were too delirious to remember."

"No," Bo said louder. "He tried to save me. He—"

Bo heard an alarm and a nurse rushed in looking concerned. She asked Agent Slattery to leave. "His blood pressure is rising, sir. We need to keep Dr. Richards calm. You can come back later." The nurse injected his IV and his body went limp.

Wait! Bo tried to say but no words came out. The peaceful drug spread from his arteries to the capillaries, stretching all the way to the tiniest cells in his fingertips and toes; Bo didn't have a care in the world.

CHAPTER

88

Finally the house was quiet.

Marisol put Arturo to bed early and paced the walls of the bedroom over and over, anxious for the men to fall asleep. But tonight was different, the men drunker and louder than usual. A couple of times she heard them brag about "the shipment tomorrow."

Marisol would escape tonight. She had one chance to get it right or Sanchez would kill them all. She peeked into the adjoining bedroom. Esther and Ruby had fallen asleep. The men had been rough tonight, and Marisol covered her ears as Esther wailed and later cried herself to sleep. Marisol wanted to tell them about her escape plans, wanted to give them hope, but she was afraid they'd let it slip. She'd wake them later.

Marisol sat on the edge of the bed and picked at her stomach wound. Dr. Vince had placed the key in the surgical scar, leaving a single suture for Marisol to grab. The scar had healed over the past couple of days. Marisol tugged at the suture but the key wouldn't budge. She pulled harder and the suture broke. Damn! Refusing to accept defeat, Marisol worked her fingernails into the wound and pulled. Searing pain forced her to stop. She shoved a washcloth into her mouth to muffle her screams, ripped open the scar, and pulled out the key. She held a towel to the bloody spot and waited for the room to stop spinning.

Marisol approached the locked door, rested her left ear against the wood panel, and listened.

Sputtering, drunken snoring rattled through the house; the men were finally asleep. She had to act fast. After a silent prayer, Marisol inserted the key into the lock, hoping she cut the X-ray pattern precisely. She hesitated with her hand on the knob. What if someone was awake in the living room? Would he kill her?

Marisol looked back at Arturo for encouragement and turned the key.

It worked!

The door opened and Marisol stepped into the hall. Soft carpet padded her feet as she sneaked into the living room. A shirtless man reeking of stale alcohol with a dragon tattooed across his torso snored on the couch. He stirred with a snort, and Marisol held her breath as he turned on his side, folding his legs into the cramped sofa. She searched the kitchen and the rest of the first level, careful to avoid the strewn beer cans, and thankfully, everyone was asleep.

Marisol slipped back into her bedroom and walked through the bathroom to wake up the other women. She nudged Ruby first, whispering for her to be quiet and wait. She walked over to Esther and tapped her shoulder. Esther sat upright and started to yell. Marisol put her hand over her mouth and warned her with her eyes to be quiet.

"Follow me," Marisol whispered to the women. "We're getting out of here tonight."

Ruby and Esther understood and followed Marisol into her bedroom. Marisol scooped Arturo off the bed, hoping he wouldn't wake up, and cradled him against her breast. Ruby placed Arturo's blanket over Marisol's shoulder and covered him. Marisol looked out the door. The man in the living room was still asleep and the house remained quiet. Through the kitchen window, she could see the orange glow of the sunrise. They had to hurry. She looked back and gestured for the women to follow.

In single file they crept past the sleeping gangster. Esther tapped Marisol's shoulder and motioned for her to step away. Using both hands, Esther carefully turned the lock and opened the front door. Cool air greeted them on the porch. They were going to make it.

And then Esther walked back into the house.

Marisol and Ruby looked at each other, puzzled.

After several tense minutes, Esther rushed out of the house and closed the front door. "Hurry," she urged.

The three women ran down the front steps and into the street. Esther flashed a toothy grin and dangled a set of car keys in front of Marisol. They all piled into the car in the driveway, and Esther started up the car and backed out.

They were halfway down the street when Esther slammed her hand against the steering wheel. She put the car in reverse and returned to the Sureños house.

"Let's go, Esther. We need to get out of here before they wake up." Marisol was starting to panic.

"Just one more minute, Marisol," Esther said, getting out of the car, leaving the door open. "I have to do this."

Marisol watched her roommate sneak up the steps, open the front door, and disappear inside the house. *What is she doing?*

About fifteen seconds later Esther emerged and sprinted to the car. She jumped into the driver's seat, slammed the door shut, eyes wild with excitement, and stared at the house.

"Come on, Esther, drive," Ruby pleaded. "We need to get away from these animals."

Esther just smiled and continued to look at the house. "Watch, Ruby. I did this for you."

As if on cue, the women heard a short whoosh followed by a fiery explosion, and the house burst into flames. They sat in the car, mesmerized by the inferno, imagining the terror of the men upstairs but not feeling sorry for them.

Finally Esther drove away. "My momma always warned us never to smoke with the oven on."

CHAPTER

89

Bo woke up hungry. Sunlight filtered into the ICU, casting abstract shadows on the wall. As he struggled to sit up, he noticed Lisa by his side.

"Don't move, Bo. You've been through a lot."

"Where's Musk?"

"I don't know. He stopped by a couple of times to check on you."

"He tried to kill me."

"No. Dick Dunner tried to kill you. Musk saved you. Your memory must be off, after the brain trauma."

"You need to call Slattery. Tell him to run a background check on Musk. There's got to be a connection. That's why he fired me."

"Okay. But Slattery is coordinating a big operation right now. Through your friend Raul, we found out that a big group of mules is coming through DIA today."

"Please call him, Lisa. I'm not crazy."

He watched Lisa dial her cell phone. The room started to spin and Bo closed his eyes and drifted off to sleep. He thought he heard her leave a voice mail.

CHAPTER

90

"I hope this is the one," Esther said, "because we're running out of gas."

"It's the closest one to the hospital, according to the man at the last YMCA," Marisol said.

Since their escape this morning, the three women had been driving around downtown Denver. Marisol was hoping to find Raul and get help. She really didn't want to go back to the hospital again, afraid they would search for them there first.

"At least it's better that being trapped in the damn house," Ruby said. She kept playing with the radio knob, changing stations, head bobbing, while Marisol helped Esther navigate the crowded downtown streets.

"I still can't believe you had the key in your belly and didn't try to escape earlier," Esther said.

"I had to wait for the right time." Marisol patted her wound. "I needed to know when Hector was returning." Marisol got out of the car, entered the YMCA, and asked for the pool. She entered the steam room, and there he was.

Raul shook his head in shock. "Marisol?"

Marisol shuffled across the YMCA pool deck, holding Arturo and trying not to slip. Arturo stared wide-eyed at the swimmers in the water.

Raul got up from the bleachers, shaking his head in amazement. "I can't believe I found you."

"Where were you? And who is this?"

Marisol introduced Raul to Arturo before describing her ordeal with the Sureños. "Sanchez found me. He called me and said he was going to kill Arturo if I didn't come back to him. I had to go," she said, "for my family."

"I understand." Raul stroked her back.

"Sanchez took me to this house. There were other women there. We escaped this morning while they slept."

"We?"

"Me and two other women. They're in the car outside. We've been driving around Denver stopping at YMCAs to ask about you. I can't believe I found you."

"Where's your husband, Hector?"

"Sanchez sent him to Mexico to smuggle more drugs. He's supposed to land today. That's why I'm here. I was hoping you could help me. Once Sanchez finds out we escaped, he'll kill Hector."

"I know who you should talk to. My brother has been working with a federal agent, a guy named Slattery. Dr. Bo trusts him." Raul pulled out his cell phone and dialed.

Marisol took Raul outside while they waited for agent Slattery to arrive. She introduced Raul to Ruby and Esther.

CHAPTER

91

A black Ford Cutlass sped into the parking lot of the YMCA and screeched to a stop. "That's Slattery," Raul said, as the agent hurried over to meet them. Raul started to introduce everyone when Slattery cut him off.

"Sorry, Raul. I have to hurry. We just got confirmation about a bunch of drug mules coming through DIA today."

"That's what I was trying to tell Raul," Marisol said. "One of them is my husband, Hector. Sanchez is going to kill him."

Slattery grabbed Marisol's hand and led her to his vehicle. "We'll talk in the car. There isn't much time." Turning to Raul, he added, "Another car is coming to get these women and take them somewhere safe while I deal with this. Keep an eye on them, Raul."

Raul nodded and offered to take Arturo to his mother's house. "We'll take good care of him, Marisol."

Slattery opened the back door and motioned for Marisol to get in. "Official policy," he said with a serious look. After getting in the driver's seat, Slattery turned to her and said, "What do you know about the Sureños?"

Marisol looked away, suddenly nervous. Was this man going to arrest her?

Slattery must have sensed her uneasiness. He said, "Look, I know you were a drug mule. Raul and Dr. Richards told me all about it. Right now all I'm interested in is nailing the Sureños."

As Slattery negotiated the crowded streets of downtown Denver, Marisol told him her story, starting with Hector losing his job and ending with this morning's explosion.

"I've been trying to nail El Piojo for a long time. I even have a picture of a louse over my dartboard at the office. We're going to get him today, I know it," the agent said with a determined look. "Do you have any idea where they took you from the airport? Where you evacuated all the bolitas? They'll probably take Hector there too."

"I know it's a couple of blocks from the church St. Francis of Assisi. If you take me there, I could show you."

"Now we're getting somewhere." Slattery smiled.

CHAPTER

92

Bo woke with sugary-sweet lips on his mouth.

"You were right," Lisa said when she finished her kiss. "I had a friend do a background check on Musk. Did you know he owns half of the MRI center? The other half is owned by a shell corporation that's controlled by the Sureños."

Bo nodded and pulled Lisa back for another kiss. "Go get him. He tried to kill me."

"I'll be back, lover."

When Lisa left, Bo buzzed the nurse to help him sit up. The initial dizziness faded and he took a big sip of water. For the first time, he looked around the room. Flowers covered every conceivable spot. Closest to him was a big note from Sheri: "Y'all get better soon. Your favorite Southern belle."

Southern?

Bo's muddled brain started to make the connection: the weird accent on the killer at the pool wasn't a Mexican dialect, it was a Southern drawl.

It was Sheri's brother. He'd seen his picture in her apartment. That's why he looked familiar! It was just hard to tell because of the gang tattoos.

Sheri's brother killed Cory?

The more he thought about it, the more sense it made: Sheri's brother had been in Limon prison. Sheri was jealous of Cory. And Sheri had access to all the computer terminals.

Could his best friend have killed his girlfriend and set him up to be fired?

He needed to find out.

CHAPTER

93

Marisol listened to Slattery bark orders into his cell phone. He beamed with excitement when Marisol found the warehouse. Since then he'd been on the phone, arranging a raid and coordinating his men. Slattery had federal agents stationed at the airport, and they were now taking positions around the warehouse.

His plan was to let the smugglers pass through customs, follow them here to the warehouse, and catch them red-handed. He gave Marisol a sly look and told her the smugglers were in for a big surprise; he had a secret weapon. Slattery smiled. "Dr. Richards found the electronic door opener to the warehouse on one of the CAT scans of the Sureños. We just didn't know where the facility was until you showed me."

After all the rushing around and the urgent phone calls, Slattery finally hung up, leaned his seat back, and sighed. "Now we wait," he said with his eyes closed. "As soon as they spot the mules at the airport, I'll be notified."

Marisol described Hector and pleaded with Slattery to protect him.

Marisol liked Slattery. She liked the way he listened to her story and didn't judge her. And she liked his bold confidence. She started to feel optimistic. Maybe her family would survive this ordeal yet.

Turning to Marisol, Slattery said, "That was a brave thing you did this morning—saving Ruby and Esther. You didn't have to do that."

"I couldn't leave them. The Sureños would have killed them."

The waiting continued. Marisol and Slattery talked. She told him about Cabo San Lucas and the pretty beaches and nice hotels. Slattery was married but didn't have kids. He never seemed to get around to vacationing. Maybe after this was over, he said, he'd take his wife to the Baja. They talked about Dr. Bo. Slattery described Bo's kidnapping and escape from the Sureños. "He had to have two brain surgeries, but I talked to him last night and he should be okay. Just to be sure, I've stationed a police officer at the hospital."

Marisol shook her head and moaned. "It's all my fault. If Dr. Bo had never read my X-rays and saved my life, this never would have happened to him." She looked out the window. "I feel terrible. He's such a nice man."

"It's not your fault, Marisol. You did what you had to do."

"What about Dr. Vince? After he dropped me off to go back to the Sureños, he said he was going to get help. Do you know him?"

"Vince is dead. He was kidnapped and killed by the Sureños."

Marisol gasped. "So much misery."

She heard the agent's cell phone ring again and watched his face redden as he listened.

"What do you mean they passed through X-ray? Dunner is dead. They shouldn't be able to get through." Slattery slammed his hand against the steering wheel. "Okay, okay. Just follow the van." She saw Slattery make another call and then hang up without talking. He snapped the phone shut.

"What's going on?" Marisol asked.

"Someone is still letting the mules get through customs with normal X-ray reports," he snapped. "And the officer at the hospital isn't answering her phone."

"Is Hector on the van?"

"No. He's on the next flight."

Marisol put her head back against the seat and tried to relax. Soon Hector would get off the plane, his belly full of cocaine, and try to walk through customs. So many things could go wrong: the bolitas could rupture and kill him, or Sanchez might be so incensed at Marisol's escape he might kill Hector out of spite. Marisol hoped the agent had the situation under control.

The waiting continued. Marisol kept her eyes closed. She heard the crinkle of the leather seats as Slattery shifted.

"Here we go," Slattery said, and Marisol was instantly awake. "The van just pulled into the warehouse." He opened the door to get out. "Now stay here while we take them down. As soon as this is over, I'll have an officer drive you back to Raul's house."

Marisol watched intently as the scene unfolded. Two groups of agents gathered on each side of the warehouse door. Slattery walked over, pulled out the electronic door opener, and pressed a button. The door opened and the men rushed in with guns drawn.

CHAPTER

94

Bo pulled himself up and let the dizziness pass. He buzzed the nurse again and asked for a wheelchair but was turned down.

"Can you at least get me a laptop? And call Officer Folletti."

A few long minutes later one of the nurses brought Bo a hospital computer and placed it on the bed stand. After several fumbling attempts on the keypad—his fingers didn't want to cooperate—Bo realized he still didn't have access to the hospital network and asked the nurse to log on for him.

He studied the radiology database. An X-ray from the airport was being read now. He checked the terminal.

He had to move fast.

Bo pushed the bed stand away and stood up. He immediately crumpled to the ground. When he looked up, Lisa was standing over him.

"What are you doing out of bed?"

"I'll explain later. Now we need to get to the MRI center."

"They say you shouldn't be up. You might bleed into your brain again."

Bo pulled Lisa toward him. Their noses almost touched. "I figured it out. It's not just Musk. Sheri and her brother are mixed up in this. Now get me in a wheelchair."

Lisa coaxed the wheelchair out of the reluctant nurse, and Bo directed her through the maze of corridors to the luxurious MRI center.

"Where are we going?" Lisa asked.

"Turn here," Bo said, but as they turned the corner, a man with a gun stepped out from hiding and pointed a gun at Lisa. Lisa backed away from the wheelchair, and the man whacked Bo on the back of the head with the pistol butt.

"I had a hunch you'd bring us more trouble," Torrero said.

CHAPTER

95

Gunshots rattled from the warehouse. Marisol remembered her first trip here, how bloated her belly felt and how disgusting the room smelled. She remembered strangling the driver with her rosary beads and wondered if God would ever forgive her. Mostly she remembered the evil look on Sanchez's face when he flashed the knife over her belly. Now it was time for him to go to jail.

The shooting stopped. Marisol hoped the Slattery was okay.

A man emerged from the adjacent building carrying a briefcase. To anyone else, he looked like a business executive. But Marisol shuddered in disbelief. This couldn't be happening. It was El Piojo. And he was looking right at her.

Marisol jumped up and leaned over the front seat to lock the doors, but she was too late.

"You bitch!" El Piojo growled. "You led the cops here, didn't you?"

The car started. Marisol tried to open her door but it was locked.

"You've caused me a lot of grief," Sanchez said as he adjusted his tie in the rearview mirror. "Now it's time for you to pay."

The car sped down the block.

CHAPTER
96

Bo rubbed the bruise on his neck, grateful that Sheri's brother missed his fractured skull. He didn't think his brain could take any more pounding. He saw the stern look on Lisa's face as she wheeled him into the MRI reading room. Sheri shrugged when they entered and said, "I'm sorry, Bo. Did Jack hurt you?"

"For the last fucking time, sister," he said, "my name is Torrero."

"I forgot. You're a Mexican now—the tattoos, the name."

"Shut up, Sheri," Jack said. "And get back to that computer. The phone's going to ring any second."

Jack set up a line of cocaine on a table and snorted it, all the while holding a shaky gun on them. Jack turned to his sister and said, "*Torrero* means 'lighthouse.' I thought you'd like the name after all the summers we spent at the Outer Banks." Wiping his drippy nose, he jumped when his cell phone rang. Bo watched him, hoping for a distraction.

Jack snapped the phone shut and said to Sheri, "Customs just sent the X-ray. Now do your thing."

Sheri sent off the normal report and turned around to face Bo.

Bo still couldn't believe his best friend was a criminal. "It's all over, Sheri. I figured out your scheme. The cops are on the way."

"Don't believe him, Sheri," Jack said. "They're alone."

"It wasn't supposed to be like this, Bo," Sheri said. "Jack—sorry, Torrero—needed my help. He owed the Sureños big time when he got out of prison last year. All I had to do was send normal reports. No one was supposed to get hurt."

292

"Why put my name on the reports?"

"You left your password lying around one day; it was easy. Just as easy as sneaking into Vince's office when he was half-cocked all the time. Besides, I didn't think anyone would read the normal reports. If you hadn't saved the bitch Marisol, everyone would still be happy."

Except Cory.

Jack paced the room like a caged animal. "Just shut up already, Sheri." Spit spewed from the corners of his mouth.

Bo noticed Lisa had stepped to the side of Bo's wheelchair and was now three feet away from Jack. His drug-addled brain didn't seem to notice.

When he roamed close to Lisa, she made a move for his gun, but Jack jumped away with quicker reflexes than Bo would have thought possible. Jack raised his gun to shoot Lisa but Sheri stopped him. "Someone will hear the shot. Let's wait until all the mules are through."

Jack put the gun down, but Bo could tell he wasn't happy about it. It wouldn't take much for him to blow them both away.

Bo needed to create a diversion. If he could distract Jack long enough, Lisa might be able to move into position and get the gun.

Jack might have killed Bo's first girlfriend, but he sure as hell wasn't going to kill his second.

Bo stood up from the wheelchair and waited for the room to stop spinning.

"What do you think you're doing?" Jack asked.

"How are those lungs feeling, asshole?" Bo asked, and Jack turned the gun on him. "I saw that panicked look when I kicked you. I'll bet you peed the pool, *Jack*,"

"It's Torrero, asshole."

Bo saw Lisa inch a step closer to Jack.

"You should have seen the look on your girlfriend's face before I knocked her over the cliff," Jack said.

Bo felt the heat rise to his head and the room started to fade. He knew he had to control his blood pressure or risk another bleed. He saw Lisa take another step.

"Why did you kill Cory?"

Jack poked the gun in Bo's chest and said, "She saw Sheri send one of the mule reports and started asking too many questions."

Bo's head started to pound. He had to keep control.

"And Sheri here has the hots for you. She thought that with Cory gone, she'd have a chance with you. She asked me to kill Cory."

Bo clenched his fists. A jackhammer blasted through his brain.

"So I did her a favor."

"You killed her?"

Another step.

"Not right away. She was so hot. So sweet. First I gave her a test drive."

Bo stood his ground, gritting his teeth, pulse pounding.

Jack licked his lips and said, "She was one hot lady in the sack, bro." He reeled back in laughter, and that was all Lisa needed. In a move that unfolded faster than Bo's muddled mind could comprehend, his girlfriend took one quick step and launched a scissor-kick right out of a martial-arts movie.

Jack turned in surprise and tumbled to the ground. Lisa wasted no time. She jumped on top of Jack, landing a vicious elbow to his nose, blood spewing, and reached for the gun. Desperate and energized from the cocaine, Jack flopped around like a dying fish, throwing his head from side to side, trying to free himself. Lisa held on to the gun, fierce determination on her face, as the two rolled around on the floor.

After being temporarily paralyzed by the quick action, Bo dived to the floor to help Lisa. He landed on top of them as a gunshot exploded, echoing in the small office.

Lisa rolled away and stood up, raising the gun over her head like a trophy.

Jack sat up, saw the gun, and collapsed back to the floor in surrender, holding his bloody nose.

Bo battled the blinding pain in his head, trying to stay conscious.

And Sheri groaned and slumped to the floor holding her right side, blood oozing between her fingers.

"Fuck," Jack said, wiping the blood out of his eyes. "I shot my sister."

CHAPTER

97

Lisa held the gun on Jack while Bo crawled across the floor to Sheri. He pulled up her shirt and cringed when he saw the entrance wound over her liver. He knew the blood staining her shirt was nothing compared the internal bleeding he couldn't see. She's going to bleed to death.

"You're not going to die on me now, Sheri," Bo said. "You're going to live and spend the rest of your pitiful life in prison." Bo yelled for Lisa to call a code. "Just dial zero."

"Hold it right there," a voice said from the door. "And drop that gun."

All heads turned in unison.

A well-dressed man with a tattooed face flashed the largest handgun Bo had ever seen. And too surreal for Bo's injured brain to comprehend, the gunman threw Marisol Hernandez into the room. If that wasn't weird enough, Dr. Musk sauntered in sporting his usual sneer.

The gunman motioned for Lisa and Marisol to sit on a couch, while Jack went to the bathroom holding his bloody face. He came out stuffing tissue in his nose, walked over to Sheri, and knelt in front of her.

"How is she doing?" he asked Bo.

"She's going to die in about five minutes unless we get her to a surgeon, you asshole," Bo said.

Jack's face twisted in anger as Bo's words registered in his drug-impaired brain. Jack jumped up and approached Sanchez, a wild look in his eye.

"I've got to get my sister out of here," he shouted.

Sanchez waved him away with his gun. "Sit down and shut up."

Jack sulked to the couch and sat next to Lisa. He mumbled to himself as he pulled the toilet paper out of his nose. His hands were shaking and his head was cocked at an awkward angle.

Jack looked over at his ashen sister and exploded off the couch with a feral scream. He charged at Sanchez, howling, "She's going to die, El Piojo!"

Sanchez never moved. His smug expression never changed. He raised the gun and fired. Sheri's brother, Cory's killer, dropped dead to the floor.

"No one calls me by that name," he said to Musk, as if he'd just swatted a fly, "Now, I have three more mules to get through."

Bo watched Musk log on to the computer. How could he do this? He was the chairman of one of the most prestigious medical centers in the country.

Sanchez's phone rang, and he listened before saying, "Pull up the X-ray on Felicia Fernandez."

"Why are you doing this, Dr. Musk?"

"Just shut up, Bo. You ask too many questions."

Sanchez turned to Bo. "So you're the famous Dr. Bo Richards, the troublemaker who's been interfering with my smuggling operation. I'll take care of you later."

"Next," Sanchez said, "pull up Hector Hernandez." He sneered at Marisol. "I think you know him, my sweet Marisol."

"I'm going to be sick," Marisol announced. She jumped off the couch and raced for the bathroom, covering her mouth.

Sanchez checked the bathroom before letting her in. "You've got one minute." He looked back to Musk. "Now. Send a normal report."

Marisol hunched over the toilet and vomited. When she heard Sanchez say Hector's name and saw his belly full of the deadly condoms, her stomach revolted. By the look on Sanchez's face, he was never going to let her husband live, not after this morning. At least Arturo is safe, she thought as she vomited again.

Marisol washed her hands and rinsed out her mouth. She could hear Sanchez yelling at Dr. Bo. The Sureños boss was furious. As soon as the mules passed through customs he would kill them all.

She was about to walk back into the room when she spotted the bottle of disinfectant on the wall. Her hotel back in Cabo used the same brand—Purell—for the guests. Some of the employees took the half-empty bottles home to use as starter fluid for fires. She had never seen it done but heard it worked pretty well. Purell was, after all, mostly alcohol.

"Time to get back out here, Marisol," Sanchez yelled.

She opened cabinet drawers, flushing the toilet to mask the noise, and smiled when she found a book of matches. She loosened the top of the Purell and pushed a tissue into the liquid, making sure the free end hung over the top. She shoved the bottle into her pants, walked back into the room, and sat next to the pretty police woman on the couch.

Bo felt Sheri's pulse trickle to a stop. He pushed her body aside and again asked the chairman, "Why are you doing this?"

"I just set up the structure, Bo. I never hurt anyone."

Until you tried to kill me the other day.

"That's enough," Sanchez ordered. "We've got one more mule to go. Look for Andre—"

Sanchez never finished his sentence. A loud knock at the door interrupted him.

"Federal agents!" the voice behind the door yelled.

Sanchez turned to Musk. "I don't believe it. It's too quick. Now go out there and get rid of him. They don't know you're involved."

Dr. Musk cracked the door and, in a reassuring tone, said, "This is Dr. Musk. I'm coming out."

Sanchez pulled out a second gun, handed it to Musk, and pushed him out the door.

"I'm the chairman of the department. Everything is okay," Bo heard Musk say before the shot.

Bo saw Sanchez smile as he shut the door. When the mafia leader turned around, a blazing ball of fire arched through the air and landed on his chest. A clear liquid stained the Mexican's shirt, and Sanchez looked down, bewildered. And then, with a whoosh, his shirt ignited and flames shot out and around his neck.

The Sureños boss didn't panic—at least not at first. Like a perfect fire drill, he stopped, dropped, and rolled. But it didn't work. The fire spread and his pants ignited. He ran into the bathroom howling.

Marisol jumped over the couch and hid. Bo grabbed Lisa and they ran out the side door of the office into the MRI control room.

They spotted Slattery on the ground and Musk running for the door. "I'm all right, Lisa," he moaned.

Lisa started to go to Slattery when the door creaked open and a charred El Piojo stood before them. A gun protruded from his burnt hand.

"Quick, into the magnet room," Bo urged.

The room started to spin, but Bo felt Lisa push him forward. As they entered the room a shot fired and Lisa dropped. Bo closed the door and looked down.

Lisa squeezed her side, a crimson stain pooling around her fingers. "I'll be all right. Just lock the door and call a code."

"It doesn't lock from the inside." He felt Sanchez pushing against the door, and with his vision fading, he knew he didn't have much time.

Bo looked around the room. He had one crazy idea, and if that didn't work, they'd both be dead.

"Crawl around to the backside of the magnet and pull the yellow tape off the new ventilation ducts," he instructed Lisa. He pushed his back against the door and watched her crawl around the gantry, her blood streaking the tile floor.

"Good. Now grab the oxygen tubing off the wall and stay on the floor."

The door started to open.

"Hurry."

"Got it."

"Listen to me. No matter what happens, keep sucking that oxygen tubing. Don't take it out for anyone, even me."

"What are you going to do?"

Bo didn't have time to answer. He felt the tension go off the door and realized Sanchez was preparing for a running start. He hobbled around the side of the scanner, kicked the ventilation duct free, and stood as close as he could get to the gantry. Lisa was on the floor and grabbed his ankles.

Sanchez burst into the room.

Bo leaned over and kissed Lisa. "I love you. Now just breathe the oxygen."

Bravely, he stood up and faced Sanchez. The drug lord smelled like burnt popcorn. His gun was out and ready. Ten feet of floor space and the gantry table separated Bo from certain death. But Bo held his ground, hoping for the best, hoping he was lucky, standing as close as he could to the bore of the magnet.

"It's over, El Piojo."

The Sureños boss twitched as Bo called him "The Louse."

"Maybe for you, Dr. Richards," Sanchez said and squeezed the trigger. Bo ducked behind the gantry as the bullets deflected into the bore of the magnetic, pinging as they lodged into the side of the MRI machine. Bo heard a faint hiss, and he smiled as he dived to the floor.

He covered Lisa with his body and took one last huge breath before a booming blast ripped through the room. The magnet exploded in a burst of smoke. The door to the control room slammed shut. Bo held his breath like no other swim practice he'd ever endured.

EPILOGUE

Two months later at the Boulder Reservoir.

"There she is." Bo jumped up from his beach chair and pointed to the water.

"I don't see her," Agent Slattery said. "They all look the same."

Hundreds of swimmers emerged from the reservoir: some standing too early, only to sink and restart their stroke; some tripping in the shallow water. With their black wetsuits and goggles, they could have been Navy SEALs, except for the fluorescent caps. Bo pointed again as Lisa pulled off her goggles and cap. She ran up the chute with the other swimmers, peeling her arms out of the wetsuit like a contortionist. She stopped and waved to Bo, motioning him over with an enormous, proud smile. The other triathletes raced by her, but she didn't care.

She hugged Bo. "I could have never done this without you." And then she kissed him and ran over to the transition area to mount her bike.

As she rode away, the DEA agent turned to Bo. "You two are sure getting along well."

"Thanks to you."

Bo owed Slattery his life. After the magnet exploded, the MRI room filled with noxious helium, killing Sanchez instantly. Bo held his breath until the agent finally opened the door and pulled him out. Lisa, covered by Bo's body and breathing pure oxygen, survived. Fortunately, her gunshot wound to the belly missed all vital organs.

After several blurry days in the hospital, Dr. Vanderworst finally let Bo go home. But not before apologizing. "It was Dr. Musk's idea to fire you," he said. The DEA agents caught up with Musk at the airport, about to board a flight out of the country, to Mexico of all places. His trial hadn't started yet, but Slattery told Bo they had enough evidence to keep the chairman in jail for the rest of his life.

As the layers of shell corporations peeled away, it became clear that this was bigger than just a drug-smuggling operation. With Musk's help, Sanchez was laundering the drug money through the MRI center, sending cash-paying "patients" through the center. No wonder it was so successful.

Slattery came over to Bo's condo a couple of times to fill him in on the case. The DEA found Hector and the other mules at the airport and arranged for them to evacuate the bolitas at the hospital—just in case. Marisol and her family were now back in Cabo—she even convinced the all-inclusive hotel she worked for to send the DEA agent complimentary tickets. He and his wife were finally going to get away this time.

Bo tried not to dwell on Sheri—how someone he thought was his best friend could have betrayed him and killed his girlfriend. He wanted to believe it was out of love for her brother, but he didn't know. And never would. Sheri and her brother were sent back to North Carolina for burial.

Over the past couple of weeks the headaches became less frequent and his vision cleared. Lisa visited almost every day. They walked along the Boulder Creek and stopped to watch the tubers float down the river. They shared coffee at the outdoor cafes on Pearl Street; Bo talked a lot about Cory, and Lisa listened, understanding. He knew no one could replace Cory, the first love of this life. But he felt something special with Lisa, feelings he didn't think he'd ever have again.

Oh, and last week, Dr. Vanderworst called and offered Bo his job back. He told the neurosurgeon he'd think about it.